LOVE AT LAST

Alfred took Casey's hand, kissed her palm, and tasted the tips of each of her fingers. His lips began to weave a spell over her body. Every fiber of her being was screaming *yes!* His fingers pulled the band from her hair so that it fell past her shoulders.

This is what he had been thinking about. The woman whose face filled his mind at every waking moment and dominated his dreams at night was finally in his arms. He pulled her close to him and brought her lips to his. Her hands caressed his back and shoulders.

"What do you want from me?" she whispered against his lips.

He tilted her chin so that he could see her face. "What do you think I want from you, Casey?" he asked hoarsely.

BOOK YOUR PLACE ON OUR WEBSITE AND MAKE THE ARABESQUE ROMANCE CONNECTION!

We've created a customized website just for our very special Arabesque readers, where you can get the inside scoop on everything that's going on with Arabesque romance novels.

When you come online, you'll have the exciting opportunity to:

- View covers of upcoming books

- Learn about our future publishing schedule (listed by publication month and author)

- Find out when your favorite authors will be visiting a city near you

- Search for and order backlist books

- Check out author bios and background information

- Send e-mail to your favorite authors

- Join us in weekly chats with authors, readers and other guests

- Get writing guidelines

- AND MUCH MORE!

Visit our website at
http://www.arabesquebooks.com

LOVE AT LAST

Rochunda Lee

ARABESQUE
BET BOOKS

BET Publications, LLC
www.bet.com
www.arabesquebooks.com

ARABESQUE BOOKS are published by

BET Publications, LLC
c/o BET BOOKS
One BET Plaza
1900 W Place NE
Washington, D.C. 20018-1211

All Kensington Titles, Imprints, and Distributed Lines are available at special quantity discounts for bulk purchases for sales promotions, premiums, fund-raising, and educational, or institutional use. Special book excerpts or customized printings can also be created to fit specific needs. For details, write or phone the office of the Kensington special sales manager: Kensington Publishing Corp., 850 Third Avenue, New York, NY 10022, attn: Special Sales Department, Phone: 1-800-221-2647.

First Printing: June 2001
10 9 8 7 6 5 4 3 2 1

Printed in the United States of America

Prologue

Casey James was the product of a single-parent family. Life wasn't easy for her and her mother, who had to work two jobs just to make ends meet. Yet, through it all, not once had their lights been turned off. Casey had never gone hungry though she may not have eaten what she wanted to eat all of the time. Casey's mother had her utmost respect. She fed her and kept clothes on her back and a roof over her head. She did all of this by herself. In Casey's opinion, she was a modern-day superwoman.

Casey grew tired of seeing her mother drag from one job to another. She even suggested getting a job after she graduated from high school to help out. But her mother wouldn't have it.

"No, you're going to college and get yourself a good education," her mother said. "I want you to have a better life than I have. So, you're going to college and I don't want to hear you talk such nonsense again."

Sometimes it angered Casey that her father wasn't around. Instead of standing up to his responsibilities, he deserted both of them. Although he left them, her mother still loved him. Casey never asked her mother if she still loved her father, but she could see it in her eyes and hear it in her voice whenever she talked about him. After all of the years had passed, her mother never said one negative word against her father to her. Casey had a mouthful of negative things to say, but her mother would cut her short and advise her not to say such things because he was still her father. How could she still love him after what he did? She couldn't understand it.

Casey never felt so passionate about anything, but she knew she despised the man who was supposed to be her father. She vowed that she would never go through the same things her mother went through. She would never give her heart to anyone because she wasn't going to put herself in the same position her mother was in.

People often asked her why she became a social worker. There were so many other professions she could have chosen, so why that one? The answer was simple. If she could help people who were going through the same things she had gone through, then she wanted to make a difference. Social work wasn't just a job for her. It was her calling. She was destined to help people who were in no position to help themselves, and to her, it was all worth it. Not too many people could say that they actually enjoyed what they did for a living. She was one of the few people in the world who could honestly get up in the morning and look forward to going to work. In her mind, if you loved what you did for a living, then it was not like work at all. She anticipated every day because each one brought something different, whether it was meeting a new child or sending one home to be reunited with a family. After a whole year of watching a family struggle to do whatever it took to get their kids back, closing the books on that case was a joy like no other. She liked that feeling.

One

"Another day, another dollar." Casey said as she shut off her computer. She zipped her briefcase while her coworker, Vicia, waited in the doorway for her.

"At least that's what they say." Vicia stepped in stride with Casey, purposefully heading for the door. "This is a job you *have* to love. It's not about the pay."

Casey shifted the briefcase on her shoulder. "As much as I hate to admit it, you're right. Money couldn't be the reason I'm here. I don't love the job. I love the kids." She pushed open the glass doors and stepped out into the fading sunlight. It was already six-thirty and once again, she was leaving the office late. This wasn't your ordinary nine-to-five job. Sometimes she found herself being called to the emergency shelter at three o'clock in the morning.

"Have a good evening, girlfriend," Vicia said as she headed to her car. "I'll see you in the A.M."

"Good night." Casey waved.

She took the stairs to the second floor where she usually parked, shaking her head. Sometimes her job depressed her, and it was hard to leave her work at the office. She found herself shaking her head more often than she wanted to. When she started working for Social Services, Casey felt her life had meaning for the first time. She had finally found her purpose in life. The flip side to saving the world was that she saw so many children who were being abused and neglected by their own families. Yet, it was Social Services' fault that their children were taken into custody, everyone seemed to feel. Social Services was always to blame for not doing an adequate job. Every time the agency was mentioned in the media, it was because of something horrible—severe child abuse or even the death of a child. The media never focused on the cases that ended on a good note. The public never knew about the babies who were adopted into good homes or children who were returned to their families. The world was so biased.

Many caseworkers had become desensitized to the plight of the families they served, but not she. She didn't think she would ever be able to look at a child who hadn't eaten a good meal in weeks and not feel anything. She'd never allow herself to be desensitized. She knew that most of her coworkers thought she was crazy, but she wasn't concerned about them. She was there to do her job, and she didn't half-step with other people's lives.

"You take your job too seriously," one of her coworkers told her. "You can't save every child in the world, so don't beat yourself up about it. Go home and get a good night's sleep."

If they only knew what she knew, they would feel differently. It was true that she couldn't save every child in the world, but she could do her best. She felt that if she were doing her best, then that was all that she could do.

Casey had become so engrossed in her thoughts that her drive home was a blur. After a shower and a quick bite to eat, she decided to lie down for the night. She was physically and mentally drained.

She quickly clicked on the television and turned the lights off before slipping under the cool covers. For some reason, she didn't like sleeping in the dark. Ever since she could remember, she slept with a nightlight or the television on. When she was a little girl, she would wake up in the middle of the night and turn the lights on to make sure her mother was still there. One of her greatest fears was that she would find that her mother had left her too.

As soon as her head hit the pillows, sleep began to overcome her. A friend had told her about how she became a volunteer mentor for a little girl who came from a single-parent family. Her friend talked about how happy the little girl was that she was spending time with her. Casey had thought about finding out more information about the program. That would be a nice way to devote some of her time since it wasn't as if she had much else going on outside of work. Satisfied that she had made that decision, she drifted into a peaceful sleep.

"Well, Ms. James, we're always happy to make new placements," said Ms. Green, the case manager at Big Brothers and Sisters of America. "We have some very needy children, and most are desperate for someone like you to spend a little time with them. Are you sure this is something you can handle right now? I know your job is pretty stressful."

"Yes," Casey said eagerly. "My job is stressful at times, but it won't keep me from honoring my commitment to a child. I honestly want to make a difference in someone's life. I know what it means to come from a broken home, and I would have given anything to have someone to do things with me. You don't know how therapeutic this will be for me."

Ms. Green smiled. "Well, I have a couple of families in mind. Let me look over their information and compare it with yours, and I'll give you a call in a couple of days. You see, we try to make the best possible matches because we want to unite people who have the same values and things of that nature. Not to mention that we have to do a background check before we can match up children with potential mentors." she explained. "After all is cleared, then we'll set up a meeting."

"That's fine. I look forward to hearing from you soon," Casey said as she prepared to leave Ms. Green's office.

"Don't worry, Ms. James. We'll get you started soon."

Casey felt good about what she was going to do. If she could keep one child from feeling the loneliness that she felt growing up, it would be well worth it. She headed to the office. There was no telling what was waiting for her when she got there. She gave a wry smile. The least she could say was that no two days were the same.

Vicia was standing in the hall when Casey walked in. "Hey, Casey, did you have court this morning?" she asked.

Casey turned the lights on in her office and leaned against the edge of her desk. Vicia followed behind her and closed the door before she took a seat.

"No, I went to Big Brothers and Sisters of America this morning." Casey took the top off of the Starbuck's coffee she had picked up on the way to the office. She didn't know that her interview at the Brother and Sister program would take so long, and to think, she wasn't through with the screening process. She figured it was better for them to be safe than sorry. How would it look for them to pair a child with someone who was a molester or a murderer?

"Really? Are you trying to get some of your kids involved in that program?" She took out a compact mirror and began primping her hair.

Casey had never seen Vicia without a mirror in her hand. It didn't matter where they went or what they were doing, Vicia was going to pop out a compact at some point. Casey didn't know how she got any work done with all of the primping she did.

"No, I'm applying to be a mentor. Hopefully, I'll get through the screening process and be paired with some lucky little girl," Casey answered.

Vicia frowned as she scrutinized her brows. "You know you have to get that approved from our supervisor, don't you?" Vicia made a kissing motion to the mirror before snapping it shut. "There could be a conflict of interest."

"I'm sure there won't be a conflict." Casey took a sip of her coffee. "Besides, you already know that if I go to Liz with this, she's going to say no. That's just how she is."

Vicia shook her head in disdain. "Of course she's going to say no. She wants to make sure you do a good job here at the agency. Well, I guess you know what you're doing." She stood and went to the door. "You don't want to put yourself in a compromising position. Girlfriend, you have to start thinking about yourself sometimes. Start loving yourself because ain't nobody gonna love you like you do."

Vicia bounded out the door with a perkiness that Casey found nauseating. Perhaps she was right. Who was going to love her when she needed it? Her lips pressed firmly together as she stared at her credentials hanging on the wall. What did it all mean? A person could have a degree in this or a degree in that, but if one didn't have people skills in this business, it was all pointless. Casey found it ironic that Vicia reminded her of how shallow a piece of paper and no socialization could be.

Vicia was an investigative worker, so she spent a lot of time out in the field. Casey had seen her in action and frankly, it wasn't a pretty sight. Talk about lack of understanding. One time Vicia knocked on the door and yelled "Social Services." When the family opened the door, she barged right in as if her agency identification were a police badge. The people were trying to explain what happened and Vicia cut them off.

"You can't fool me," she snapped, "and you can't fool this agency." She began slinging out business cards as if they were Chinese throwing stars. "Somebody is lying about what's going on in here, and it ain't me."

Casey could see that Vicia's tactics were getting her nowhere. She was dominating the conversation and half listening to the people's side of the story. Eventually, Casey was able to calm everybody down and get to the bottom of the situation. It turned out that everything was a misunderstanding. They were able to give the family a warning and go about their business. Vicia was upset as they left the residence.

"Next time," Vicia said, "let *me* do *my* job."

"Well, I was only trying to help."

"Next time, *don't.*"

Vicia was an okay person, but she didn't really want to have anything to do with the families she was supposed to help. Casey turned on her computer and caught up on phone calls. Somehow, she knew that it was going to be one of those days. She received a call to go check out a family for possible abuse. It was a priority one, which meant she had to see the family within twenty-four hours. There was nothing on her schedule for the rest of the day, so there was no need to put it off.

Her car radio blasted as she headed to the address written on a sheet of paper in the folder. She always played something to calm her nerves before going on an investigation. Even after four years, her stomach still knotted up when she had to investigate. The thing about it was that she never knew what was going to be on the other side of the door. It never ceased to amaze her as to how much abuse was going on right in Houston. She could only imagine how bad abuse was nationwide.

The house, if one could call it that, was located on the outskirts of Harris County. Casey pulled into the dusty driveway that led to the shanty. There were piles of trash in front of the house, and she thought she caught a glimpse of an outhouse in the back. *I didn't think people still used those!* Her eyes scanned the yard for possible dogs. She placed one foot on the ground and called out to see if any dogs would run from under the house. When she felt it was safe, she closed the gate and headed to the front porch. The porch was made of rotting wooden planks, so she had to judge where she stepped.

The door was open, but the screen was hooked. She didn't know what the purpose of that was since there were large holes in the screen. The weak cries of an infant could be heard, and she noticed that a woman just sat by and let the baby cry. Casey rapped on the door. The woman continued to sit on a couch, which was cluttered with beer cans and food wrappings.

"Are you Mrs. Lipton?" Casey asked.

The woman spat chewing tobacco on the floor before answering. "Dat depends on who wants ta know."

Casey resisted the wave of nausea that overcame her. "Mrs. Lipton, could you please come to the door? My name is Casey James and I'm with Social Services."

Mrs. Lipton continued to sit on the couch. It seemed as if she hadn't bathed in weeks. Her hair was all matted and unkempt. "Go 'way," she yelled at the door. "Ain't no reason for you ta be here."

Casey's teeth clenched as the infant's cries grew louder. "Mrs. Lipton, I just need to come in and speak with you regarding your children. We've received a report that something isn't right with them, and I'm here to help."

The large woman moved from the couch with such speed that Casey nearly jumped back. "Who called you?" she asked angrily. "It was my sister, wasn't it?"

"I can't give you that information," Casey said firmly. Her heart felt as if it were about to beat out of her chest.

"You tell her dat she'd better leave us be or else," Mrs. Lipton threatened.

Casey noticed fingerlike bruises on Mrs. Lipton's wrists and forearms. One of her eyes was blackened underneath.

"Please, Mrs. Lipton. We can work this out if you'd just let me see the children. I just want to make sure that they're okay."

The woman hesitated before unlatching the hook. "Thank you," Casey said as she stepped into the house. "Where are the children?"

Mrs. Lipton went back to the couch and refused to answer any questions. Casey was left to roam the house. When she found the children, she already knew what had to be done.

She immediately called her supervisor from her cell phone and told her about the situation. She advised her to take both children into custody. Casey pulled a form from her briefcase and handed it to Mrs. Lipton.

"Mrs. Lipton, I'm sorry, but we're going to have to take your children into custody. If you follow our plans, you can eventually have your children back."

The woman took the paper and finally broke down. "It's not my fault," she said calmly. "He beats me. Take the children. It's best for them right now."

Casey went to the back of the house and prepared the children to leave. Just as she was gathering them she heard a loud bang at the front of the house. Heavy footsteps were coming toward her. As she rounded the corner, a bulky man stood in front of her.

"Just what do yew think yew're doin'? My kids ain't goin' nowhere. I suggest yew put them back where yew got them from, gal." He glowered at her with bloodshot eyes and reeked of alcohol.

Gal? Who the heck was he calling a gal? This man was truly from the sticks, and he looked as though he might do just about anything. Casey's breathing became ragged. This man was three times her size. "Sir, I'm afraid I can't do that," Casey said with as much authority as she could.

"Oh." His eyes bulged out of his round head. "Yew can't, huh? Well, we'll have to see about dat."

The children immediately began to cry when they saw their father. Mr. Lipton snatched both children from her and advised her to get out before she received bodily harm. Casey didn't need to be told twice. She immediately bolted from the house to her car and called for police assistance.

Mr. Lipton wasn't too pleased to see her come back with law enforcement, but after an hour of talking to him, he turned the children over to the police The

Lipton case took her all morning to get settled. After getting the children examined by the clinic, she had to drop them off at the emergency shelter and get started on foster care for them.

The oldest child cried and cried to be returned home. Though the child couldn't say too many words, he kept saying, "home, momma." It nearly broke her heart. She kept telling herself over and over that removing these children was the best thing that could have happened to them, especially with their father being an abuser. Yet, even through the sadness, she was happy to see the Lipton children safe. Hopefully, with a little encouragement, Mrs. Lipton would get the help she needed as well. Casey clicked her tongue as she began typing up notes from the case. How could anyone stay in an abusive relationship? A lot of women fell for the line, "I won't hit you anymore, I've changed." It was the typical cycle of abuse.

Minutes later, there was a tap at the door. Casey glanced up from her laptop as Liz poked her head in the door. Though most of her coworkers considered Liz a fickle person, she was good at her job, and she didn't take any mess. She didn't mind writing people up. People judged her harshly because they thought she didn't support her workers. She didn't mind going to bat for a worker if he was right. But if he was wrong, Liz was that first to cut him up into little pieces. That's what Casey liked about her the most. She was known as fake, but to her, she was real.

"Good mornin', Liz said. As usual, she was on the money with her tailor-made suit and Via Spiga shoes.

Casey already knew something was up because Liz rarely came to her office unless it was something important. The manila folder in Liz's hand told her that it was a possible case.

Liz plopped the folder down on Casey's desk. "Well,

I know it's been a busy morning, but we've got a new one. This one is pretty sad. If you haven't heard it on the news, it would surprise me." She rubbed the back of her neck and sighed. "A family of three was returning from a weekend visit to San Antonio when they had a head-on collision with another vehicle. The car was totaled. It was amazing that anyone survived. Both parents were killed instantly, but their five-year-old daughter was thrown from the car."

Casey's breath caught in her throat as she listened to all of the details of the case. The poor little girl escaped with minor scratches. She was still at the hospital.

"Neighbors said they didn't know of any relatives. The family rarely had any company and mostly kept to themselves," Liz continued. "See if you can find any relatives. If not, I guess we'll have to try to get her adopted."

Casey found out which hospital the little girl was in and headed over. Her name was Dara Willingham. Casey went by the clothing room and picked out a change of clothes for her and a teddy bear. Dara was probably looking for anything that would comfort her, though nothing could replace her parents.

When Casey arrived at Texas Children's Hospital, Dara hadn't yet been discharged. Casey stood outside of her room and took a deep breath. How did you tell a child that she was never going home? Casey had done it hundreds of times, and each and every time she found it hard.

She tapped lightly on the door and pushed it open. She found the cutest little girl standing near the window looking out. Her hair was parted down the middle with two long plaits on each side. She was neatly dressed in a blue denim short jumper and a pink T-shirt. Her big brown eyes were red from crying.

Casey sat in a chair near the bed and introduced herself.

Dara walked up to Casey and stood in front of her. "Are you here to take me to my mommy and daddy? I've been here all alone, and I haven't seen them."

Casey gritted her teeth. Her fingers grasped the arm of the chair tightly. Why hadn't anyone told her anything about her parents? Casey tried to hide her uneasiness. She patted her lap and Dara climbed on and sat down.

"Dara," she paused, trying to keep her voice steady. After clearing her throat, she continued. "Do you remember being involved in a car accident?" She watched Dara nod yes.

"Well, your mom and dad, uh—" Her voice cracked. "Were hurt really bad in the accident." Dara's eyes filled with tears, and Casey struggled to keep from crying. "The doctors couldn't fix their hurt." Dara's fists rubbed her eyes.

"Do you understand what I'm saying, Dara?" Dara shook her head no, but Casey knew she understood. Her fat little arms wrapped around Casey's neck as she sobbed. "I know this is tough for you, but you're going to be fine." Casey held Dara close as she discreetly wiped tears from her eyes.

"I want my mommy," she sobbed. "I want my daddy."

"I know," Casey said. "I know."

Unfortunately, she had to take Dara to the emergency shelter until she found a foster home for her. She was in the system not because she had been abused or neglected, but because of a freak accident. Casey vowed to do everything to make the little girl's transition as smooth as possible.

* * *

She leaned back in her chair, staring at the words she had just typed on the computer screen. This case was going to be difficult for her. She could see it already. Rest wouldn't be a friend until she knew she had done all that she could to help this little girl. This was the first case she had that she found herself crying on. Her fingers went back to the keyboard with the determination to finish inputting her notes. The next thing she had to do was find someone in Dara's family to take care of her.

"Hey, it's quitting time," Vicia called out to her. She was about to pass by her office but backed up when she saw Casey wasn't budging. She shook her head as she always did. "You can't get involved in these cases. Honey, just do enough to earn a paycheck. That's what I do." She walked into the office. "If you allow yourself to be engrossed in every one of your cases, you'll be crazy. Don't let other people's problems consume you." Vicia placed her satchel on Casey's desk.

"It's not that I'm involved," Casey lied. "I just want to finish these notes while they're fresh on my mind." Vicia made it seem like a crime to show a little compassion and concern.

"Let's go have a drink," Vicia suggested. "You've had a hectic day and so have I."

Casey's fingers never left the keyboard. "Nah, I'll pass this time." She could hear Vicia smacking her lips in disbelief.

"I'm not taking no for an answer. You're so uptight. Besides, I'll treat." She could see Casey considering so she continued her sales pitch. "We won't be out long. It'll be fun."

Casey looked from the screen to Vicia. "Only if you promise me one thing."

Vicia smiled, pleased that Casey was about to see things her way. "Sure, you name it, and it's done."

"Lose the compact." Casey laughed.

The bar was crowded at the local night spot, Bennigan's. It was nicknamed Blackigan's because so many black people went there. Vicia refused to sit at a table and careened Casey to the bar. Apparently, this was her hangout because the bartenders all knew her by name and knew her favorite drink.

"What would you like?" The bartender slid a napkin and a glass of water in front of Casey.

Casey took the glass and placed a straw in it. "Water's fine."

Vicia pretended she was about to fall off her stool. "Girl, I said let's go have drinks. We could have had a glass of water at the job." She halted the bartender. "Nab, give her a glass of Frexienet."

"I'm not really a drinker," Casey protested. "I don't want something with a bad taste or anything that's too strong."

"Trust me," Vicia said with a wink. "You should like this."

Casey ventured to taste the drink. It wasn't as bad as she thought it would be. Actually, it was kind of nice. Casey watched as Vicia quickly guzzled two drinks.

"Stress relief." Vicia laughed as she held up her glass and swallowed.

Casey was starting to feel like a third wheel. It seemed as if she hadn't come with anyone. Vicia knew just about everybody who walked in. Vicia was busy flirting with the bartenders and conversing when she suddenly stopped midconversation. Casey followed Vicia's gaze to a man who was sitting on the other side of the bar.

"Now that's what I call good-looking." Vicia nudged Casey's arm. "Don't you agree?"

"He's okay." Casey gave a haphazard glance before sipping her drink.

"Girl, p-lease," Vicia said with intoxicated exaggeration. She threw her head back in a flirtatious gesture that was supposed to be directed toward the man on the other side of the bar. "He is fine." She immediately pulled out her compact and checked her makeup.

Casey glanced in the man's direction. He probably thought he was Mr. Important. He was attractive, but she wasn't about to fall in cahoots with Vicia. His brown eyes met hers briefly before she focused on her drink. She took a sip while watching him over the rim of her glass. Mr. Important was busy talking on his cell phone. He was likely to be talking to his wife or a girlfriend. Guys like him always had a woman nearby. She took a glance of everyone sitting at the circular bar. It was amazing that almost everyone had a cell phone. She chuckled to herself. Most of these people probably didn't even have their phones activated.

"He looks like he has a good job," Vicia whispered to Casey. "I bet he's a businessman."

Casey frowned. He was probably fronting. "Why do you say that? Just because he's wearing a suit doesn't mean he's a businessman. He could be coming from a funeral or anything."

"Nah, he probably owns the funeral home." Vicia giggled. She flagged down the bartender. "Send him another of what he's having and tell him it's on me."

"You're gonna get enough of that," the bartender said to Vicia. "That man is not interested in gold diggers." He laughed.

"How do you know what he's interested in?" Vicia asked. "Has he been here before?"

"Yeah, I've seen him before, but I don't know much about him," he said as he filled up the glass to take to the man.

"That's okay, I'll find out for myself. Go ahead and give it to him," Vicia urged.

The man looked in Casey's direction and smiled. Casey's eyes went to the bartender. She could feel the man looking her direction, watching her. She took another sip of her drink. His smile was rather inviting.

Casey watched as the bartender went over to the man with another drink. He looked up at Casey and smiled again. The bartender motioned toward Vicia, and the man made a declining motion with his hand and said a few words to the bartender. Shortly thereafter, he returned with a message for Vicia.

"He says he's at his limit for tonight, but thanks anyway," the bartender said with a smirk that might have ended in a laugh if he hadn't walked away so soon.

Vicia's nose immediately went up in the air. "Well, he wasn't my type anyway."

"Wait a minute. A few seconds ago, he was all that and now he's not your type." Casey laughed. It was hard to believe that Vicia had gotten shot down—dissed!

Vicia began to pout. "I guess he feels good about himself, since he's leaving." She idly swirled the straw around in her drink and mumbled something inaudible to Casey.

Casey couldn't believe what a sore loser Vicia was. She sat there pouting as if she had just lost her best friend. Her whole demeanor had changed because this man refused to give her the time of day. How could she let someone she didn't even know dictate her happiness? Was she really that shallow? With one glance at her slumping shoulders and drooping eyes, Casey surmised that she was. Shortly after Mr. Important left, the bartender went over to Casey and discreetly slid her a white napkin. He glanced at Vicia and laughed before going to wait on other customers. Vicia was too busy pouting to notice Casey unfold the napkin, which had Mr. Important's name and phone number neatly printed on it. Alfred was his name. *Alfred what? Why didn't he put his last name on it?* She folded the napkin and attempted to slide it into her pocket. Vicia's eagle eyes noticed the paper in her hand.

"What is that?" Vicia asked.

"What is what?" Casey pretended she didn't know what she was talking about. She slid off the stool and prepared to leave.

"What did he just give you?" Vicia nodded toward the bartender.

"A napkin." Vicia was starting to irritate her. Apparently she had one too many drinks. Casey attempted to step away from her seat, but Vicia made her flop back down again. Vicia pried the paper from Casey's fingers.

"Who is Alfred?" Vicia thought for a moment before her fingers snapped. "Oh, I get it. He wanted you and not me. Well, doesn't that beat all?"

"Look, it's not a big deal." She took the paper from Vicia. "See?" She crumbled it in her hand and threw it on the counter. "It's nothing. Let me call you a cab. You've had enough for one evening, and we've both got to get up in the morning."

Vicia reached under the bar and picked up her purse. Her accusing demeanor had somewhat diminished. "Yeah, you're right." She placed a hand on

Casey's shoulder. "Let's get out of here. I do have to get up early."

Vicia leaned on Casey as they left the restaurant. Casey was still kind of leery about letting Vicia drive home in her condition, but Vicia assured her that she would be all right. She even apologized for her behavior at the bar. Casey sat in her car until Vicia cranked up and drove off. Her conscience was eating at her so badly that she followed her a little way down the street until she was sure that Vicia could make it home.

When she saw that Vicia was all right she turned her car around. Her mind began to stray to Dara. She groaned in frustration. How could she keep her mind off her job? It was starting to get pretty pitiful that her life revolved around work.

Normally, she was used to a quiet atmosphere because she was alone most of the time, but at that moment, the silence was maddening. She turned on the radio to drown out all the silence. The station was playing songs for lovers on the Quiet Storm. For the first time in a long time, Casey felt a void in her heart. The singer was telling his lover how much he missed her and longed to feel her in his arms again. Her fingers went to the buttons to change the station, but for some reason, she couldn't change it. She wanted to listen to the words and find out what was so spectacular about love that people begged their lovers to come back or not to leave. She didn't get the point.

For years, she lived what she thought to be the ideal life. She had her mother and father, a nice home with a picket fence, and a dog she named Muffin. One night her father said he was going to the store, and never came back. It wasn't until her mother had gone to the bank to withdraw some money that she realized he had been planning to leave for some time. He left them penniless, with a mortgage to pay. Eventually, they had to give up their home and move into a one-room apartment. She couldn't count the number of times she woke up in the middle of the night to hear her mother sobbing. For years she watched her mother faithfully pull back the curtain every day and look out the window, hoping that her father would return. The thing that annoyed Casey the most was the fact that she knew her mother still loved him. There was no way she was going to give all of her love to someone only to have him slap her in the face. No, that wasn't the life she wanted for herself.

As she drove down her street, she wondered if she were ever to fall in love, what the man would look like. Ironically, the only face that came to mind was that of the man from the bar.

Two

Following her court appointment for Dara, Casey decided to leave work early and take a little time for herself. She could feel herself becoming stressed. She had never left work early in her four years of being employed at the agency. Liz wanted to know if she was feeling all right. After being assured that nothing was wrong, she told Casey to take all the time she needed. She didn't see Vicia in the office. She asked Liz if Vicia had called in. Liz told her that she had called in and said that she wasn't feeling well. Casey breathed a sigh of relief. At least Vicia made it home safely.

At first, Casey felt an overwhelming sense of guilt for leaving work with nothing in particular to do. She kept telling herself that there was nothing wrong with taking a little time off without having anything planned. When the holidays rolled around, she always volunteered to work because she had nothing to celebrate. When the calendar read skeleton crew for a holiday, everyone already knew Casey would be on that crew. It had gotten to the point where they stopped asking if she was going to be off. After a pep talk, her guilt was soon replaced with relief. She was going to the beauty shop to get her hair and nails done. She hopped in the car and caught a glimpse of her hair in the rearview mirror. She was also in need of a wash. Besides, she knew she would catch up on the latest gossip from Paul, her beautician and best friend. Her car whizzed in and out of traffic, as she tried to make it to her appointment on time.

Paul was waiting by the door when Casey arrived. He motioned to his watch when he saw her pull into a parking spot. As soon as she stepped inside, he led her to his chair. She couldn't believe that she didn't have to wait. He was usually so swamped with clients that she had to sit for at least forty minutes before he started on her hair.

"Girlfriend, I can't believe you're on time. Usually I have to find out if you're still coming or not," he said, as he ran his fingers through Casey's hair. He swiveled the chair around so he could get a better look at her hair. Scissors in hand, he began clipping away split ends. Most women considered him to be another man gone to waste. He was tall and handsome with eyes that matched his caramel skin. Heck, if he were straight, women would fight over him like dogs on a bone.

Casey sat in the chair while Paul, or Punkin, as he called himself, prepared to perform another hair masterpiece. He was the sole owner of the popular beauty shop, Dignified Divas. He was a hair guru—a hair master! Punkin was her best friend. She wouldn't trade him for the world. Although he was gay, he was like a true girlfriend. Punkin told everything the way it was, and he didn't bite his tongue on anything. It didn't matter if feelings were hurt or not—you were going to hear about yourself.

"Hey, I can't help it if my schedule is not my own most of the time." She watched him in the mirror as he snipped here and there.

"Did your coworker make it home all right?" he asked.

"I guess so. She called in this morning saying that she was sick. As much as she drank last night, I'm not surprised."

"And to think she got mad at you over a phone number. Honey, I think you better cut her loose." He made a cutting motion in the air with his scissors. "She sounds like she can't be trusted. Anybody who gets mad over a man they don't know has serious problems." He resumed trimming her hair. He deliberately combed a section of hair down in front of her face so he couldn't see her expression.

"I just think she had too much to drink." Casey didn't know why she was defending Vicia, because deep down inside, she knew that she irked her at times.

"Well, you know what they say. When people drink, it gives them courage to say things they wouldn't normally say. I'm sorry, I didn't get by this weekend. What did you end up doing?" He parted her hair to reveal her face. "Don't tell me you curled up with a good book."

Casey laughed as he let her hair fall back in her face. "No, I hung out for a little while Saturday night. You know, the usual."

Punkin smacked his lips. "We have got to add more spice to your life. What you need is a Mr. Goodbar." He directed her to the sink to wash her hair.

"I don't need a Mr. Goodbar. Too much candy will give you cavities." Casey closed her eyes as he massaged the shampoo into her scalp.

"Cavities! Honey, I guess I must be toothless 'cause ain't nothin' like a chocolate-covered—"

"Uh," Casey interrupted. She wasn't sure she wanted to know what the rest of that sentence was.

"I'm almost afraid to ask what you did this weekend." Punkin was massaging her scalp so well that she thought she would fall asleep.

"Everywhere I went there was a fight. Girl, there was more slappin' going on than that wrestling show, *Smack Down!* It was much better than watching pay-per-view."

Casey laughed. "You are too silly."

Punkin placed a wet finger to his chin thoughtfully. "Hmm, not silly. Maybe a little off at times, but never silly." He laughed.

"You are a complete riot."

"Well, you asked. And you know Punkin tells it like it is." He began rinsing the shampoo from her hair. He studied her face as he did so. She was too attractive to have shut men out of her life the way she had. Sometimes she was such a mystery to him. She laughed all the time, but the laughter didn't quite reach her eyes. She almost seemed as if she were the walking shell of a person. He'd find out what the mystery was soon enough.

"Don't I know it?" Casey asked.

"Yes, you do." He glanced at the clock on the wall. It was almost four. Pretty soon the nurse would be dropping off his sister, Rene. "You know Rene will be here at any moment, and you know what that means," Punkin said with wariness in his voice.

"Yes, I know only too well," Casey answered.

Rene was a handful. No one really knew why she fell off the deep end. The doctor said she had a nervous breakdown, and she hadn't been the same since. She went around having conversations with people who weren't really there. When she decided to have a conversation with someone real, they had no idea what she was talking about.

Punkin put a hand on his hip. "Do you know what

that heifer did last night?" He didn't wait for Casey to respond before he continued. "I was in bed sleeping and around three this morning, something told me to just open my eyes." He flashed his fingers in the air. "I guess it was the Spirit, child. But anyway, I opened my eyes and there Rene was standing over my bed with an open Bible in her hand."

Casey laughed. "What? What was she doing?"

"Girl, your guess is as good as mine. Anyway, there she was standing over me quoting scriptures." He shook his head.

"Why was she preaching?" Casey tried her best to keep a straight face, but Punkin was making it difficult.

"I don't know. I guess she was trying to perform an exorcism on me or something."

Casey couldn't stop the laughter from bubbling out. "Not the exorcist."

"Honey, if her head had started spinning I would have run straight through the wall. Then she started asking me if I knew who had her social security benefits."

"Her benefits? Where did she get that from?"

"She accuses everybody of stealing her social security. My hands are just full with her."

"I can't believe this. That might be why you're crazy now. She's probably been performing rituals on you every night, and you didn't know about it." Casey laughed.

"That might be why I turned left instead of right." He laughed. "Honey, ain't no telling about that girl. Sometimes I think she's just acting out to keep my feathers ruffled." He blew the subject off with the wave of his hand. "That's my sister though, and ain't no sister like the one I got."

Punkin always complained about something Rene

was doing, but he wouldn't trade her for the world. Casey envied the closeness of his family. She wouldn't have minded having that kind of relationship. Sometimes she wondered where her father was. Did he ever think about the lives he ruined? Maybe it was best that he left them. She and her mother got along just fine without him.

He didn't believe in horoscopes, but sometimes they were so accurate that it was scary. It was kind of weird since he was just reading yesterday's forecast that told him he would meet his soul mate. It also told him to seize the moment because opportunities come along only once in a lifetime.

He folded the paper and threw it aside. His soul mate. He thought his soul mate was his ex-wife, but apparently she didn't feel the same. His expression darkened as Kelly's face manifested in his mind. She was a lesson in life that he could have done without. He glanced at the framed picture that hung on the wall in his study. It had been three years since his divorce, and he had yet to take their wedding picture down. Well, there was no time like the present. He went to the wall and removed the picture. After looking at it one more time, he threw it in the trash can, frame and all.

After his divorce, he buried himself in his work. Kelly had married him for all of the wrong reasons—money being reason number one. He grimaced as he thought about how much of a fool he had been. The one thing he cherished from his marriage was his daughter, Christie. He had hoped they would have another child, but Kelly flat out refused to have more children. She said that she wasn't losing her figure just because he wanted another baby. In fact, the only reason she "gave" him a child in the first place was that *he* wanted one. Kelly insisted they hire someone to watch Christie because she wasn't going to be sitting around all day changing dirty diapers. She couldn't find time to change dirty diapers, but she had time to go on rendezvous with her lover. Alfred finally got fed up with her attitude. He ended up writing her a check to maintain her lifestyle and sent it with her divorce papers. The only thing he warned her about was if she tried to take him to court for "her share" he would fight her tooth and nail, and she would lose.

Three years had gone by, and he could count on one hand the number of times she had visited Christie. All of the encouragement in the world couldn't help Kelly be an active parent. The only time she came around was to show off some expensive gift she brought Christie from her most recent escapade. He hovered over the trash can staring at the remnants of his past. A picture could say a thousand words, but what about the words it didn't say? They were so happy then, or so he thought. Every time he glanced at the picture, he could see Kelly's face with an artificial smile staring back at him—mocking him.

Alfred vowed not to make the same mistake twice. Since he was single again, there were plenty of women who tried to stake a claim, but he wasn't having it. He had been proposed to twice and other women were trying to be Christie's fill-in stepmother. He had changed his home number several times because women were tracking him down and calling him. One woman went as far as pretending her car had broken down and that she needed to use his phone. Such trickery. Well, he wasn't going to fall into that trap again. The next woman he met would have to love him for who he was and not for what he could provide. More importantly, she would have to love his daughter as if she were her own.

That's why he couldn't understand what he had done the other night. He thought about the woman from the bar. She seemed out of place sitting there with a drink in front of her. Her heart-shaped face was framed by long tresses, which bounced with every move she made. Her brown skin was smooth, as if she wore no makeup. She was totally different from her friend, who happened to be a little on the loud side, sort of like Kelly. He couldn't count the number of times she had to check her face in the mirror. Her hair was so stiff that a hurricane probably wouldn't move it. And then when she offered to buy him a drink, he was compelled to decline. He wasn't inviting any more Kellys into his life.

He sat behind his desk and turned on his laptop. His fingers grazed the keys, but it was hopeless. Work, work, work. That's all his life amounted to lately. He felt guilty for not being able to spend more time with Christie. He was the only person she had, and lately he'd been so busy that he hadn't spent as much time with her as he would have liked. He'd have to think of a way to make it up to her. He pushed himself away from his desk. The study seemed to be closing in on him, and he had to get some fresh air. The fragrant smell of apple pie drew him toward the kitchen. But the jingle of the keys in his pocket prompted a quick change of his mind.

"I'm stepping out for a minute," he called out to his housekeeper before walking out the door. He didn't know where he was going, but he did know that he wanted to get out of that house. Anything was better than focusing on the loneliness that had just popped out of nowhere.

Three

When she got home, she took off the pumps that were killing her feet and wiggled her toes to get the blood circulating. She turned on the television to catch up on the news. Why did it have to be so depressing? The news anchors had a habit of announcing some dreadful situation and would then break out with a smile and say, "And now for the weather." There were bits and pieces of information about a possible serial killer running loose in the Houston area. His style was wooing single women, then attacking them once he got to know them. In all of his victims' homes, the police found cream-colored cards with matching envelopes. They were all cards that expressed how much the killer cared for the victims. The media dubbed him the "Calling Card Killer." That was the last thing she wanted to hear. To know that some psycho was running around town killing people was very disturbing.

Looking at all of the news on television reminded her of Dara. She hoped she could get her placed with a family member. She changed into a comfortable pair of jeans and a shirt. It made no sense to take off from work early and not enjoy every moment of it. She stuck her feet into a pair of slides to show off her fresh pedicure.

She had a craving for something Italian. Though she didn't like going downtown, she didn't mind going to Josephine's for fresh Italian cuisine. Thirty minutes later, she found a parking spot directly across from the restaurant. She was pleased to see that the umbrella-covered patio tables were still out on the sidewalk. The smell of food met her as soon as she stepped out of the car. It had been about four years since she had been to Josephine's, around the same time she started working for the state.

The restaurant was getting crowded so she walked briskly in order to save a patio table for herself. She didn't know why she took a menu since she always ordered the same thing. Still, she scanned the menu and ordered the usual, shrimp primavera over angel hair pasta. Though it was a warm evening, there was a breeze that kept her cool. Dusk was upon them, and the waiters busied themselves lighting candles at every table. Casey glanced around and saw couples at almost every table. Lucky for her, she brought along a good book to read. After propping her feet up in an empty chair across from her, she flipped the book open and waited for her order.

Several pages later, the waiter brought her dinner. It was almost a tragedy to have to eat something that was so beautifully garnished. It was like eating a masterpiece. She should have invited Punkin to join her, but knowing him, he had other plans. She was used to dining alone. Her eyes closed as she savored her meal.

Alfred casually strolled down the sidewalk, heading to his favorite restaurant. Hopefully he'd have somewhere to sit or else he would have to order something to go. He paused to open the door for an elderly couple when he spotted the woman from Bennigan's sitting alone. His horoscope had been wrong—as usual. Opportunity did knock more than once in a lifetime. Part of him felt rejected because she hadn't called him, and the other part told him to put his phone number in her hand.

He closed the door and headed up the opposite end of the sidewalk. He wondered what he was doing. Why was getting to know this woman so important to him? What about the vow he made to himself and to his daughter? He had to think of his daughter's happiness. He paced in front of his car, keeping an eye on the patio. His feet stopped moving as he noticed the way her head tilted to the side as she read a book. From what he could remember, the soft features of her face could soothe the savage beast. Every move she made was totally feminine and graceful. She had barely glanced in his direction the previous night. Going over to her would be a mistake.

He headed back to the restaurant with every intention of going inside, but one glance in her direction, and all plans were off. His feet moved of their own accord. The next thing he knew, he was standing at her table.

"I hope I'm not interrupting." He noticed the surprise in her eyes. For a moment, he felt she was going to tell him to get lost. "Is there a dish that you'd recommend?" *My approach is getting a little rusty.*

Her private world had been shattered by the sound of the commanding voice over her. She looked up to see a face wearing a familiar striking smile. It was a face that she thought she'd never run across again. How ironic that she would bump into Mr. Important again. Only this time, he wasn't wearing the crisp suit. More than likely, he was another one of those bad brothers in a pretty package. He was probably just as smooth talking as he looked. She quickly assessed from the sleeveless pullover vest he wore with no shirt underneath that he was confident in his looks. Khaki walking shorts and a leather belt, which perfectly matched the Cole Haan shoes he wore, suggested that he invested a lot in himself. He probably spent more time in the mirror than she did. She didn't have time for that. He was just the opposite of what she wanted or needed in her life.

She dabbed her mouth with her napkin. Suddenly, she was self-conscious about the clothes she had thrown on in haste. Her tongue grazed her teeth to make sure there wasn't anything in them.

"I'm having the shrimp primavera. The lasagna tastes pretty good too. I guess it depends on what you're in the mood for."

He nodded toward the chair in which she had her feet propped. "Are you waiting for someone? I don't want to intrude."

"No, I'm just relaxing." She hoped he wasn't about to ask to have a seat. She didn't know if she could endure one of those I, me, and my conversations. Everybody talked about what they had or what they were and then you got to know them and none of it was exactly as they said.

"Do you mind if I join you?" He glanced at the packed restaurant. "I might have a long wait for a table. Besides, it's not fun eating alone."

"Actually . . ." She hesitated. He did make a valid point. It wasn't fun eating alone. She chose not to follow her first mind. "I don't mind at all. Have a seat." She removed her feet from the chair.

"Thanks." He was relieved that she allowed him to sit down. He hadn't been on the dating scene in a while, and he wasn't sure if his approach was still what it used to be. *Guess I've still got it!*

"I would shake your hand," he said, nodding toward her plate, "but I can see you're busy. Anyway, my name is Alfred."

"I'm Casey." She noticed the small look of triumph on his face. He could have a seat, but there was no need for him to get too comfortable. She closed her book and placed it underneath her purse.

As soon as he walked up to the table, the waiter was there in a flash. He hadn't opened his mouth or motioned for attention, but the waiter brought out a bottle of wine and poured it for him.

"Will the lady be drinking?" the waiter asked.

"Yes," he answered.

"I'll be back with your dinner, sir." The waiter disappeared.

Alfred noticed the suspicious look on Casey's face. "As you've probably guessed, I dine here often."

"I see," Casey said, drily. She had just met the man and already he was deceiving her.

He didn't know if the way she responded was good. She had probably labeled him as a liar. Under any other circumstances, he wouldn't care what anyone thought of him, but there was something different about her. He didn't know what that difference was, but he was more than willing to find out.

"You can't blame a man for wanting to dine with a lovely lady, can you?" He smiled.

She shrugged. "I wouldn't know about that. I'm not a man," she said with an edge of iciness in her tone. She hoped that her cold shoulder would freeze that smile right off his face. Instead, she heard a hearty laugh.

"She has a sense of humor as well," he said softly. "I saw you when I got here, and I wanted to meet you. It's that simple." He watched her face for a change of expression. He quickly assessed that she was definitely the kind of woman who didn't take kindly to deception, even if there were good intentions behind it.

"If you say so," she replied nonchalantly. *He probably uses that line all of the time. Who does he think he's fooling?*

He allowed himself to relax in the chair. "Correct me if I'm wrong, but I think I saw you last night at Bennigan's."

"Yes, I was there with my coworker." She busied herself swirling pasta around her fork to keep from gazing into his eyes, which seemed as if they could see straight to her soul. She could feel them on her face and hands. She didn't know where it was coming from, but suddenly she was nervous.

"I left my number for you. Did the bartender give it to you?"

"Yes," she answered.

He took a sip from his glass as he weighed her answer. He wanted to know why she hadn't called, but he didn't want to look as though he was starving for attention. The waiter appeared with his order and asked Casey if she needed anything. When she refused, the waiter disappeared.

"The primavera is my favorite too," Alfred confessed.

Casey shook her head. She knew he was a smooth talker when she saw him. He could probably talk some women right out of their clothes, but not her. She was too sharp for that. As much as her nerves were bundling inside her, she remained cool on the outside. Thanks to her job, she was able to mask her feelings well. "Tell me something, Alfred."

"What would you like to know?" he asked between bites.

"Do you invite yourself to dinner like this all of the time?"

His laugh was so rich that it was almost contagious. "Quite contrary to what you might believe, I've never done this before."

Somehow, she believed he was telling the truth.

The next thing Casey knew, it was three hours later, and she found Alfred to be one of the most charming men she had ever met. This, in and of itself, was enough to throw her off balance. The egotistical man that she expected to see turned out to be a down-to-earth kind of guy.

When the check came, Alfred insisted on paying for her dinner.

"I couldn't let you do that," Casey protested.

"No, I want to," Alfred said. "Besides, you've given me something tonight."

"What's that?"

"Good company and a very engaging conversation." He smiled. "I haven't had that in a long time. Thank you." Not even his ex-wife had given him an engaging conversation. She could only talk about the latest gossip and what was in style for the season. It was a pleasant change, not discussing his job or things along those lines. This woman was pleasingly different from any woman he had ever met.

If he was trying to make her blush, he was doing a good job. "Ditto," she answered.

"Thanks again for allowing me to dine with you," Alfred said as he waited for Casey to get into her car. He already knew he wanted to see her again.

"Thanks for dinner." Casey smiled. She watched his fingers trace his neatly trimmed goatee.

"Why don't we do this again sometime?" He stuffed his hands into his pockets, nervously jingling the keys.

"I'm not sure when I'll be free again." She wanted to say yes, but knew she wasn't ready to open up to anyone. She still had a lot of things to deal with and inviting potential problems into her life wasn't the smart thing to do.

"Can I call you?" he asked.

Remember, he's the opposite of what you want or need in your life. You're asking for trouble down the road. Don't fool yourself, girlfriend! Remember how your mother suffered. Her fingers gripped the steering wheel tightly.

"I had a wonderful time, but I don't think so. It's nothing personal. I just don't make it a habit to give my number to every man I meet." She forced herself to look into his face so that he would believe her.

"Not even to one who you've shared a lovely dinner with?" Her silence answered his question. He stared at her for a moment before saying anything. "Are you sure you won't reconsider?"

"I can't." Her words were soft with a hint of regret.

His eyes lowered in defeat. He wasn't going to be reduced to begging this woman for her phone number. Things happened for a reason. Maybe he saw her again because he was feeling down, and she came along just to lift his spirits. Maybe he did the same for her. He couldn't ask for more.

"Very well then." He stood to his full height and stepped back from the car so he could see her face. "I really enjoyed talking with you."

"Likewise." She put her car in gear and gave him a little wave before driving away.

He watched as her car turned at the intersection. How many times was this woman going to pass him by? He hoped this was the last. He had known her for less than twenty-four hours and already it seemed as if she were leaving with a piece of him. How could that be?

Four

"And just what happened to you last night, Ms. Thing?" Punkin asked. "I called you twice, and you weren't home. Don't tell me somebody has gotten herself a life." He laughed.

"I've always had a life." Talking to Punkin always put a smile on her face. "It's just not as colorful as yours."

"Whaat-eva!" he drawled. "So, I'm curious, where were you?"

"You act like I can't make a move without you." She laughed. "But if you must know, I went to Josephine's for dinner."

She went to the bookshelf and pulled Dara's file and began punching holes in correspondence relating to her case.

Punkin gasped as if he couldn't believe she went to Josephine's without him. "How are you just going to burn off to Josephine's and not even bother to ask if I wanted to go? I mean really." He paused for a dramatic affect. "Just leave Punkin, why don't you? I hope you had a good time. You know I love that place, but Punkin does not care."

She never understood why he sometimes referred to himself in the third person. In that way, he kind of reminded her of her father. He would always wait until he was under the influence of alcohol and say, "You know your daddy sho' loves you. He cares about you a lot." That was when he was her *daddy* and not just her biological father.

"I thought about you." She laughed. "But I did enjoy my meal. Do you remember me telling you about the guy who sent his number to me at Bennigan's?" She noticed the red message light come on. Someone had called while she was on the phone yapping with Punkin. The day had officially started.

"The one you called Mr. Important?" Punkin asked.

"Yep, he's the one. Anyway, I ended up seeing him at Josephine's last night, and we had a nice conversation."

Punkin thought his heart was about to stop. Did she actually say that she entertained male conversation last night? He stuck a finger in his ear and wiggled it around to make sure he was hearing correctly.

"There is a God!" he sang. "Hallelujah! Casey was getting her mack on. So when is the official date?" he asked with excitement. Maybe she wouldn't end up a nun after all.

"Well, we had a wonderful conversation. He seemed like a nice guy, but I wouldn't give him my number."

Punkin's eyes scanned the beauty shop. He could have sworn he heard that horrifying music that played whenever a monster was about to attack someone. "But you did get his number, right?"

"No, I told him I wasn't interested right now."

"Aughhh!" Punkin squawked. The ugly monster had sprung from the closet. "You did what? You might as well start working for Blue Bell because you are definitely one Popsicle if I ever saw one."

"I am no such thing," she rebutted. "I just don't have time for—"

Punkin cut her off. He had heard enough of her

excuses. "Yeah, yeah, I know. You don't have time for a relationship. You're not the one to play games. Well, sometimes games are fun, as long as you know how to play by the rules." His tongue clucked in a condescending manner. "Girlfriend, I'll holler at you later. My first client has walked through the door."

"All right then, I'll talk to you later." She hung up the phone. Punkin just didn't understand her. She wasn't willing to trust her heart to just anybody.

The message on her voice mail was from Mrs. Fletcher, one of her foster mothers, and it just about made her morning. She was willing to care for Dara until more information was known about her family. A search on Dara's parents revealed no previous history with Social Services. The officer working on the case promised to get back to Casey if any new details popped up. Hopefully, she would know more about Dara as the day wore on. She would deal with that later. Right now, she had to get Dara out of that emergency shelter.

Dara ran to meet her as soon as she walked in the door. She held on to Casey as if for dear life. Casey gave her a tight hug.

"I don't want to be here anymore," she wailed.

"I know, Dara. I'm going to take you to a nice lady, and she'll make sure you're all right."

She told Dara to wait for her until she finished some paperwork and then they would leave. After checking her out of the shelter, Casey took Dara to her car and told her about Mrs. Fletcher. When they arrived at the foster home, Mrs. Fletcher immediately fell in love with Dara. There was no doubt in Casey's mind that Dara was in good hands. Casey thought her heart would shatter into a million pieces as Dara begged her not to leave. She kept her composure long enough to make it to her car.

By the time she got back to her office, her head was throbbing. She had been on this case but a few days, and she was already losing sleep. How could she sleep knowing that the only thing that Dara could call her own was the teddy bear Casey had given her?

The court appointed Brenna Jennings as a child advocate for Dara. Casey had worked with Brenna before, and she was a wonderful worker. Brenna was a compassionate woman who would do everything in her power to help Casey get to the bottom of the case and make sure that Dara was taken care of. Knowing this helped ease some of the tension Casey was feeling.

Casey was skeptical about answering the phone because every other call was from a reporter trying to get inside information on Dara's story. When the phone rang again, she was expecting another reporter, but it was Brenna.

"I think I've got something you can use," Brenna said in an excited tone.

Casey could hear paper shuffling on the other end of the line. She grabbed the nearest pencil and pad and readied herself for the information. "I sure hope it's news I can use. What have you got?"

"Are you ready for this?" Brenna sounded like a game show host. Sometimes Casey found it hard to keep up with her. "You won't believe what I had to go through to get this information. I mean I had the hardest time and had to pull all kinds of strings to get it so fast."

Casey listened to Brenna ramble on and on. She didn't want to be rude so she forced herself to endure the whole shebang about how good it was to know people in all the right places.

Her pencil drummed on her desk. Casey listened

as Brenna recalled another case in which she had to use her friends in high places to find out information. After ten minutes of unnecessary information, Brenna finally got to the point.

"We've got somebody, and I think you're gonna love this." She giggled.

"What?" The lead of Casey's pencil rested on the notepad.

"I think I've found an uncle. All I know is his first initial, which is A, and his last name, Willingham. I've got the phone number and address."

Casey was ecstatic. Half of the battle was won. Now all she needed to do was win the war. She eagerly took down the information and tried to decide whether to call Mr. Willingham or to drop by his house.

Forty minutes later, she found herself driving down a winding street. She checked her directions to make sure she was going the right way. Had she known her drive was going to take more than forty minutes, she would have made a phone call instead. Cows were grazing in fields on either side of the road.

"If I had known I was going out to the country, I would have stayed at the office," she griped to herself and pulled the sun visor down to block out the bright sunlight. Even with the AC blowing, it was still hot. All she needed was to get hot and sticky and then have to get out of the car at some dusty farm with cows and chickens.

She sure hoped Dara's uncle wasn't some spittoon-spitting hillbilly who hadn't the slightest clue as to how to take care of her. "Please don't let this be a waste of time," she prayed.

Suddenly, a high white brick wall replaced the barbed-wire fence that kept the cows away from the street. She found herself becoming annoyed by the massive structure because she couldn't see what was on the other side. Finally, she spotted the brass numbers on the wall. She glanced at the address she had scribbled on her notepad to make sure she was at the right place.

After several cars passed by, she steered into the driveway, which matched the brick wall. There was a massive gate at the entrance. She let down her window to press the button on the call box. Before her fingers could touch the button, the gate began to swing open. She put her car in gear and inched through the gate. The brick driveway was lined with tall trees on either side. This was a far cry from the farm she was imagining.

She tried to suppress the glimmer of hope that was about to arise, because she didn't want to be disappointed if Dara's uncle couldn't or wouldn't take care of her. Whoever Dara's uncle was, he loved being isolated. Casey couldn't see a thing for all of the trees everywhere. Her breath caught in her throat when she finally came to the clearing. She wasn't aware of stopping her car and gazing at the immaculate home that was before her.

The only place she had seen a house like this was on television. She loved everything from the pure white brick to the arched windows, pillars, and stone lions that guarded the entrance to the double doors with Tiffany-stained windows. Not many things impressed her, but this was one that did. She parked her car in the circular drive and headed toward the main entrance.

Alfred stood at the base of the stairs, calling for Christie. This would be the only day of the week that he could spend some quality time with her. He promised to take her to Moody Gardens in Galveston to check out the aquarium and to ride the latest I-Max ride.

"I'll be there in a minute, Dad," Christie yelled from upstairs.

That meant another twenty minutes. Women! He never knew what took them so long to get dressed, but he always liked the results. His daughter was no exception. He sat on the bottom step and waited for Christie. This was going to be the best part of his day. He woke up with a bad attitude and didn't want to admit that it was because of a bruised ego. A brush-off was something he hadn't experienced in a long time. Thanks to Casey, he'd been caught up to speed. He spent the night reliving every word she said to him. It didn't take long for him to grow fond of the way she smiled and the melodic sound of her voice. *Oh, well, I may as well get over it. She's gone for good.* Eventually, he might have found out that she was like all the others, but somehow he doubted that.

"I'm ready, Daddy." Christie bounded down the stairs taking two at a time.

"How many times have I asked you not to run down the stairs like that?" Alfred chided. The last thing he wanted was for her to fall down those stairs and hurt herself or worse.

"Sorry." She grabbed his hand and pulled him to the door.

"Just don't do it again," Alfred said softly. How could he stay angry with her? She was the apple of his eye.

"Oh, I forgot my sandals. I'll be right back." She ran back to the stairs.

"Uhh!" he groaned. "I'll be outside." Alfred called after her.

He opened the door to see a woman standing in front of his house looking around. She was leaning over smelling the roses. She moved from the roses to the azaleas, touching other plants along the way. He softly closed the door and stood on the steps watching her in silence. He'd know that woman anywhere, but the question was, what was she doing at his house? He chewed his bottom lip as she leaned down to pick up an azalea that had broken off and fallen to the ground. She began twirling it around in her fingers.

He moved to the garden, where she still had her back turned to him. "You wouldn't happen to be stealing any of those flowers, would you?"

Startled, she dropped the flower as she spun to face him. "I, uh, what are you doing here?"

"Since I live here, I might ask you the same question." He hoped she wasn't another one of those women who resorted to dire tactics to get next to him. Things were starting to seem pretty strange, especially since she gave him the brush-off the night before.

She picked up the flower and passed it to him. "I shouldn't have taken my time about coming to the door. It's just that I've never seen a garden so beautiful."

He stood there looking at the flower, spinning it between two fingers. It was funny how he never really noticed the vibrant colors of every flower in the garden, until now. It was as if a veil had been lifted off his eyes, and he was seeing it all for the first time. Why hadn't he noticed it before? Without saying anything, he stepped closer to her and tucked the flower behind her right ear.

Her fingers went to her ear, touching the flower he had just placed there. When her eyes met his piercing gaze, she struggled to say something. There was a giddy feeling that rested in her chest. There was a warmth that washed all over her from head to toe, and she didn't know where it was coming from, but she did know it was because of this man she had been trying to forget. The only thing that came to her defense was her reason for being there. Suddenly, she pulled out a business card and handed it to him. She immediately thought about the Chinese throwing stars and immediately wished she hadn't done that.

He scanned the card, and confusion began to show on his face. What in the world did Social Services want with him? He knew he hadn't been spending much time with Christie, but he never abused or neglected her.

"I don't understand." He moved back a couple of steps. *God, am I such a bad father that someone reported me to Social Services?* His mood began to darken as anger set in. "I know Kelly is behind all of this." He crumpled up the business card. "You tell her that if she's out of money that's just too bad and don't try to get my daughter because it will never happen. Of all the treacherous things," he muttered.

"Wait, I'm not here for you," Casey said. "Well, I am here for you, but not like you think," she explained. There was a loud slam of the front door as Christie bounded down the steps.

"Daa-dee, I'm ready," Christie sang out as she ran over to Alfred.

"Christie, go back into the house. I'll come get you when I'm ready." Christie was about to complain until she noticed the stern look on her father's face. Kelly was going too far. She didn't care about Christie. All she was concerned about was money. He quickly turned back to Casey. He took a couple of deep breaths to calm himself. "Exactly what is this about?"

"This is concerning your brother, Aldrich, and his wife, Layla." From her tone, she was sure Alfred would be able to tell that she was about to lay some dreadful information on him.

She watched as his countenance changed from upset to perplexed. "What about my brother?" His voice was soft.

Casey couldn't answer him fast enough before he asked her again in a stronger tone. "I'm sorry to have to tell you this, but your brother and his family were involved in a fatal accident."

He turned a pale gray. She thought she was looking at a ghost. She held his forearm firmly. "Are you okay?" she asked.

He removed his arm from her grasp and stepped away. "What—how did this happen?"

Casey didn't like being the bearer of bad news, but she often found herself the one who dropped the bomb on people. "Your brother, his wife, and their daughter, Dara, were on their way to Houston from an out-of-town trip when they had a head-on collision with another vehicle." She could hear him suck in a deep breath.

He turned his back to her. "Did they all—" His voice broke. "Did anyone survive?"

She stood facing his back, not knowing what to do. She gently touched his shoulder. "That's why I'm here. Your niece is the only one who survived." She tried to get him to face her but he kept looking away. "We want to know if you know of any family members who might be willing to care for Dara. If not, then we'll have to look into adoption."

He stood with his palms opening and closing into tight fists. "She's family, and she belongs here with us." He stared up at the sky. "If only my brother would have put our differences aside. It's too late," he mumbled in exasperation. "My niece belongs here."

"Does Layla have any family that you know of?"

She waited for him to answer. The man had already received some horrible news. There was no need to bombard him with questions and rush him to answer.

"Last I heard, her mother and father were living in Los Angeles. I'll get their number for you. I'll be right back."

Casey watched his retreating figure. A few moments later an older woman came out and gave her a number neatly printed on a piece of paper.

"He's taking this a bit rough," the woman said. "I'm sure you understand. He did say that he wanted his niece here with him."

"Well, tell him I'll be in touch."

This man seemed as though he had a lot of problems. First, an ex-wife and now his estranged relationship with his brother. Did he not have a healthy relationship with anyone? Maybe she did the right thing by not getting to know him better.

Five

There were times when Casey thought she didn't make a difference in the lives of the kids she served, but Dara's case was different. Hopefully, she was going to be placed with a family member who cared about her and would see that she was well taken care of. That still didn't supersede the fact that Dara's parents were no longer with her. Alfred planned to have a memorial service for her parents on Saturday. If Casey found out the details of the service, she would probably go to support Dara and to see how well she interacted with her uncle.

Casey checked her watch to make sure she wasn't running late for her appointment with Ms. Green at Big Brothers and Sisters. She was cutting it kind of close, but traffic was running pretty smoothly for the morning rush. She wondered how Alfred was adjusting to having to care for two girls instead of one. Apparently his relationship with his ex-wife was a strained one. He seemed pretty adamant about her not getting their daughter. She found herself wondering why they divorced. Was it his fault or hers? Maybe his ex got fed up with something he had done and left. But how did he end up with his daughter? Chances were that money dictated who the better parent would be.

Ms. Green smiled as Casey entered her office. "You haven't changed your mind on me, have you? I've been trying to get you back in the office for some time now."

Casey chuckled. "No, I've been busy working on some things. I've made a commitment, and I plan to stick by it."

"Great," Ms. Green said as she opened a manila folder. "I think we've found the perfect match for you. As a matter of fact, she should be arriving in a few minutes. I didn't think she would be able to make it today because her family has had some extenuating circumstances in the past few days."

"I see." Casey said. "How old is she?" She hoped her little sister liked her and that they could finalize everything today.

"She's nine years old."

"Nine," Casey said. "What do nine-year-old little girls like?"

Ms. Green noticed Casey's look of apprehension. "Don't worry. You two will do just fine. She'll tell you what she likes."

"I just want us to get along well," Casey said.

"You will, you'll see." Ms. Green glanced at the door. "Oh, here she is now." She stood to greet them.

Casey turned to see a familiar face standing in the doorway. She couldn't hide her surprise.

"Thanks for bringing her, Mrs. Lincoln. This is Casey James, the big sister I was telling you about." She turned to Casey. "Casey, this is Christie Willingham."

"It's nice meeting you," Casey said to Christie and Mrs. Lincoln. "Are you Christie's grandmother?"

Mrs. Lincoln smiled softly. "No, but I feel like she's one of my own grandchildren. I work for Mr. Willingham, but Christie calls me Aunt Maggie."

"I know you," Christie said with a smile. "You were talking to my daddy."

Casey smiled. "Oh, I see you remember me. You think we'll have fun together?"

"Yes, I think so," she said coyly.

After almost an hour of talking and going over paperwork, Casey was officially Christie's big sister for one year. She should have been happy about it, but she knew her supervisor would make her drop the program if she found out. She planned to tell Liz about it, but not just yet.

Alfred was happy his flight from Dallas returned early. This would allow him to finalize the arrangements for his brother and sister-in-law. He still couldn't believe Aldrich and Layla were gone. Then he thought of his niece having to endure such a loss and having to live with strangers in the meantime. Yet, somehow, he knew she was in good hands. Casey wouldn't let anything happen to her. Why did he feel that he could trust Casey? What he liked most about her was that she seemed genuine in her efforts to help Dara. *You're just fooling yourself. She's just doing her job. It has nothing to do with her caring anything about you or your family.*

Aunt Maggie told him about Christie being a bit lonely since his work required him to be away most of the time. He planned to cut his schedule the first chance he got. When Aunt Maggie first mentioned the Big Sister program to him, he was dead set against it. The only reason he changed his mind was that Christie seemed excited about joining. As soon as his schedule permitted, she was getting out of that program. Besides, when Dara came to stay with them, Christie wouldn't be as lonely. If only Christie's mother were concerned about her, there would be no need for Christie to have a big sister.

He parked his car in the garage and entered the house through the side entrance. Aunt Maggie was busy preparing dinner when he stopped by the kitchen to retrieve a bottle of water.

"Hi, Aunt Maggie. Where's Christie?" he asked.

Aunt Maggie placed the top on a pot before answering him. "She's in her room. Do you want me to get her for you?"

Alfred opened the water and took a swallow. "That's okay. How did the Big Sister thing go?"

"It went well. She said something about knowing the woman who's going to be her big sister. Her name is Casey James."

Alfred's expression went blank. This woman was definitely up to something, and he didn't know what it was, but he didn't believe in having this many coincidences. Life just wasn't that strange. He had quickly forgotten her concern for Dara. She would help him get custody of Dara, and that was it.

"I don't want Ms. James as Christie's big sister. Call them tomorrow and ask them to change it."

"Why not? Christie really seems to like Ms. James."

"I'll talk to Christie." Alfred purposefully headed upstairs to Christie's room. He found her watching television.

"Christie, I'm going to see if Ms. Green can find you another big sister."

Her eyes widened. "Why would I want another big sister? I like Casey."

"Well, I'm sure they'll give you someone else you like."

"I might as well quit." Christie pouted. "Why do you want to change my big sister? She promised to take me to Six Flags, and I wanna go."

"I can take you to Six Flags." Alfred had no idea she would be this adamant.

"But it's mother-daughter day, and you can't take me. Aunt Maggie is too old to be my mom." She clicked off the television. "You already know my *real* mother won't take me."

Alfred stood with his mouth clamped shut. He finally broke the silence. "If it means that much to you, then fine." He closed the door behind him as he left her room.

Casey James had better not let his daughter down, because if she did, she would have to deal with him.

Six

Casey went to visit Dara at Mrs. Fletcher's home. She was running around playing with a new puppy she had received. Casey informed Mrs. Fletcher of the services planned for Dara's parents on the coming weekend. Mrs. Fletcher promised to take Casey to the services once she received all of the details. Dara was so busy playing that she didn't notice Casey ease out.

Mrs. Fletcher lived in the same subdivision as Casey's mother. A smile played on her lips when she thought of her mother. Finally, her mother was happy. After her father ran out and left her to struggle on her own, she went to college and earned a degree in accounting, graduating when she was forty-eight years old. Now her mother had time to visit places she never had the opportunity to go.

Casey opened her appointment book and noticed a red circle on the calendar. She had to pick her mother up from the airport that evening. She had gone on a cruise with her best friend, Ressie. It was a good thing Casey had checked her appointment book because she had completely forgotten about it.

After making a quarterly visit to one of her clients who lived near the airport, Casey decided to go and wait for her mother's flight. She bought a couple of magazines from the bookstore near the gate where she had to pick up her mother.

She sat in the waiting area, thumbing through the pages of one of the magazines. She was deep into an article when the doors opened and the passengers on her mother's flight began filing out.

She watched as the passengers poured into the terminal. Several of them were carrying laptops. She chuckled to herself; they probably hadn't typed a thing on those computers. Some people liked packing them just to make others think they were important. She moved closer to the door so that her mother could see her when she came out.

She could hear her mother and Aunt Ressie cackling before she saw them. Her mother ran up to her as if she hadn't seen her in years. She gave her a big hug, and they headed to baggage claim.

On the way to drop off Aunt Ressie, her mother told her about all of the places they had visited and what kind of food they had. She convinced Casey to spend the night since the next day was Saturday.

"You know, you work too hard," her mother told her at the dinner table. "Not that there's anything wrong with hard work. When do you plan on taking a vacation?"

Casey shrugged. "I don't know. I've never thought about it."

Her mother sat there looking down her nose at her the way she always did when she was about to scold her. "That's just pitiful. You're too young for this. And when do you plan to settle down and give me some grandkids? You're not getting any younger. What are you waiting around on? A man is not going to fall on your doorstep."

Casey pushed away from the table and put their plates in the dishwasher. "Mom, I've already told you,

I'm not getting married. You can still have grandkids. I'll adopt." She started the dishwasher and returned to the table with a dish towel.

"Look at this nonsense you're talking. You like to pretend like you don't need companionship. Should Mr. Right come along, don't pass him up because you're afraid."

"I'm not afraid of anything," she denied. She began wiping off the table.

"Then why haven't you brought anyone by for me to meet? I can't believe that you haven't had anyone interested in you." She took the dish towel from her daughter's hand and motioned for her to sit.

Casey groaned. She should have known her mother was going to start grilling her about not having anyone in her life. "Mom, why is it so hard for you to understand that I don't want all of the complications that come with a relationship? I'm happy by myself."

"Girl, life is complicated," her mother snapped. "You might think you're happy, but you don't see what I see when I look at you. You could be a heck of a lot happier."

"I'm not getting into any relationship just to be deserted. That's not happening to me twice in my lifetime."

Her mother leaned back in her chair with a new understanding. "Oh, so that's what this is about. Not every man in the world is like you think your father was. Don't deny yourself happiness based on what your father and I went through. Let go of the baggage, or you'll never live." She pushed away from the table and stood. "I'm going to bed. Jet lag is starting to set in. I'll talk to you in the morning."

Casey couldn't help thinking that her life was missing something. Was that something she lacked love? How could she have let the thought enter her mind?

Her mother loved her and supported her in all of her decisions. Wasn't that enough? She sure hoped so. The thing that unsettled her the most was that she never second-guessed her happiness. She could honestly say that she was content—until she met Alfred. The feeling she got whenever she was in his presence was enough to make her question that happiness.

He stared at the phone ten minutes before deciding to pick it up and make the phone call. After Christie's outburst earlier that evening, he felt he had to do something. If Kelly had an ounce of love for their daughter, she would do this one thing for her. If she agreed to take Christie to the mother-daughter day at Six Flags, then he could possibly take Christie out of the program all together.

The phone rang three times before she answered. He explained the significance of the mother-daughter day to Kelly and how much it would mean if Kelly would take her.

"You would make her one happy girl," Alfred said. He felt he had to make a sales pitch just to get her to do something with her own child.

"Would that make her daddy happy too?" Kelly asked.

"Yes." Alfred bit his tongue so hard he thought it would bleed.

"Tell her that I'll be there to pick her up next Saturday. And I'll see you to," she drawled. "After all, I've got to get something out of the deal, and it might as well be you."

"Good-bye, Kelly." Alfred clicked the phone off. She was really starting to irk his nerves. Would she ever change?

Alfred couldn't believe she was the same woman he married. He couldn't resist the urge to go outside and get a breath of fresh air. He left the study and headed down the darkened hall to the front door. After sucking in a deep breath of air, he focused on the garden he never really noticed until the other day. It was amazing how people didn't take the time to appreciate the things most important to them. He cringed when he thought about how little time he'd been spending with Christie. After receiving the news of his brother's death, he canceled their trip to Moody Gardens. He kept promising that he would make it up to her. How many times had he told her that he would make it up to her? The only reason he wouldn't be out of town the next day was his brother's funeral. If it weren't for that, he would be with Christie. Not wanting to think about it, he sat on the steps, gazing up at the stars.

Though he wasn't willing for them to go there, his thoughts went to Casey James. He could vividly see her standing in the garden touching the flowers. It was as if she belonged there, as if she brought new meaning to the word *home*. Why was he so adamant about her not being around his daughter? Was he afraid that Christie would end up getting hurt? For some odd reason, he knew deep down inside that it wouldn't be Casey James who would hurt his daughter; it would probably be her own mother. If there was anyone to be hurt by Casey James, it was likely to be him.

Seven

Casey sat on the couch eating a bowl of Frosted Flakes. The television was tuned to the Saturday morning cartoons, which she ignored. She nervously glanced at the clock. It was almost time for the service for Dara's parents to begin. There was a certain uneasiness that rested in the pit of her stomach. She hoped Dara would handle everything okay. Mrs. Fletcher called to let her know that they were on their way to the mortuary, and she would call when they returned.

A knock at the door jarred her. She went to the door and looked through the peephole and saw Vicia. She thought hard about not answering the door because she really didn't appreciate people dropping by her house unannounced. Besides, Vicia had never been to her house before. She must have gotten her address from the computer system at work. She sighed, but opened the door anyway.

"I just happened to be in the neighborhood and thought I'd stop by," Vicia said.

"Come in and have a seat," Casey said. She stood to the side and allowed Vicia to walk in. There was no need to be rude to her.

"I see you have a cozy place here. This is really nice," she said, looking around.

Casey sat opposite her in a chair. "Well, I try. So, what were you doing that brought you to my side of town?"

Vicia stammered before she spoke. "Ah, well, I wanted to check out that new mall they built and since I was so close, I just wanted to say hello." Vicia pulled out her compact and began checking her hair.

"I see." Casey eyed her suspiciously.

Vicia put away her mirror. "I heard you found a relative for the little girl who was involved in the accident."

"Yeah, I found an uncle. You wouldn't believe who he is," Casey said. Maybe Vicia wasn't up to anything. Maybe she just wanted someone to talk to. Casey was sure that, with that personality of hers, it was likely that she didn't have many friends.

Genuine interest was in Vicia's eyes. "Who?"

"Do you remember the guy from the restaurant? The one you bought a drink for?"

"Yes, I remember him." Her tone darkened. "He's the uncle?"

"Yes," Casey said. "If all works out, I'm placing Dara with him."

"So what does he do?" Vicia asked. Her left palm had been itching all day, and her grandmother used to say that was the sign of money. Maybe this was her lucky day.

"I think he's a Realtor." Casey stood. "Where are my manners? Would you like something to drink? I've got juice and soda."

"Sure, juice would be fine." Vicia began rubbing her itching palm on her jeans. "Realty can be a shady business. The question is, can he afford to take care of that little girl? You know," Vicia added to sound concerned, "we have to do whatever is in the best interest of the child."

Casey handed her a drink. "I don't think that's a problem at all. He's done pretty well for himself." Casey returned to her seat. "My only concern is that he won't have time to spend with Dara or his daughter, Christie. He's always traveling somewhere from what I understand."

"How sad," Vicia said in deep thought. In her mind, she was calculating figures. She listened as Casey continued to go on and on about how concerned she was for the little girl.

"Yeah, it is sad, especially since the funeral just started a few minutes ago." Casey glanced at the clock. "I know this has to be hard on Alfred. After all, he did lose two family members and now he is facing the possibility of caring for their child."

"Where is the funeral?" Vicia asked.

"At Carothers Mortuary." She couldn't shake the feeling that had overcome her. "So," Casey continued, "after the home study is done, I'll be able to place Dara with them."

She noticed Vicia's trancelike gaze. "Are you all right?"

"Oh," Vicia snapped back. "I'm fine. I was just thinking about how good that would be for the little girl. Have you started your Big Sister program yet?" She watched Casey's eyes brighten. How could she be so interested in all of this volunteer work? Vicia wondered. If she wasn't getting paid, she wasn't working. Money was the only gratification she needed.

"Yes, as a matter of fact I have. The thing that's so ironic about all of it is, I've been paired with Christie, Alfred's daughter. Can you believe it?"

Vicia nearly choked on her juice. "What? Have you told Liz about this?"

The gleam in Casey's eyes faded. "No, I haven't

mentioned it to her yet. I'm going to wait and see how things go and then I'll tell her."

Vicia gave her empty glass to Casey. "Well, I've got to be heading out. I'm supposed to be meeting a friend of mine for a bite to eat and then I'm heading to the house." She opened the door and stepped out.

"Oh" Casey said, "this was a short visit. But, I'm happy you stopped by."

After walking Vicia to her car, Casey began to wonder why Vicia left so abruptly. She had seemed so standoffish since they went out for drinks that night.

"Oh, well," she said to herself, "some people you can never get figured out." She walked back into the house and closed the door.

Every time the door opened, he glanced to the back of the room. He didn't know who he was looking for, but he couldn't help feeling that someone was missing. His arms tightened around Dara and Christie. As much as he explained things to Dara, he didn't really think she knew the significance of what was going on. One thing he did know was that he wanted her to be happy again.

After the service was over, and they prepared to leave the cemetery, he walked Mrs. Fletcher and Dara to her car. She seemed like a nice woman and some of the uneasiness about who was caring for Dara was erased.

A middle-aged couple approached him. They wore crisp suits and reeked of old money. The woman who had silver shoulder-length hair seemed vaguely familiar. The man who accompanied her also had graying hair. When Alfred thought about it, they both seemed familiar. They reminded him of his own grandparents.

Dara spotted them and immediately ran to meet

them. "Granny! Paw Paw!" she yelled as they lifted her into their arms. They hugged and kissed her as if it were going to be their last time seeing her.

They went over to meet Alfred. The woman shook Alfred's hand and held it firmly. "I'm sorry about your brother," she said. "This is hard for us all. I know you hadn't spoken to him in several years, but he loved you. In spite of everything that happened between the two of you, he realized his mistake, but his pride wouldn't let him ask your forgiveness."

Alfred was at a loss for words. He didn't know how to respond to what Mrs. Wynne had said. Mr. Wynne patted him on the shoulder in consolation.

"It's all right, my boy. It wasn't your fault, you didn't know. Aldrich finally came to grips with it and got over it. He fell in love with our Layla, and he cherished the ground our daughter walked on."

Alfred could feel years of pressure and pain lifting from his shoulders. Why hadn't his brother come to him? Why did they have to go so long before resolving their conflicts? They missed out on so much and now it was too late. He felt robbed and cheated.

"You don't know how much I appreciate you saying that," Alfred said. "I'm sorry about Layla."

Mr. Wynne spoke. "The only thing we ask is for you to let Dara live with us. She's all we have. She knows us and loves us. We've kept her every summer since she was born. Please, don't fight us on this. Let Dara live with us."

At that moment, Alfred knew he couldn't keep Dara away from her grandparents. She had a bond with them, whereas she had never spent any time with him. He was a complete stranger to her.

"I'll be in touch," Alfred said. Mrs. Fletcher went to the Wynnes and waited for Dara to say her goodbyes.

"Thank you for bringing Dara." Alfred shook Mrs. Fletcher's hand. He waited as they got into the car and gave Dara a wave good-bye as they drove away.

"Let's go," he said to Christie, who was standing at his side. "Aunt Maggie is waiting for us at the car."

He opened the door for Christie and Aunt Maggie. Before he could open his door, someone pulled alongside his car. Dark tint on the windows prevented him from seeing who the driver was. Whoever it was barely let the car come to a stop before throwing it in park and opening the door. A woman wearing a black suit and dark sunglasses emerged.

The woman walked over to him and extended her hand. "Hello, my name is Ms. Blake, and I'm with Social Services." She was silent for a moment. "I'm sorry we had to meet under such circumstances. Ms. James wasn't able to come out to observe the service today, so I'm here in her place."

He took her hand and shook it lightly. The woman's hand lingered for a moment. He tried to imagine what her face looked like without the oversize sunglasses. He had seen her somewhere before, but he couldn't put a finger on where.

"It's a pleasure to meet you," he said with a bit of an edge in his voice. It was hot outside, and he wasn't too fond of funerals. He was more than ready to leave.

"How did the child handle the funeral?" she asked.

He stared crossly at the woman who was busy rambling around in her purse. *"Dara,"* he corrected, "handled the service just like any five-year-old who just lost her parents would." *Who is this woman? She doesn't even know Dara's name.*

"Yes, *Dara,"* she said dryly. "Anyway, did she have any problems separating from you when the foster mother prepared to leave with her?"

Alfred could feel his temper about to explode. How could this woman be so insensitive to their situation? He watched as she checked her face in a mirror she pulled out of her purse.

"Ms. Blake, I think I'd rather wait for Ms. James to discuss this situation with me. But, overall, Dara handled the funeral the best way she could. Now, if you would excuse me." He opened his car door. "I've got to be going."

Vicia watched as Alfred's car turned out of the parking lot. Who did he think he was brushing off? She was *Vicia Blake*, and Vicia always got her man. She would just have to resort to Plan B.

Eight

Casey dropped by her mother's house to check her mail. Though she had been out of her mother's house for five years, she still used her mother's address for all of her important documents. She was surprised to find her mother still at home since she usually went to church on Sunday mornings.

Her mother called out telling her that she was in the kitchen. She found her mother draining the last cup of a pot of coffee she had brewed. Casey pulled out a chair and sat at the table.

"I thought you'd be at church," Casey said.

Her mother shook her head. "Nah. Me and Ressie caught the bus to Louisiana. You know we do the casino thing every now and then. I just got back this morning." She sat next to her daughter.

Casey frowned. "Why don't you ever let me know when you leave like that? Anything could have happened to you, and I wouldn't have known a thing about it." She threw her car keys on the table. "A simple phone call is all I ask."

Her mother eased her mug onto the dining room table and eyed her daughter. "What's with you this morning? I guess you fell out of the wrong side of the bed."

Casey rubbed her eyes. "I'm sorry, Mom. I didn't

mean to snap at you. I've just had some things on my mind lately."

"Well, why don't you talk about it? Talking can sometimes help you solve your problems."

Casey explained how she had been totally engrossed in Dara's case and how she was Christie's Big Sister. Her mother listened intently as Casey went over every detail.

"Are you sure this is what you want?" her mother asked. "You know the consequences of doing such a thing."

Casey focused on the floral-print tablecloth that draped her mother's dining room table. "I know it sounds strange, but for some inexplicable reason, I feel like Christie needs me."

Casey's mother laughed softly. "What can you give a little girl who has everything?"

"Something she's not getting at home—my time," Casey answered.

"Yes, but why this little girl? There are plenty of other children in the Houston area who need you more than she does." She knew her daughter inside and out. She had other reasons for wanting to be with this particular girl.

"Mom, I don't choose who I get. Besides, just because a child comes from a wealthy family doesn't mean she doesn't go through the same problems as the next child." Casey could feel head begin to throb. Since her mother hadn't made any more coffee, she went to the kitchen to grab a Coke. She had to get her caffeine one way or the other.

"Yes, but is this situation worth jeopardizing your job?" Her mother joined her in the kitchen.

"I know this is risky, but I'm going to talk to Liz about it."

"If you feel that you can make it work, then go for

it." She smiled softly. "You're a smart woman, Case. You've always accomplished everything that you've set your mind to, and I'm sure that this situation is no different. Just don't be disappointed if your boss doesn't approve."

"I'll try to make her understand that my commitments don't just involve the children in our agency, but children in general." She propped herself against the kitchen counter as she tried to read her mother's expression.

"Are you sure this is worth losing your job over? That could very well happen as I'm sure you know."

"Trust me, Mom. I know what I'm doing."

"I sure hope so." Her mother left Casey to her own devices. She had always been a stubborn child and little had changed. One thing she could say about Casey was that she always learned from her mistakes.

Casey tried convincing herself that she wasn't worried about what Liz would say about her being a big sister to Christie. Liz would understand once she explained. She checked her watch. It was still early, so she decided to see what Christie had planned for the day. She knew it wasn't time for their outing, but she wanted to establish a bond before they jumped into spending time with each other.

Casey waited as the phone rang. Mrs. Lincoln's voice came through the receiver. Casey explained that she wanted to drop by to visit Christie for a little while if she was home. Mrs. Lincoln seemed excited to have her come out.

"Oh," Mrs. Lincoln exclaimed, "Christie would enjoy that. As a matter of fact, I think it will make her day."

Mrs. Lincoln went on to say that Christie hadn't really been doing anything lately. She believed she was pouting over her father not taking her to Moody Gardens.

"He's always so busy," Mrs. Lincoln said. "Sometimes poor Christie gets lost in the shuffle." She sighed. "But soon Dara will be here, and they'll both be a lot happier."

Casey found herself gritting her teeth. She was quite sure that Alfred Willingham could afford to take a little time away from work to spend with his only child. He was just as bad as her father. The only difference was the simple fact that his daughter lived with him.

"Do you have any suggestions as to what we could do today?" Casey asked, trying to lift some of the anger out of her tone.

"Well, let's see," Mrs. Lincoln said. "Why don't you bring a bathing suit? Maybe the two of you can sit out by the pool and get to know each other."

"Okay." Casey agreed. "I'll be there around noon."

How sad that Christie had to sit alone in that big house. Alfred was just a jet-setting gigolo who left his daughter at home while he picked up women. At that particular moment, Alfred Willingham was in the same category as her father and that didn't say much for him.

Nine

It had been a while since Casey had gone swimming. After digging around in her closet, she found a bathing suit she had bought last summer for a pool party. She never had a chance to wear it because she got called in to work. She scrutinized the bright blue halter bikini top with the matching scoop bottom. She found a white sarong with turquoise floral print that matched perfectly.

Casey was sure the water would feel great since it was hot outside. Houston hadn't had rain in more than a month. When she arrived at the Willingham estate, the gate was already open. Mrs. Lincoln opened the front door as soon as Casey parked her car. Casey opened the back door and retrieved a large tote bag, which held her bathing suit, sunscreen, and a large towel.

Casey smiled at Mrs. Lincoln as she reached the door. She extended her hand to say hello, but Mrs. Lincoln embraced her instead.

"Come on in, child," Mrs. Lincoln said. "I'm glad you could make it. Christie's upstairs getting dressed."

"Thanks, Mrs. Lincoln." She stood in the foyer looking up at the high ceiling, which had a beautifully detailed ten-armed chandelier. "That's breathtaking," Casey said still looking at the ceiling.

"It is beautiful, isn't it?" Mrs. Lincoln agreed. "Lord knows I could never afford a Waterford Crystal chandelier in my home. Heck," she said, chuckling, "that's the price of a car. One thing I can say about that Kelly, if nothing else, she had expensive taste."

Casey followed Mrs. Lincoln as she headed down the hallway. Every room she passed looked unused with the exception of the study. A large desk was cluttered with papers and books. A bell went off, and Mrs. Lincoln stopped.

"Oh, goodness. That's the timer. Wait here while I go check on the food." She scurried off to the kitchen.

Casey looked around the study at the books lining the shelves. She stepped behind the massive desk to look out of the window, which overlooked the pool. This room was a sharp contrast to all the others. It was elegant but simple. As she was about to step away, a glare from the trash can caught her eye. She leaned over for a closer inspection. A silver frame was lying facedown on top of a pile of papers. She picked it up and saw a wedding picture of Alfred and his ex-wife. He wore a black tuxedo and his wife was no less than what she expected. She was gorgeous in a beaded white gown with a long train. He truly seemed happy. She returned the picture to the trash and waited by the door.

"Hi, Casey. Aunt Maggie told me you were here." Christie came padding barefoot down the hall. She hugged Casey around the waist. "Aren't you going to change?" Her nose wrinkled as she took in Casey's shorts and tank top. "You aren't going to swim in that, are you?"

Christie was really a straightforward little girl. "No, actually I need to change into my suit."

Christie took her by the hand and led her back

into her father's study. "You can change in here. My dad isn't home so no one will come in. I'm going out to the pool." She began running down the hall. "See ya in a minute," she yelled before disappearing out the door.

Casey eyed the tote bag. Whether Alfred was home or not, she would have preferred changing somewhere else. Knowing him, he was out of town, leaving his housekeeper to raise his daughter. Mrs. Lincoln wasn't a spring chicken anymore, and she was bound to retire soon. What was he going to do about Christie then, not to mention Dara?

She stood by the door, stepped out of her shorts and pulled on her bikini bottoms. Poor Christie, she thought. Maybe Dara would bring more enjoyment to her life. Casey removed her shirt, placed it in the bag, and fished in the tote for her top. *How can someone's job be so important that he totally neglects his kids? Just when is Mr. Willingham home anyway? Probably just long enough to change clothes and leave again.* She continued digging around in her bag for her top.

"It's got to be here," she said to herself. She pulled out the towel, the sarong, sunscreen, and a couple of books she brought along in case she wanted something to read. "I know I put it in here."

She could hear a male's voice outside the door. She began digging around furiously in the bag.

The doorknob began to turn. In a panic, she ran across the room to the desk. The door seemed to be opening in slow motion. The only thing she could think of was to duck behind the desk to keep from exposing herself.

Alfred whistled a tune as he stepped into the study, closing the door behind him. He paid no attention to the clothes that were lying on the floor by the door.

"Boy, it good to be back home," he said as he headed toward his desk.

"Stay right there." Casey's head popped up from behind the desk. She could only imagine what she must look like.

Alfred froze. "What's going on?" He began heading toward her.

"Don't come any closer," Casey said in a high-pitched tone. She felt foolish kneeling behind his desk, wearing nothing but a bikini bottom.

"What are you doing back there?" Alfred's eyes peered over the top of the desk. He then noticed the clothes strewn by the door. He picked up the bathing suit top and held the stringy material between his fingers. "Is this what you're looking for?"

Heat began to sear her cheeks. "Yes," she answered. "Could you please throw it over here?"

Alfred gave a sly grin. "You sure you don't want me to bring it over? I'm sure I can help you put—"

"That won't be necessary," Casey interrupted. "Just throw it over."

"Suit yourself." He threw the top, and it landed on the front edge of the desk. He propped himself against the door. It was going to be a sight seeing her get out of this one.

"You did that on purpose!" Casey said.

"No, I didn't. That top is light, I could only throw it so far," he said, defending himself. He folded his arms across his chest, waiting.

"Can you please step out?" Casey asked.

Alfred's silence was her answer. She cursed to herself. The only way she was going to get her top was to get it herself. She held one hand across her chest as she stretched across the desk and snatched her top off it.

"The least you can do is turn your back," Casey snapped.

Alfred studied her for a moment before turning his head in the other direction. He could vaguely see her pulling the straps over her shoulders from his peripheral vision. He could only imagine what a full view would be like. *Here I am, in my own home with a beautiful woman that I can't touch.* He was breathing so hard he thought he was going to hyperventilate.

"Are you finished yet?" he asked almost impatiently. He was only giving her a few more seconds, and then he was looking.

"Yes," she snapped. "No thanks to you." She walked near her bag and snatched the sarong from the floor.

Alfred sucked in his breath. Why did this woman have to come to his house in a two-piece bathing suit? Why did he have to be alone with her? He began to ache in places he had almost forgotten he had. It was starting to torture him.

She was too busy grumbling under her breath to notice Alfred staring intently at her. "That's just what I get," she complained. "I try and I try to be nice and do all of the right things and what does it get me? Nothing." She began fussing with the sarong. Her fingers were all rubber, and she couldn't tie a knot to save her life. This man had a way of unraveling every piece of sanity she had.

"Let me help you," he said huskily.

Somehow, she couldn't find the strength to argue with him anymore. She looked in his eyes and could see something burning in them she had never seen in a man's eyes before.

"How's that?" he asked as his lips lowered to touch hers.

She wanted to pull away, but her feet wouldn't

move. A wave of delight washed over her as his tongue darted in her mouth tasting hers. His arms pulled her closer to him, and Casey found herself wanting to be there.

There was a thud at the door as Christie bounded in. They broke apart quickly.

"Are you ready yet?" Christie asked before she spotted her father. She ran over to him. "Daddy, when did you get back?" He scooped her into his arms.

"I just got back. I was on my way out to see you, but I got detained," he said, looking at Casey.

She quickly looked away. *What was that all about? Didn't you tell yourself that he's like your father? Maybe becoming Christie's big sister wasn't such a good idea after all.*

"I'll be out by the pool," Casey said as she gathered her things and walked hastily out of the study. She continued chastising herself until she reached a lounge chair. She knew exactly what she needed to cool her down. After climbing up the stairs to the diving board, she bounced three times before doing a perfect dive into the pool.

After a quick shower, Alfred changed into a pair of swimming trunks and headed downstairs.

"Um, I haven't seen you swim in a long time," Aunt Maggie said as Alfred passed by the kitchen. "But who can stay in when there's such beautiful scenery outside?" She gave him a wink.

"You're right, Aunt Maggie, the scenery is exceptionally beautiful today." A smile crossed his face. Aunt Maggie was a real character sometimes.

"By the way," she added. "Quincy is out by the pool waiting for you."

A smile crossed his face. Quincy was his best friend.

It had been a while since he'd hung out with him, as they both had hectic schedules.

Quincy was waiting just outside the door when Alfred stepped out. They greeted each other with a manly hug and quickly separated.

"It's good to see you," Quincy said, taking in Alfred's swimming trunks. "Going for a swim?"

"Ah, yeah," Alfred said a bit uneasily. "I was thinking about taking a quick dip."

Quincy followed Alfred's gaze to Casey, who was floating on her back with her hair flowing about her like a large halo. "Well," Quincy said, "if I had a mermaid swimming in my pool, I'd take a dip too. Who is she?"

"Oh, that's just Christie's mentor from Big Brothers and Sisters of America," he replied. It didn't matter how nonchalant he was, Casey's kiss was still fresh on his lips.

Quincy watched as Alfred's gaze never left Casey. "Don't tell me she's another one of those fake breakdown stories." He went over to one of the lounge chairs and straddled it. "You always have all the luck. How did you manage to get her?"

Alfred sat on the concrete next to Quincy's chair. "I didn't ask for her. She ended up being Christie's mentor and that's all there is to it." His eyes couldn't meet his best friend's because he knew that was a complete lie.

Quincy's gaze returned to the pool. "If you say so."

"She's also my niece's caseworker. Layla's parents want Dara."

"What are you going to do?"

"I don't know. Outside of Christie, she's the only other family that I have. I want her to know her father's side of the family."

"Well, she could visit. I'm sure her grandparents wouldn't mind that."

"What do you think I should do?" Alfred didn't know if the only reason he wanted custody of Dara was that she was the last of his family or that he wanted what was best for her.

"Only you can answer that, my friend."

They both watched as Casey and Christie took turns diving. If Casey was aware they were watching her, she didn't show it. She and Christie busied themselves racing around the pool, splashing water everywhere.

Aunt Maggie came out with a pitcher of tea. She poured Alfred and Quincy a glass before disappearing back into the house. Both men sipped their tea in silence.

"It seems like Christie likes her a lot," Quincy commented. "She never liked any other woman who showed up on your doorstep."

"Yeah, I know." Alfred studied his glass.

Quincy touched Alfred's shoulder. "Who knows, maybe Kelly will spend more time with Christie in the future."

"She's supposed to take Christie to this mother-daughter outing at Six Flags this weekend, but she'll probably find a mouthful of excuses for that too." He downed the rest of his tea.

"You see," Quincy said. "I must be a psychic because I told you she'd probably come around."

A grunt was Alfred's only reply. How could he tell Quincy that the only reason Kelly was taking her own daughter on an outing was that she thought something would be in it for her? Suddenly, a bell went off in his head. He forgot to tell Casey that Christie's mother was going to take her to Six Flags. That would be his reason to give her a call next week.

Alfred continued to watch Casey and his daughter

laughing and talking. Yes, this woman was much different from any other woman he'd ever met, and that was a good thing. His mother always told him that when you found a good thing, you should hold on to it. Once he knew for sure that Casey was that good thing, that's exactly what he planned on doing.

Ten

Casey couldn't shake the confusion that rested on her shoulders. She was convinced that Alfred was a replica of her father, yet she found her thoughts wandering back to him. She was embarrassed when she recalled some of the thoughts that had crossed her mind about him. She caught herself gaping when Alfred climbed out of the pool, his body glistening with beads of water. Not only was he good-looking, but the man had a body and a brain! Why was her mind in the gutter?

She had had such a wonderful time with Christie the day before. She was convinced that being a mentor in the Big Sister program was the right decision. Aunt Maggie told her that she hadn't seen Christie that happy in a long time. Casey smiled as she thought of all the fun she and Christie had had.

The ringing phone made her mini-vacation disappear like a puff of smoke. She sighed as she picked it up.

"Social Services," she answered in a crisp tone.

"And what kind of *social services* do you provide?" the deep voice asked.

The voice sent tingles up her spine. The smile she thought was gone for the day resurfaced. "Who is this?" she asked, knowing very well who it was.

"Someone who would like to get to know you better," he replied. "Have lunch with me."

"I'd love to, but I'm swamped."

"Okay. Why don't I pick you up for dinner tonight?"

Casey paused in consideration. What would one date with the man hurt? It wasn't as if he were asking her to marry him. *One date and that's it.* "All right. That sounds good to me." *What's wrong with me? I used to know how to stick to my guns, but now, I'm getting soft.*

"Great," he said with surprise. He didn't expect her to accept so easily.

Casey quickly gave him directions to her house, and he told her he would see her around eight. She turned her chair around so she could see outside. What in the world was she doing? She was breaking all of the rules. The thing that scared her the most was that she really didn't care.

Punkin could have jumped for joy when he found out Casey was going out to dinner. "Honey, this is a real Kodak moment, okay? Ooh, your momma is going to have some grandkids yet," he sang into the phone.

"Punkin, it's not a big deal. We're just going out."

He made a gagging sound into the phone. "Don't try to sell me any of that 'it's no big deal' junk. There has to be something special about this man that makes you want to go out with him. Do you like him?"

"Punkin, I don't know how I feel about him. Honestly, I'm afraid." She was starting to feel something for Alfred, she just didn't know what.

"Afraid of what? Honey, you've got to live for yourself. You can't base your relationships on your parents' relationship."

"What should I do?" Casey stepped into her walk-in closet, searching for something to wear to dinner with Alfred. She took out a blue silk capri pants set.

"If he's anything like you describe him, I'd give him a chance," he answered. "It's not as if you're seeing anyone else. Don't deny yourself happiness."

Casey spread the outfit across the bed. "What makes you think I'm not happy?"

Punkin laughed as if that was the funniest question he had ever been asked. "Girlfriend, you spend a majority of your time working. When I do try to get you out of the house, you always have a mouthful of excuses. I never understood why you never got out and met someone. You are too young to be this lonely. Alfred could be the therapy you need."

"So now I need therapy?" Casey laughed.

"Yes, therapy. Go out with him and have a good time. Where are you going?"

"He didn't say. He called and asked me to dress casual."

"What are you going to wear?"

"You remember the capri set I bought at the Galleria?"

"Yes, I remember that outfit. Girl, I thought you didn't want any extra attention from him. That outfit fits like a glove. A tasteful glove, but still a glove."

"It's not that tight, Punkin, it's just tight in all the right places."

"You go, girl. Anyway, you'd better start getting dressed. I don't want you to be late for your date."

"It's not a date," Casey corrected.

"Is he coming to pick you up?"

"Yes."

"Is he paying for dinner or whatever?"

"Yes."

"Then it's a date. Talk to you later."

As she knew he would be, Alfred was right on time. He drove up in his black Lexus at two minutes till eight. At eight o'clock, her doorbell was ringing. When he caught a glimpse of Casey, he beamed with pride. She was a beautiful woman. A man would have to be a fool to let her get away. Alfred played a jazz CD as they drove to a popular downtown night spot.

"That's a nice CD. I'm a big fan of jazz myself," Casey said.

Alfred smiled. "I like this group because they blend jazz with a bit of R and B. It's much different from the jazz they play in elevators."

"You're right."

Just as the CD was getting better, they pulled into the restaurant's parking lot.

They went to the bar while they waited for their table. Casey couldn't help noticing how nicely Alfred's jeans fit. Apparently she wasn't the only one who appreciated it, because two ladies had been checking him out since they'd arrived. Actually, it made Casey feel good to know that she was on the arm of such a prized possession.

After dinner, Alfred wanted to go dancing. The floor was packed with people grinding to the music. Casey was surprised to see so many people out on a weeknight. It had been a while since she had a chance to get her groove on.

The deejay was live on the radio, hyping up the party. "I'm about to take y'all back—way back!" He put on an old school classic by Earth, Wind, and Fire.

"That used to be the jam," Casey said as she began to drag Alfred onto the floor. He was surprised that she initiated the dance. He watched the curves of her hips as she swayed to the music. She didn't know the intoxicating effect she was having on him. Before long, they were both exhausted from dancing through several fast songs. The deejay decided it was time to cool down, so he put on a slow song.

Alfred held Casey close. This was the part he had been looking forward to the most. It was as if her body was made to fit his. She was what his life had been missing.

Casey's head rested on Alfred's shoulder. She could stay there forever. His embrace felt so right. She felt safe in his arms. What made him so hard to resist? She found herself enjoying his soft caresses to her back. She lifted her head to look at him. A burning intensity was in his eyes as he returned her gaze.

"Why are you looking at me like that?" Casey asked.

Alfred kissed her. "Do you really want to know the answer to that?" he asked.

"Yes, I want to know."

He traced her fresh-kissed lips with a finger. "I'm not one to play games and go all around the corner just to get across the street. But I'm feeling something for you that I haven't felt in a long time. The thing of it is, I'm not sure if you feel anything remotely close to what I do."

Casey had to beat down the resistance to blot out everything relating to a relationship that Alfred was talking about. Her first instinct was to run in the opposite direction, but what was there waiting for her? She already knew the answer to that: loneliness. On the other hand, if by chance she did allow herself to become involved with Alfred, what was waiting for her there? Heartbreak.

The natural smile she wore all night became a forced one. She felt rigid in his arms, and her movements were stiff. He should have known she wasn't interested. Once again, Alfred felt he was wasting his time.

Why was it so hard for her to let go? Casey wondered. Had her father's desertion shaken her up so badly that she couldn't function in a normal relationship? As much as she wanted to love and to be loved, she couldn't at the moment. What made Alfred so different from her father? Nothing. He was still a man, and he was allowed to make human mistakes.

Alfred decided to leave the club early before it got too crowded.

"Hey, how about a stroll through Transco Towers?"

Casey's eyes lit up. "I've never been there. Is it really as pretty as people say?"

"Why don't we find out?" He smiled. *Why don't I just take her home? She's not interested in me at all. Maybe she has someone else.*

Transco Towers was a business park by day and a romantic's paradise by night. There was a tall waterfall that lit up as soon as the sun went down. Visitors could walk inside the fall and look up to the top of the fountain. It was a frequent site for newlyweds who wanted to take their wedding pictures.

A large lake was filled with ducks that weren't shy of visitors. Some couples strolled hand in hand, while others took carriage rides. Alfred had to circle twice around the park before having any luck with a parking spot.

"Wow, this is nice," Casey said, looking at the waterfall. "I can't believe there are so many people out at this time of night."

"Yes, it is nice," Alfred said. "Let's take a carriage ride."

Alfred flagged down a carriage and helped Casey get inside. Alfred sat next to her, wrapping his arms around her. Casey closed her eyes, enjoying the night air and Alfred's warmth.

"Tell me why you're afraid of a relationship," Alfred said. "Has someone hurt you so bad that you want to shut yourself off from every man?" He could feel her body tense.

Her heart was beating so fast and hard, she thought it was going to jump right out of her chest. "Yes, someone did hurt me."

Alfred held her closer. "I'm sorry," he said softly. "But I can't apologize for another man's mistakes. At the same time, you can't blame me for what someone else did."

"It was my father," she said.

He lifted her chin so that her eyes could meet his. "I'm not sure I'm following you."

She toyed with the thought of telling him about her family. She had never told anyone but Punkin about her father's desertion. Somehow, after all those years, she felt it was her fault her father left. Maybe she wasn't the daughter her father wanted her to be.

"What do you mean?" he urged.

"One day, my father told me and my mother he was going to the store, and he never came back. I haven't seen him since." She turned her head and watched the streetlights go by.

Alfred leaned his head back, picking out stars in the sky. "Casey, I've been hurt too, and at one point in time, I was about ready to live like a monk. My only concern was providing my daughter with the kind of life that she'd been accustomed to and preparing her for the future."

He swallowed hard, thinking of the right words. Pressuring Casey would push her away from him, but at the same time, he wanted her to know how he was feeling.

"I vowed not to allow another woman into my life

until Christie was a grown woman. I actually planned to do that." He touched her chin and gently turned her face to his. "But I recently met someone who is starting to change my mind."

Her heart was beating wildly. No one had ever told her anything like this and frankly, she was afraid. She knew what she wanted to do—run. This couldn't be. This man was telling her that he felt something for *her*, a woman who her own father didn't want.

"No." Her eyes glistened with unshed tears. She hoped it was dark enough for him not to see the pools that had formed in her eyes.

"Yes," he said. "That woman is you, Casey. That woman is you."

"How can you feel something for a woman whose own father didn't want her?" Casey asked in a strained voice.

"I'm not your father. He made a mistake that I don't plan on making—he let you go."

"This is a bit much for me." That was the only thing that came to her mind.

Alfred's fingers left her chin. There was an impregnable silence. The only sound was the repetitious clopping of the horse's hooves on the pavement.

"I think everything happens for a reason," he said. "Maybe it was fate that we met."

Casey shook her head in denial. "I don't believe in fate, Alfred."

"Well, maybe I can make a believer out of you," he answered.

"We'll see." She didn't know if she wanted to be a believer. She was quite sure her mother was a believer. Look what happened to her.

As much as he enjoyed Casey's company, he didn't want to keep her out too late. Casey stifled a yawn as she reclined in the seat. She was definitely no night owl. How long had it been since she'd had so much fun?

Alfred took the long way back to Casey's house. He didn't want such a wonderful outing to end so soon.

Casey wondered if he could make her believe in fate. What if he was the man who would change how she felt about relationships? She couldn't resist looking in his direction as the thought crossed her mind. He was everything a woman could possibly want in a man and more. He made it through her mental checklist almost flawlessly. Alfred was the kind of man women only read about in romance novels. Yet, there he was with *her*. He was a hero trying to rescue a damsel in distress who didn't feel she needed rescuing.

"Thanks for a wonderful evening," Casey said before unlocking her front door.

Alfred smiled. "No, thank *you* for a wonderful evening."

He leaned closer to her. That familiar look of pain crossed her face before her eyes closed, waiting to feel his lips next to hers. Alfred hesitated before kissing her lightly on the forehead. He knew that if he kissed her lips, and she responded the way she had before, it would be hard for him to walk away.

She couldn't hide the disappointment in her eyes. Alfred paused before opening the car door, chancing one glance at her before departing. He thought about asking her out again, but decided it would be too much, too soon.

"Good night," he called out to her. He could never forget the picture of fear that crossed her face. If only he knew what to do to make her open up to him.

"Good night," she answered. Why did it seem as if she was seeing Alfred for the last time? It almost felt as if he were saying good-bye instead of good night. She shuddered at the thought.

Alfred wove through the empty streets with thoughts of Casey heavy on his mind. He had seen so many women like her before. They had been hurt so badly by someone that they couldn't allow themselves to love again. Many of them were lost causes, beyond learning to love again. He refused to believe that Casey was a lost cause. Yet, he couldn't risk investing an enormous amount of time in her if she could never reciprocate his feelings.

He sped up as he started up the entrance ramp on 59 South. It was still early in the game, but he knew that he was falling hard for Casey. It was time he learned to protect himself. When he really thought about it, he had just as much to fear as she did. What if he woke up one day and realized that he loved her? Would she feel the same way? Chances were she wouldn't because the entire time, she would have been too afraid to let go and let love take over. As a matter of fact, he was going to give her some space. It took two people to make a relationship work. If Casey felt anything for him, she would have to come to him. Otherwise, he would make himself scarce when she came to spend time with Christie.

Alfred gripped the steering wheel firmly. "I'm not chasing after you, Casey. You have to let me know that this is something that you want just as much as I do."

He turned on the radio and listened to the Quiet Storm on Majic 102. A man called in and wanted to make a dedication to his longtime girlfriend.

"Hi, this is Vance," the caller said. "I'd just like to tell my girlfriend—or rather my ex-girlfriend—that I still love her. We broke up a couple of weeks ago, and my life hasn't been the same. I did everything to make her happy. I worked twelve hours a day, paid her bills." His voice broke. "I just don't understand how she could do me like this."

"I feel you," the deejay said. "We've all been there. What would you like to dedicate to your woman?"

The caller paused, trying to choose the perfect song. "I'd like to dedicate 'Special Kind of Fool' by Basic Black."

"I'll put it on for you right now," the deejay said. "Stay strong, my brother, because at some point in time, we've all played the fool." He spoke to the other listeners. "And if you have a dedication to make to that special someone, give us a call."

The lead singer crooned in a pain-filled voice, "I can't stay, and I can't go . . ."

Those few words perfectly described how Alfred felt. He couldn't stay with Casey, yet he couldn't go. There was a twinge of sympathy in Alfred's heart for the guy who had called in. Although he didn't know all of the caller's story, he sounded sincere. The man's plea probably fell on deaf ears. If he kept things up with Casey, he too would probably be calling in making dedications to someone who refused to listen. As fond as he was of Casey James, he wasn't about to be a special kind of fool.

Eleven

As soon as she heard Alfred's car drive away, Casey raced to the phone to call Punkin. It was two o'clock in the morning, but she needed someone to talk to. Tears streamed down her cheeks as she dialed the number. She was starting to think she needed a psychiatrist to help her deal with her hang-ups.

"Punkin?" she croaked when Punkin picked up the phone. "Punkin, it's me. Wake up."

Punkin, who hadn't long been asleep, forced himself awake. "Casey?" he said groggily. "What's wrong? Why are you crying?"

"I don't know," she wailed. "I just had the most wonderful time with a man most women only dream about, and I don't know what to do." She paced around the room.

There was a short pause on the other end of the line. "What do you mean you don't know what to do? Do what comes natural, girlfriend."

Casey finally sat on the couch. "Running is what comes natural. What's wrong with me?"

"Honey, there is nothing wrong with you," Punkin counseled. "You are just like everybody else. A lot of people are afraid of what a commitment may bring, including yours truly."

"But what if—"

"There are no buts," Punkin interjected. "If this man has love to offer, take it. You can't spend the rest of your life running away from love. Eventually, love is gonna get ya."

"I'm not ready," she whined.

"Casey, you already know what to do." He yawned. "Let's talk about this in the morning. You know Punkin needs his beauty rest."

Casey managed a smile. "Yes, I know he does. Thanks, Punkin, I'll talk to you later."

"I sure hope you don't mean that literally. I don't know if I can take any more of these late-night phone calls."

After a quick shower, Casey changed into an over-size T-shirt. She lay in bed watching the blades on the ceiling fan turn round and round. She wanted to be happy. She wanted the ideal life—marriage, kids, a house with a white picket fence. She knew that nothing in life was guaranteed, but she wanted as much of a guarantee as possible.

It was too beautiful a morning to be leaving Houston. Yet, there he sat, in a window seat flying first-class to New York. Alfred hoped that it was as beautiful a day in Manhattan as it was in Houston. One business trip after another was starting to get old to him, and it was taking its toll on Christie.

He peered out of the window, barely able to make out the cars moving below. His daughter was waiting for him at home, but somehow, he felt he was missing something. He and Christie lived in a big house with too many empty rooms. It wasn't that he didn't enjoy being home, because he did. His home was missing something, or was that *something* a *someone*?

His heart warmed as his thoughts returned to Casey

James. He would never forget the look on her face when she told him about her father's abandonment. He had never met a woman that he truly felt he could spend the rest of his life loving—until she kept popping into his life. He honestly believed that he would never know true love.

Casey was just enough to get under his skin.

He glanced over at the woman sitting next to him. She was attractive, heavily engrossed in reading a book. He stared long enough to see the title, *Heavenly Kisses*—a romance novel. Was she reading for pleasure or did she just not have a life? He didn't notice a wedding ring on her finger. She was probably the type who spent a lot of time dismissing guys because they weren't good enough. She probably woke up one morning and realized that she was lonely. That's usually the way it went—beautiful and lonely.

The author of the book was Kelsey Anderson—he had never heard of her. Yes, he decided, this woman was probably desperate for companionship. She was reading a book because she didn't have a love life and wanted to live vicariously through the characters.

A passenger on her way to the lavatory stopped beside the woman sitting next to him.

"Oh, my goodness, aren't you Kelsey Anderson?" the woman asked with her hand to her chest. "I can't believe it. I have all of your books. Can I please have your autograph?"

"Why of course," Kelsey said in a silky tone.

She scribbled her name on a napkin and handed it to the woman. After signing the autograph, she returned to her book, shrugging off curious glances from other passengers.

Alfred couldn't help feeling guilty for his thinking. It was a good thing people couldn't read thoughts, because he would have looked like a fool. He felt bad for stereotyping the woman next to him.

Twenty minutes before the plane was to land, Alfred realized that he hadn't been nervous about flying at all. His mind had been so occupied with thoughts of Casey that he hadn't had time to worry about his flight. He made a mental note to thank her when he saw her again. *I guess that settles it.*

To his surprise, the airport wasn't packed. As he called home to let Christie and Aunt Maggie know that he had arrived in New York, he thought how nice it would be to call home to a wife to let her know that he made it safely to his hotel. He missed that, not that Kelly ever looked forward to his calls. He knew Casey would be eager to hear from him. He never thought he would be thinking about marriage again, but Casey brought out those thoughts in him.

He stopped by the reservation desk of his hotel to check into his room. After receiving his card key, he took the elevator to the top floor. He opened the door to his room and threw his luggage on the bed. The plush carpeting, the elegant furnishing, and the large fruit basket went unnoticed as he headed to the balcony and slid open the glass door. He stared out over the city, yet he saw nothing in particular. Lately he had been so temperamental, which was something totally out of character. He was usually the level-headed one—the one in control. Where was that man now?

In the short span of a few weeks, his life had been turned inside out. It all started when he met Casey. His brother and his wife had died tragically, leaving behind their daughter. His fist tightened around the railing on the balcony. Dara was only five and would require a lot of attention. Heck, he hadn't been giving his own child as much attention as she needed.

He went back inside the room and closed the balcony door. He picked up the phone and called back to Houston. He already knew what had to be done. After hanging up the phone, he prayed he'd made the right decision. He hoped Casey wouldn't think any less of him for the decision he made.

The menu on the dresser caught his attention. He propped two fluffy pillows under his head as he scanned the items. As hungry as he was, everything was starting to sound good. His heart jumped at the sound of the ringing telephone. Maybe it was Casey calling him to say hello.

His hope was dashed out when he heard Kelly's voice on the other end of the line. As usual, she was out of money and begging for support. She played on his senses all the time, and he knew she was taking advantage of the situation, but surely he couldn't turn his back on the mother of his child. How could he allow her to suffer? How would that look to his daughter to see her mother living a terrible life while they had one of luxury? He promised to send Kelly some money, and once again, she promised to spend more time with Christie. He wanted to believe her for Christie's sake.

Twelve

"That woman is you, Casey. That woman is you." She smiled when she thought about him telling her she was the woman who changed his mind about being alone. He was right; he wasn't her father, and he shouldn't have to pay for her father's mistakes.

"We're having a unit meeting in fifteen minutes." Liz stopped by Casey's office to inform her. "We might as well get it done since all of you are in the office this morning."

"Okay," Casey said. "I'll be down to your office after I check my messages."

Fortunately, there was only one message on her voice mail, and it was from Alfred.

"Hi, Casey, it's Alfred. First, I'd like to tell you how much I enjoyed your company last night. I had a wonderful time. With that said, let me get to the other reasons I'm calling you." He paused. "Uh, Christie's mother decided to take her to the outing at Six Flags this weekend. I apologize if this has inconvenienced you in any way. Second, I've had second thoughts about Dara."

Casey stared at the telephone as he dropped one bombshell after another. She was starting to feel as though the night before was indeed good-bye. She listened as he struggled for what he thought to be the right words.

"Well, she knows nothing about me. She may as well live with a complete stranger since I haven't seen her since she was born. I couldn't do that to her. Layla's parents want her to live with them, and when I saw how much she meant to them, I knew I couldn't stand in their way. I think this is the best thing for Dara."

He was breaking every tie she had to him. He didn't want her around his daughter, and he didn't want her working with him as Dara's caseworker. Why didn't he just say that he didn't want to be bothered with her? Was she really the Popsicle Punkin called her?

"Well, that's all I wanted to say. I'm out of town, and I won't be back until the end of the week. If you need to get in touch with me, just leave a message with Aunt Maggie, and I'll call you as soon as I get the chance. Later."

Later? What did he mean later? What happened to I'll call you tonight or tomorrow? Later? Later was so indefinite. Why didn't he leave her a number so that she could call him herself? What was up with having Aunt Maggie as a middleman? If she hadn't committed to the Big Brother and Big Sister program, she wouldn't even bother trying to keep her visits with Christie. It was a fine time for him to call off their visit to Six Flags. Casey wished she had known that before she went out and bought the tickets. Maybe they could use them another time—if there was another time.

Just when she was thinking about opening up to him, he backed away. She snatched her notebook off the desk and went to Liz's office. All of the workers in her unit were there, except Vicia, who didn't get to the meeting until ten minutes after it started.

Liz spent thirty minutes briefing everyone on new

changes that were going to affect their unit. Casey focused on her shoes. Why didn't Liz just e-mail everyone about these changes? She had other pressing issues to deal with.

"And that's a wrap," Liz concluded.

Casey didn't look up until she heard Liz cutting off the meeting. Everyone began filing out and heading back to their offices.

"Don't leave yet," Liz said to Casey. "I need to speak with you for a moment."

Vicia was the last person to leave Liz's office, but didn't look in Casey's direction when she left. Liz motioned for Casey to take a seat and closed the door after Vicia had gone.

Liz sat on the edge of her desk, crossing and uncrossing her feet. "First," she began, "let me say that you're the best worker I've ever had the pleasure of supervising. You're hard working and a cautious social worker. That's why I found it hard to believe that you would deliberately go against agency policy regarding conflict of interest."

Casey's eyes widened. She knew she should have gone to Liz sooner. *But who told her?*

"Liz, I don't know what happened."

"Casey, I'm sure you had a good reason. I don't doubt that. If this information had come from the bottom up, I would brush it off, but it didn't. I was told about this from *my* supervisor."

Casey was quiet. Who told their program director? She knew there would be consequences, but she didn't know they would come this soon. "What did she say?"

"Well, someone made a really big stink about this, and she was about ready to throw the ax at you. I convinced her not to be too hasty. You're a good worker, and I can't let you go out like that."

"So, what am I to do in the meantime?"

Liz reached behind her and picked up some papers. "These are for you."

Casey examined the papers. "These are leave forms."

"Exactly," Liz said. "You have two months' time that you haven't taken. It's going to take my supervisor some time to examine your situation and while she does, you'll take a mandatory vacation."

"What about my cases?" She couldn't leave the kids on her caseload hanging.

"Don't worry. They've been evenly distributed. No one knows about this situation. They all think you're finally taking a much-needed vacation."

She knew she liked Liz for a reason. "Thanks."

Liz gave a nervous laugh. "Don't thank me yet. Go straighten up your office and take your vacation. I'll call you when I hear something. Until then, no news is good news."

There was nothing in Casey's office to clean up. Like her life before Alfred, everything was neat and in order. Maybe taking a vacation would be a good thing. Maybe she could pursue something that had been on her mind since she had become a social worker. She knew one thing, she wasn't going to sit around twiddling her thumbs while Social Services made up its mind about whether she could keep her job.

"So, in other words," Punkin said, "someone ratted you out."

"Yes, and I don't know who would do a thing like that." She held out her hand as Punkin applied a coat of jasmine nail polish to each finger.

"Could Ms. Green have told them?" he asked as he concentrated on her nails.

"Why would she?" Casey leaned closer so she could see how the polish looked. "Besides, she only had the number to my office."

"Well, who else besides *me* did you tell?" He screwed the top on the nail polish.

Casey thought for a moment. She didn't make it a habit to tell her business to other people, but she did remember telling Vicia. But Vicia had no reason to go to their director about the situation. Or did she? Punkin's mouth hung open when Casey told him.

"But why would she do it?" Casey asked. "I've never done anything to her."

"Well, honey, her name says it all. Vicia is short for *vicious*. Some people don't need a reason to be devious." He fluffed a pillow before leaning back on the couch. "There are plenty of people who don't want to see others do better than them. You have to do like Punkin does." He raised up and shimmied his shoulders. "Shake da haters off." He laughed.

His laughter died when he realized Casey was serious. "I know this is your livelihood, but you can't spend all of your vacation worrying about your job. You're a lot better off than most people. You've got your mother and your best friend who are behind you one hundred percent."

A glimmer of hope returned to Casey's eyes. "You know I've always wanted to start an adoption agency."

"Well, there you have it," Punkin said. "All you have to do is do it and the perfect time for you to make connections is through Big Brothers and Sisters of America's annual party."

"What?" Casey looked at Punkin as if he had just lost his last marble. Punkin had come up with some wild ideas before, but this one was at the top of the list. "Why would I want to go to the party?"

"*Hello?* A lot of children in that program are foster children or they are in state custody. Heck, they need adopting too. Your agency can focus on adopting children who are past the *cute* stage."

"You know something? You're right. I thought that party was for the bigwigs—a fund-raising event. Not just anybody can waltz in there."

Punkin was feeling the excitement that Casey was going to start her own business. He paced around the living room as he always did when he was cooking something up.

"Just let me handle getting us in. You start concentrating on finding a location and making contacts." He stared at his image in the gold-framed wall mirror. "Stand back and watch Punkin work his magic."

"Okay, Mr. Magician, this is something that I have to see." Casey stood next to him, watching him watch himself in the mirror.

"I'm on the case, honey, and when I call you in a couple of days, tickets in hand, you call me Mr. Prime Time and treat me to dinner at Josephine's." He extended his hand. "Deal?"

"Deal." She shook his hand. If Punkin worked this out, he would indeed be Mr. Prime Time. He had been known to pull a few strings when he needed to. "And get away from that mirror, you're starting to remind me of Vicia."

"Let me hurry up and move." He laughed. "Have you thought of a name for your agency?"

"Yes, I have." She had had the name picked out for years, but never told anybody. "Home Sweet Home Adoption."

"That has a nice ring to it," Punkin said thoughtfully. "Tomorrow, get busy looking for a location for your business."

A business. Casey James was about to become a businesswoman. Home Sweet Home had been born. She was about to be her own boss. Yes, Home Sweet Home did indeed have a nice ring to it.

Thirteen

Casey stepped out of the shower and dried off. After dressing and pulling her hair back into a ponytail, she went to the kitchen and retrieved a sports bottle of Ozarka.

"Okay." She pulled a chair away from her dining room table and sat gingerly on it. "Where is my business going to be located?" She opened the newspaper to the Lease section.

For the last few days, she had been searching for the prime location for Home Sweet Home, but nothing seemed to jump out at her. None of the locations listed were ideal. She threw the paper aside in agitation. Since her unofficial vacation began, she had given herself one month to get moved into a building and get the ball rolling on contracts with the state and county. She had gotten some proposals together and submitted them to both the state and the county. She wouldn't know anything about them for a couple of weeks. She was keeping her fingers crossed. The only problem she was having was finding a good location for the agency. There was only one solution to her location problem. She had to find a Realtor.

The first name that came to mind was Alfred Willingham. She hadn't heard anything from him since the day of her meeting with Liz. Yet, he said he wanted to get to know her. Feeling like a fool wasn't something she was used to, but that was how she felt. She had actually been buying into the line he was selling her. The only way she knew to deal with it was to suppress it, and that wasn't an easy thing to do. Maybe Christie and her mother were enjoying themselves at Six Flags. At least she hoped so. If Christie's mother was anything like herself, they would be riding the Serial Thriller right about now. Casey shook her head. She was doing the exact thing she didn't want to do—thinking along the Alfred lines.

"Maybe I'm just tired," she said, consoling herself. "After I've rested for a while, I'll be able to get into a working state of mind. I need a . . ." The ringing phone interrupted her thoughts.

"Yes." Casey answered the phone after the third ring.

"What took you so long to answer the phone?" Punkin asked.

"I knew it was you, and I know how you like to let the phone ring as if you just know I'm home." Casey laughed.

Punkin arched his brows questioningly, as if Casey could see his facial expression. "Now that you're semi-unemployed, where else are you going to be? Your main objective for the past week has been to try and get your business off the ground. So again, where else are you going to be? It's not as if you're going out partying or something."

Casey moved to the living room and stretched out on the sofa, holding the cordless phone to her ear with her shoulder. Although her friend was kidding with her, it was true that she hadn't done too much of anything outside of trying to tie up loose ends and focus on her company.

"I happen to be very content with my life as it is.

Just because you're more of a party animal than I am doesn't mean that I don't go out and have fun," Casey said. "You need to quit trying to get me on the fast track."

"Yeah, yeah. You haven't been having too much fun since I don't know when. Anyway," Punkin said, eager to change the subject. He wasn't in the mood for Casey to get on a soapbox about her night life, and he definitely wasn't in the mood to start lecturing her on spicing up her life. He would save that lecture for another time. "Has your Mr. Willingham made it back to town?"

"I don't know. I haven't talked to him." She made an annoying sound to indicate that she didn't want to discuss it any further. There were more important things she had to concentrate on. Thoughts of Alfred Willingham could wait until another time. Obviously he wasn't thinking about her since he hadn't bothered to pick up the phone and say hello.

"Honey, what is up with him? Has he fallen off the face of the earth or something?"

"Apparently so," Casey said.

"The last time I checked, phones worked both ways. Why haven't you called him?"

"Yes, they do for the Vicias in the world, but not for me," she snapped. "When I call there, I will be calling because of Christie, not Alfred."

"Fine then. What else is new?"

"Nothing. Just trying to find a location for Home Sweet Home. You don't happen to know any Realtors, do you?"

"Not off the top of my head. What about Alfred? Isn't he a Realtor?"

"I don't want him to help me," Casey quickly replied. "I need someone else."

"Why did I know you were going to say that?"

Punkin said with sarcasm. "Do you live to make things difficult? I'll ask my client. Her husband is a Realtor, but I wouldn't trust him any farther than I could throw him," he said, eyeing his client. "They are two of a kind—always trying to get over. She's under the dryer now. I'll go ask her and give you a call back."

After hanging up, Casey stared at the folded newspaper. It was imperative that she find a location, and soon. The sooner, the better. She circled a couple of ads in the paper that sounded like suitable locations. They were in prime areas and were bound to be expensive. She kept her fingers crossed, hoping that Punkin's client could recommend someone. She mulled over the newspaper until the phone rang.

"Casey?" Punkin's voice chimed into the phone.

"Yeah."

"Well, the first name out of her mouth, other than her husband's, was Alfred Willingham the Third." He laughed into the receiver. "She says he's the best in the business. Something about his family having generations of Realtors and them being connected just about everywhere."

"Give me the names and numbers of the other companies." Casey readied her pen and paper as Punkin rattled off the telephone numbers.

"I'll give you Alfred's just in case you change your mind," Punkin said.

"I have enough, thanks," Casey answered.

"Just write it down," he insisted. "You might actually need the number." He gave her the number. "Did you write it down?"

"I got it. Why do you always ask if I wrote it down? You make me feel so elementary."

"You have the habit of trying to remember, and then you'll call me back asking for the number again. That's why I ask. Just one of my pet peeves."

"Well, let's not get started on peeves." If she ever needed a brother, Punkin always stepped in to fill in the shoes.

"From what my client says, Alfred is one hot-lookin' number," Punkin said. "Quit running from the man."

"There's nothing to run from. You never cease to amaze me. All I asked for was a Realtor, and you come back with all of this extra information. How do you do it?" Casey laughed. Punkin always knew the scoop on everybody.

"Well, when I asked her to recommend one, I asked for a single, attractive, well-established Realtor for my best friend. I emphasized that he must be single. That's how I found out. Any more questions?"

"Why do you always do that? You make me sound so desperate. I'm not looking for anyone right now," Casey said.

"Well, looking or not, you need a man! I'm sick of you being in that house all of the time. You need someone to take you out on the town and show you a *good* time, and you *know* what I mean."

"I haven't the slightest clue as to what you're talking about," Casey lied.

"Whatever." Punkin could feel a dead-end conversation coming on.

"How did you manage to get tickets to the Big Brother and Big Sister affair at the last minute?" Casey asked.

"From your girl Marva," Punkin answered. "Marva is the one to pull the strings."

"I didn't know she was into the Big Brother-Sister thing. All I knew about was the annual soirees she throws."

Marva was Casey's sorority sister. Her annual parties were the event of the year. Anybody who was anybody attended. It was the prime opportunity to network.

People in all professions and backgrounds mingled under one roof.

"Honey, do I know more about your sorority than you do?" He laughed. "Maybe I need to be an honorary member. Heck, with as much money as I donate every year, I should be."

"Don't start with that again. You know I'm in a sorority, not a fraternity." She smiled softly. Sometimes she thought Punkin was serious about joining a sorority. The way he complained about it, she was starting to believe it.

"It's a darn shame to be judged by what's between, or shall I say what's *not* between, your legs. It's discrimination, I tell you. Anyway," he let out an anxious breath. "Consider calling your friend. I'm sure he'll help you out a lot quicker than someone you don't know."

"We'll see." She was willing to say anything just to get Punkin off her back about Alfred. Why was everybody so willing to marry her off? It wasn't as if they had to live with whomever she chose to marry. It was she who would have to deal with Prince Charming or Prince not so Charming. But either way, she was going to make a decision on her own terms and not someone else's.

Alfred hoped he would get back to Houston before Christie's mother picked her up for Six Flags. He wanted to make sure that he was there in the event that Kelly didn't show up. He was keeping his fingers crossed because Christie was really looking forward to the outing.

Every day he was in New York, he hoped that Casey would go through the trouble of getting the number to the hotel from Aunt Maggie. He called home daily to see if he had any phone calls, but none of them were from her. Alfred felt that Casey needed some space, but he was suffering on the other end. Could he just let her walk out of his life? *Do I have a choice?*

Unfortunately, he missed the last flight out of New York, and he had to catch the first one this morning. He had the misfortune of taking a coach seat between a man with a hacking cough and a woman who could have been a talk show host in another lifetime. Every time he turned around, the woman was asking him something. He tried several times to close his eyes and sleep, but no, she wouldn't let that happen.

"Do you know anything about stocks?" the woman asked.

Alfred, who was leaning back with his eyes closed, turned and glared at the woman. He put on his most polite voice. "No, I sure don't," he lied. He really looked at her for the first time. She wore a red suit, with red hose, and red pumps. She looked like a red pepper. She was too hot for his taste. The red lipstick against her fair skin looked to him like some kind of blob sitting on her face.

Mr. Hack to Death was busy coughing without so much as lifting a hand to cover his mouth. He was breathing as if he were about to have an asthma attack at any moment. Alfred reached in his shirt pocket and pulled out a mint and offered it to the man.

"So what are you trying to say?" the man said in an offended tone. "You sayin' I got bad breath?" He coughed.

Alfred bit his tongue. The last thing he wanted was an altercation. "No, that's not what I'm saying. I was just thinking that maybe a mint would help soothe your throat and perhaps ease your cough."

The man's hands went up in agitation. "What are

you, some kind of doctor or something?" he snapped.
" 'Cause if you're not, I don't need your advice."

"Fine," Alfred said through clenched teeth. "Just
cough in the other direction."

"That was very rude of him," Ms. Blob sitting next
to him said. "You were just trying to help."

The seat belt sign lit up before the captain came
on to make an announcement. "We've just turned on
the seat belt sign. There's a bit of thunderstorm activity over Louisiana, and we might encounter turbulence for the next fifty miles or so. We're going to
fly around most of the activity, but I'll keep you
posted."

The plane began to bob and weave. Alfred could
feel himself getting queasy. He didn't like flying, but
turbulence was what he disliked the most. He leaned
forward and peered out of the window. The sky was
covered with dark clouds. He had flown through
storms before, but there was something different
about this flight.

The flight attendants were serving drinks when the
pilot asked them to return to their seats. Alfred closed
his eyes and thought about Christie. He couldn't wait
to get back home to her. The next thing on his
agenda when he returned was to set things straight
with Casey.

He gripped the armrests tightly as the plane hit a
bump. He opened his eyes just in time to see one of
the flight attendants hit the ceiling as the plane began
to drop.

Fourteen

Restlessness was beginning to settle in on Casey. Thanks to the uncertainty of her employment, she had nothing but time on her hands. She glanced out the window to find her neighbor's dalmatian, Petey, climbing the fence again. That dog was seriously confused. He must have thought he was a cat. The dog successfully made it over to her side of the fence, although he was still on a chain. Casey went out the back door and over to the fence where Petey was gasping for air. He attempted to bark hello, but nothing came out.

She rubbed his coat. "Petey, why are you trying to commit suicide? Life isn't that bad on the other side of the fence, is it?" She laughed. Petey's tail wagged as she lifted him up and gently dropped him in his backyard. He began to run around happily in circles. She'd asked her neighbors to move him from the fence, but they hadn't done it yet. The last thing she wanted was to look out of her window and see that Petey had choked to death and was hanging over her fence.

A rumble in her stomach reminded her that she hadn't eaten lunch yet. She went back inside to the kitchen and turned on the mini-TV that sat on the counter. Track and field was on NBC. The races would determine who would represent the United States in the Olympics in Australia.

The anchor was bringing the baton home when a special news bulletin interrupted the program. Casey was hardly interested in the news until the reporter mentioned that there was an airplane flying in from New York that had made an emergency landing at Intercontinental Airport. There were two fatalities and an unknown number of injuries. Fire trucks and ambulances lined the runway as passengers slid safely from the emergency exit of the plane.

She noticed that David Downs was covering the story. He was one reporter she had come to loathe. He could be very insensitive at times and was only concerned about telling his version of the story. Casey had the displeasure of working with him on several occasions. Unfortunately, it was for one of her cases. She'd never forget this particular case as long as she lived. Being a relatively new worker, she had the tendency to judge with her heart and not her head. After working with a single mother who was supposed to be rid of an abusive boyfriend, Casey allowed the child to be returned home. Her eyes closed as she remembered that it wasn't a week after the child went back home that he ended up beaten to death. It was a media fiasco. David was all over her case. He questioned her judgment, her motives, and even questioned whether she should keep her job or not. He went on the air and bashed her and Social Services. A few weeks later, *20/20* did a cover story on the poor job Social Services was doing across the nation.

David began to interview people in the airport who were waiting for other flights. He then showed statistics on accidents that had taken place at the airport over the past five years. She was sure this wouldn't be the last of that story.

Her thoughts immediately went to Alfred. Her hand went to her chest. She took a deep breath. Alfred was probably already back at home, at least she hoped so. She didn't know when he was returning from New York. He hadn't called to see how she was doing, so why should she check on him? *This is different. The man could have been on that plane and could be seriously injured.*

She picked up the phone before she had second thoughts. Aunt Maggie answered in a cheerful tone. Casey asked about Christie, and Aunt Maggie said that she was waiting for her mother to pick her up, but she hadn't arrived yet.

"I sure hope Kelly comes," Aunt Maggie said. "When Alfred returns today, he's going to expect Christie to be gone. Kelly's going to have hell to pay if she doesn't come through."

A sense of alarm went through Casey. "When does his flight leave?" she asked calmly.

"Oh, he caught an early flight this morning. He should be home soon."

Casey thought hard about telling Aunt Maggie that Alfred could have been on the plane that had made the emergency landing, but she wanted to be sure before alarming anyone. Before she got off the phone, she asked Aunt Maggie to tell Christie hello.

She tried calling the hot line for information regarding the flight, but the line stayed busy. Without further hesitation, she grabbed her keys and headed out the door.

At the airport, television crews were doing live coverage of the emergency landing. Casey went to the temporary information area for family members of those on the flight.

"Are you a spouse or an immediate family member?" the airline representative asked.

"Uh, yes, I'm a, his—Alfred Willingham's wife," Casey said.

She was sent to a room where other people were waiting for news on the condition of their loved ones. Everyone talked among themselves. She overheard a man telling someone that the plane dropped five hundred feet.

David Downs was suddenly in the room with family members. She shook her head in disdain. He had no respect for privacy. People were distraught and a few were in tears. Did this deter David? No. He insisted on getting his story. He was busy interrogating a woman who broke down crying. Eventually, he got tired of trying to talk to her and yelled, "Cut" to the cameraman. He stormed in the opposite direction until he spotted Casey, who was in a corner observing his horrible attempt at getting a story.

"Well, well," he sneered. "If it isn't Ms. Send a Child to His Doom. Long time no see." He sat in the chair next to her. He summoned the cameraman over. "Apparently you know someone from the flight, so who is it?"

Casey blew a breath of frustration. "Look, David, you've made my life miserable enough. So why don't you go crawl under a rock somewhere and get a life."

David's face went pale. He actually seemed as if he couldn't believe that she was hostile toward him.

"So what happened?" Casey asked. "Why aren't you with one of the three major stations anymore?" David stood and tried to hold on to what dignity he had. "You must have finally put that big foot of yours in your mouth," she said. "That's good for you. You finally got a chance to see what it feels like to be in the hot seat."

David looked as if he could strangle her. Instead, he opted for an exit. "Come on, let's get outta here.

There's no story here." He walked away with the cameraman in close pursuit.

She clucked her tongue. The station he worked for didn't even give him an experienced cameraman to work with. He had truly gone down.

A man entered the room and called for Mrs. Willingham. Casey was so deep in thought that she didn't respond until the man called the name again.

"I'm sorry, Mrs. Willingham," the man said. "I know this is a tough time for you. Could you come with me please?"

What is he going to tell me? Where are we going? Something must be terribly wrong. She followed closely behind the man until they reached another room. When he opened the door, she spotted Alfred in the corner with his feet propped up and his head back. A bandage was taped across his forehead.

"We're happy you showed up, Mrs. Willingham," the man whispered. "He refused to go to the hospital, and he tried to convince us he could drive."

She was relieved to know that Alfred was all right. "I'll make sure he gets home safely."

"Mr. Willingham, your wife is here," the man said to Alfred.

Alfred's head hurt something terrible. Knowing that Kelly was there made it hurt even worse. The airlines must have called her. He could feel her hovering over him. When her hand gently took his, he slowly opened his eyes. He could have jumped for joy when he saw Casey's face looking down into his. It was like waking up and seeing an angel instead of the devil. How did she know? *It doesn't matter how she knows, she's here. She's here because of me. She cares.*

"Hey there," she said, leaning over him. "I thought I lost you for a minute." She glanced over

her shoulder and saw the airline representative still
hovering near.

"Well, Mrs. Willingham," Alfred said, smiling, "I
couldn't leave you like that, could I?"

She stared down into the brown eyes that intrigued
her so. "Could you?" she asked.

"Never," he said finally.

The airport staff insisted that Alfred be pushed in
a wheelchair and escorted them to passenger pickup.
Alfred waited as Casey got her car and drove around.
They helped Alfred into the passenger seat. He reclined the seat and held his hand over the bandage
on his forehead. For a moment, he had thought everything was lost.

"Are you sure you don't want to go to the doctor?"
Casey asked. She didn't know what the bruise looked
like under that bandage. He might need stitches.

"Nah, it's just a bump." He winced as he spoke.
"I'm parked in the garage."

Casey laughed. "I know you don't think you're driving. You can come back to get your car later."

"Yes, doctor." He settled back into the seat. Every
once in a while he would glance over and watch her
maneuver through traffic. He focused on the smooth
skin revealed by the crocheted tank top that exposed
her midriff. He was willing to bet that she couldn't
pinch an inch of fat anywhere on her body. He was
no longer aware of the pain throbbing in his head.
A smile crossed his lips as he looked at her hair,
which was pulled back into a ponytail. What he would
give to run his fingers through that hair. He groaned
in agony, but Casey thought he was in pain.

"We need to talk," he said.

Casey took her eyes off the road for a moment and
looked at him. "About what?"

"You." He paused. "Me, us."

Why was she so intimidated by the word *us? Us!*
Was she ready for *us?* Where would *us* take her?

"I heard there were two fatalities on the flight,
Casey said. "Do you know who they were?"

"Don't run away from this, Casey," Alfred pleaded.
"Do you mind if I go by your place to change clothes?
I don't want to go home like this and worry Christie
and Aunt Maggie. I didn't mention anything about
the flight to them."

"Sure," she answered. She began to think about
what he wanted to discuss. Her palms began to sweat.
All of a sudden the air was suffocating. She lowered
the window to get some fresh air. She nervously began
chewing her bottom lip.

He noticed her demeanor change. She was scared
as all outdoors, but he didn't care. Scared or not,
they were *going* to discuss where their relationship was
headed, and she was *going* to tell him where he stood.
Today would be the beginning of a lifetime or the
beginning of the end.

If her nails weren't done, she would have chewed
them to pieces. The very man who could upset her
entire life was in her shower. She tried to act as normal as possible. Other than Punkin, he was the first
man ever to visit her home. After giving the house
the twice-over, Casey forced herself to sit still. She sat
in the chair fidgeting and wringing her hands. *Just
calm your nerves. He just wants to talk and so do you.
This is your chance to ask why he hasn't called you.*

She swallowed hard when she heard the bathroom
door open. Her jaw almost fell to the floor when Alfred walked into the room wearing nothing but a
towel around his waist. Beads of water rolled down
his chest.

"Could you check this bandage for me?" He seemed as if he weren't aware that he was standing in front of her half naked.

Her first thought was to remain glued to her chair, but she ignored it. She stood and pulled back the bandage. Alfred was staring intensely at her. She stood on her tiptoes to get a better look.

"It's just bruised," she said as she pressed the bandage back in place.

He took her hand, kissed her palm and tasted the tips of each of her fingers. His lips began to weave a spell over her body. Every fiber of her being was screaming *yes!* His fingers pulled the band from her hair so that it fell past her shoulders.

This is what he had been thinking about. The woman whose face filled his mind at every waking moment and dominated his dreams at night was finally in his arms. He pulled her close to him and brought her lips to his. Her hands caressed his back and shoulders. *Do you know what you're getting yourself into? Think, girlfriend, think!*

"What do you want from me?" she whispered against his lips.

The passion that filled his eyes began to dissipate as he held her at arms' length. He tilted her chin so he could see her face.

"What do you think I want from you, Casey?" he asked hoarsely. Casey's silence fueled the anger that was building inside of him. "What do you think I want? To get you into my bed?" He watched Casey step away.

"That's why I'm asking, Alfred." Her eyes met his briefly before looking away.

"I'll be honest with you. Yes, I want to make love to you. I'm not going to stand here and lie to you and say that I'm not attracted to you." He removed the towel from his waist. Her eyes immediately dropped to the floor. Heat began to rise to her cheeks.

He closed the space between them. "Look at me," he commanded. "Yes, you arouse me. Yes, you excite me. You and *only you*." He shook his head. "It's so much more than making love to you. What is it going to take to get that through that head of yours?"

He picked up the towel from the floor and headed to the bathroom. "I'll be dressed in a minute," he called over his shoulder.

Casey fumbled around in the living room, arguing with herself. Yet, she was thoroughly aware of his movements in the bathroom. Being in his arms felt right, and that's where she wanted to be. She felt as if she belonged there. She kept asking herself what she was afraid of, and she couldn't come up with a legitimate answer, although she couldn't forget how her mother was treated by her father. She knew that relationships weren't easy and this one would be no exception to the rule.

Do what comes naturally. I sure hope you're right, Punkin. She headed toward the slightly closed bathroom door. *Once you go in, there's no turning back.* She felt as if she were floating down the hall instead of walking. As she neared the door, her knees began to wobble. Casey swallowed to moisten her dry mouth. *If I'm so ready for this, then why am I about to shake myself to death?* She stood outside the door, listening for any sound on the other side. The only thing she heard was the interminable drumming of her own heart.

Hesitant fingers pushed the door open. Alfred, who was still undressed, was examining the bruise on his forehead. It was then that he noticed Casey standing in the doorway. One look was all that it took, and he knew there would be no denying anymore. He took

Casey into his arms and held her close. Though it had been minutes, it seemed like forever since he held her. Having her close was the fix he had been needing. His hands slid to her back and slowly pulled the tank top over her head.

"This is your last chance to change your mind," he warned in a ragged tone. His hand kneaded the soft skin of her back. The last thing he wanted was for her to feel pressured into making love to him.

Casey held him closer. "I don't want to change my mind. I want you."

"I'm all yours," he said.

Casey successfully hid the nervousness that rested in the pit of her stomach. Her fingers slid across his broad, well-defined chest. His skin was hot to the touch. She left a trail of kisses from his neck to his chest. She was pleased to hear the soft moan he released from his throat. When her eyes met his, she saw a familiar burning intensity. They seemed to be saying, "You've gotten this far, now what?" She didn't falter from his gaze and answered it by allowing her eyes to soak in his body from head to toe.

Alfred could hardly contain his excitement. This was a different Casey James. She was bolder and in control. He didn't want to wonder how things would be after that day. The only thing on his mind was what was happening at the moment. Tomorrow would have to wait. Casey didn't wait for Alfred to remove her jeans. His eyes followed the pants as she slid them to the floor. His breath caught in his throat for a moment. He could never have imagined that her body was so beautiful. There she stood in front of him wearing nothing. A flat stomach; long, muscular legs; shapely hips and ample breasts completed the package.

Casey led Alfred to the bedroom and after taking the necessary precautions, Alfred's hard body covered hers. She had never allowed a man to possess her this way. She never would have dreamed that she would be willing to give herself to any man. What was it about Alfred that made her want him to possess her body and soul? Her arms tightened around him as she prepared to welcome him inside of her.

Alfred was surprised to find that his entry was delayed. A look of concern crossed his face. "Why didn't you tell me?" He kissed her forehead.

"I want this to happen. I didn't tell you because I knew you would have second thoughts about it." She held him closer. "Don't back out on me now." She kissed him fervently on the lips, molding her body to his.

With a low moan, Alfred acquiesced. The pain was bittersweet. With eyes closed, Alfred's voice coaxed her to touch him, explore him, and that she did. She felt uninhibited and free to express herself any way she pleased.

Alfred stroked her hair as they lay limp in each other's arms. He lay awake, listening to the rhythmic sounds of her breathing as she slept. It was too soon to express words of love to her. Yet, he knew love was what he felt.

He touched her gently on the shoulder. "Case, are you awake?" he asked. He waited for her to respond. When she didn't stir, he kissed her on the cheek. "I love you, Casey James."

"I love you too" came the sleepy reply. She burrowed deeper into the covers, returning to a peaceful sleep.

Do you really mean that, Casey James, or are you just dreaming? He silently prayed that she meant it, since he was determined to be her first and only lover for the rest of their lives.

Fifteen

The following weeks were the best she'd ever experienced. Alfred's work schedule was still busy, but she saw it as a chance to spend more time with Christie. Casey found herself becoming attached to the girl. While Alfred was out of town for the weekend, she took Christie to visit San Antonio.

They stayed in a plush suite at the Marriott Hotel, which was right on the river walk. From their balcony, they could look down on the river and had a clear view of the rest of the city. Fortunately, a cool front had come in and instead of the sweltering one hundred and seven degrees they had been experiencing all month, it was a dry ninety-seven degrees.

They drove just outside of San Antonio to the Natural Bridge Caverns. After waiting an hour and a half to buy tickets, they finally got to go on a tour. Neither of them had visited the caves before, but Christie knew a lot about them. After their tour, they went to the other side of the park to the Natural Bridge African Safari. Tourists could drive their own vehicles through the park and feed the animals.

As they drove, an ostrich poked its head through the passenger's window. Christie cringed as the ostrich searched the car for food. Casey laughed as Christie threw the pellets out the window. They stopped along the way to take pictures of different animals.

A visit to Fiesta Texas wrapped up the weekend, and they headed home. Christie slept most of the way back to Houston. She woke up about thirty minutes from her house. She glanced curiously over at Casey.

"Do you like my dad?" Christie asked out of the blue.

Casey hid the surprise the question brought. "Of course I like your father. He's a nice person," she answered carefully.

"No, I mean do you *like* my dad?"

"Whoa, where are these questions coming from?" Casey cleared her throat. She never thought about how Christie felt about her and Alfred. Maybe she didn't want her in her father's life.

"He likes you," she said.

Casey laughed. "What makes you think that?"

"Because he acts all funny whenever you're around, and he smiles a lot." She fumbled with the necklace Casey had bought her at the Natural Bridge Caverns. "And he never lets me leave with anyone other than Aunt Maggie."

Christie continued fingering the rose quartz that was suspended from her necklace. Suddenly a smile crossed her face. "I wish you were my mother. We could have fun all of the time and do things like we did this weekend."

Casey was at a loss for words. No one had ever told her anything like that. She glanced over at Christie, but held her tongue. The only way that would happen was if she were to marry Alfred, and marriage was something she wasn't sure she wanted.

"You always do what you say you're going to do. You love me more than she does." Hurt and anger were in Christie's eyes. "I don't want her to be my mother anymore."

Casey was relieved to drive through the gates that led to the house. She pulled in front of the house and parked the car. She turned to face Christie, who refused to look in her direction.

"Let's talk." Casey tried unsuccessfully to get Christie to face her. She could see from the passenger mirror that tears rolled down her cheeks. "Hey." She reached over and gently turned Christie's face toward her. She wiped away the trails of tears with her thumb.

"I know your mother hurt you. At the same time, she's still your mother. I can never take her place. I care a lot about you, and your mother loves you too."

Christie was busy shaking her head, trying to blot out Casey's words. Her hands covered her ears. She refused to believe that her mother cared anything about her. She even went as far as to say that her mother never wanted her.

"It's true," Christie said. "Her and dad were arguing and I heard her say that the only reason she had me was because he wanted me. She doesn't love me, and nothing you can say will change my mind." She flung open the car door and hopped out. "Nothing!" She slammed the door and stood with her arms folded across her chest.

"Christie," Casey reasoned, "you still have your father. He'll always be here for you when you need him."

Christie pretended not to hear her, but she knew she was listening. "When do I ever see him? He's always working and never has time for me."

"Your father works hard, and he wants to spend more time with you."

Christie's expression showed that she didn't believe

a word Casey was saying. "Then why doesn't he?" She sobbed and took off running toward the house.

Casey called after Christie, but she didn't stop running until she reached the house and disappeared inside. One step forward and a couple of steps backward. It made no sense for Christie to feel like this when she had both parents.

Casey had no idea what to do. She was about to follow Christie into the house when she heard Alfred's Land Rover pulling up. She walked briskly toward the truck. Alfred seemed tired, but he had to have a talk with his daughter. Christie was hurting all of the time, and he had no clue because he was never home.

"Alfred, you need to have a talk with Christie," she said before Alfred could put one foot on the ground.

"What's going on?" He opened the back door and took out his luggage.

"That's just it, Alfred," she said with frustration. "Do you ever know what's going on with Christie?"

Alfred couldn't believe what he was hearing. "Are you telling me that I don't know my daughter?" he asked.

"Hello?" Casey said sarcastically. "Maybe if you stayed home sometime, you'd know how she feels. Instead of working so much, you need to spend some quality time with her. Before you know it, she'll be grow, and you'll wonder where all the time went."

Alfred cut her off. This wasn't the welcome he was expecting. On Friday, everything was as ripe as rain and two days later, it was chaotic.

"Take a look around you, Casey," he snapped. "All of these material things aren't cheap. I work hard to provide my daughter with this lifestyle and in order to maintain this lifestyle, I have to work. You don't have any children, so you don't know what it's like to be a parent." He slammed the truck's back door. "I can't believe she's trying to tell me how to be a father," He mumbled as he picked up his luggage. "I'm a good father! I'm not the best father in the world, but I'm still a good father."

Casey stood with her mouth opening and closing. She was nothing short of blowing her fuse. "You're right, Alfred. I'm not a parent. But I bet you didn't know Christie overheard you and Kelly arguing." Alfred began to walk away, and she followed him. She was going to get her point across, and he was going to listen.

"She heard her mother say that the only reason Christie was here was that *you* wanted her. She doesn't think her mother loves her and probably doesn't think you do either for that matter."

Alfred's luggage hit the ground. "That little girl knows I love her," he yelled, pointing toward the house. "I will do anything in the world for her, and she knows that."

"Oh, really?" she asked. "Well, I told her that you work hard and you want to spend more time with her, but she asked why you don't. If you will do anything in the world for her, start with something simple. Give her some of your time."

"What do you want me to do? Have my child living on the streets? I'm not going to put her in that situation. I work because of her."

Casey threw up her hands and began backing away. "I'm willing to bet that this"—she motioned toward the house and cars—"*lifestyle* doesn't mean as much to her as it does to you. She would probably trade all of it like that"—she snapped her fingers—"for a little of your time."

"I'll be the judge of that," he said, hotly. "I'm her father, and I'll decide what's best for *my* daughter."

He picked up his things and walked toward the house. As far as he was concerned, that was the end of the conversation. Where did she get off trying to tell him what to do with *his* daughter? If he didn't know any better, he would believe she was trying to tell him that he was no better a parent than Kelly and that was the furthest thing from the truth. Kelly didn't put clothes on Christie's back or shoes on her feet. She wasn't the one who fed her and kept a roof over her head. He was the one to do those things. And if he didn't love his daughter, he wouldn't worry about being a provider for her.

At first Casey just stood watching him head to the house. She thought maybe he would turn around and finish their discussion. When she saw he had no intention of coming back, she waved him off and went to her car. She couldn't make him spend time with his own daughter, and he basically told her that it was none of her business. She could respect that. He didn't have to worry about her dipping into his business ever again. She had nothing else to say about the matter.

As she drove down the streets, Casey's anger turned into pain. Alfred had never snubbed her before. Did he really not want her to be concerned about Christie? *Yes, silly! He basically told you to butt out. If that's what he wants, that's what he'll get.*

"What was all that yelling about?" Aunt Maggie asked.

"Nothing," Alfred said as he threw his luggage on the floor by the door and went to the kitchen. Aunt Maggie was close behind.

"That didn't sound like *nothing* to me. Christie ran in all upset earlier. What's going on?" Aunt Maggie watched as he went into the refrigerator and poured himself something to drink. His whole demeanor screamed anger, and since she had practically raised him, she knew when he was upset.

"What's going on is, I don't need someone who doesn't have any children telling me what I should do with my daughter." He pulled out a chair and sat at the table.

"I see," Aunt Maggie said. "Would that someone happen to be Casey?"

"Uh-huh," he grunted.

"Well, sometimes someone on the outside can see something you can't see from the inside. Could that be the case?"

"I don't know, Aunt Maggie. Maybe." He stood abruptly. "I'm going to lie down for a while."

As he headed upstairs, his legs became heavier and heavier with each step he took and so did his thoughts.

Sixteen

Alfred took Quincy up on his offer to meet for drinks and buffalo wings at Bennigan's. He sat at the bar, waiting for Quincy. It was ironic that the last time he was there, he saw Casey for the first time. He had to admit that she was right about Christie. Casey was right about everything she said. It just hurt to hear the truth. He was almost certain that he had damaged their relationship. His pride wouldn't let him pick up the phone and call her.

He spotted Quincy coming through the door. He motioned for him to join him at the bar. Quincy sat next to him and ordered a beer.

"How's it going?" Quincy asked. "I haven't heard from you in a while." He took a long look at Alfred. Something was up with him. He seemed down, and he looked as though he hadn't shaved in days, which was totally unlike him.

"It's cool," he answered. "I've been hanging around the house, spending some time with Christie."

"You okay?" Quincy asked. He had been trying to get in touch with Alfred for the last few days, but he never returned his phone calls. "I hate to say this, but you're looking kind of rough, my brother."

"Yeah." Alfred tried to sound lighthearted, but he

knew Quincy could see right through him. "I've been busy."

Quincy looked at him in disbelief. "Oh, yeah? Well, you've always had a busy schedule, and you managed to keep your appearance intact." He laughed. "Man, you can't compromise our Kappa standards. We have a reputation to uphold."

"Right, right," he said in a better mood. "I'll be back on the job soon."

"Glad to hear it. You know the benefit is coming up soon. Why don't you go? Get out and mix and mingle," Quincy said.

"I sure hope this isn't one of your ploys to play matchmaker," Alfred said. He was game to attend the benefit, but he didn't want a surprise date. He was having trouble enough keeping up with his current situation.

Quincy studied him in mock disbelief "Man, I can't believe you would think that I would try something like that *again*. I haven't tried matchmaking in more than five years." He looked at Alfred out of the corner of his eye. "Besides, you and Casey make an attractive couple." He figured that was the right button to push. For him to look as ragged as he was, Quincy sensed a woman was the root of the problem.

Quincy could always tell when something was wrong with him. There was no use trying to avoid the subject. Maybe Quincy could shed some light on his situation.

"I don't know about that." Alfred finished off his beer. "We kind of fell out."

A look of surprise crossed Quincy's face. "When?"

"Last Sunday." Alfred turned to the boxing match on the silent screen, buying time to respond.

"Man, what happened?" Quincy set his beer on the bar. "I thought everything was going pretty good."

He hoped another one didn't bite the dust. He knew Alfred liked Casey a lot, and he didn't want to see him go through more changes.

"It was, until last week." Quincy listened as Alfred told him all the details of the argument.

"I don't think she was saying that you are a bad father," Quincy said. "She was probably upset because Christie stormed out on her, and she panicked. Actually, I agree with her that Christie needs more of your time. I think you know that too."

"I know," Alfred said. "I never knew Christie overheard that argument between me and Kelly. I didn't know because I'm never home, and I don't sit down and talk to her as much as I should."

"Well, you know the problem, so all you have to do is fix it. So what are you going to do about Casey?" Quincy went to turn up his glass before noticing it was empty. "Wanna buy me another drink?"

Alfred, who was lost in everything he had just said, failed to respond.

Quincy called the bartender over and ordered a beer for himself and Alfred. He swiveled his stool around to face Alfred. "How do you feel about her?"

Alfred shrugged. "I care about her," he answered.

"You care about her or you love her?"

He avoided answering the question. "When you first met Marva, what was it like? I know you liked her, but was it like, like love at first sight? Did you know she would be your wife?" Alfred gave Quincy his full attention.

Quincy beamed as he thought of Marva. She was everything he could possibly want in a woman and more. Besides Alfred, she was his best friend. Whatever he wanted and needed in a woman, Marva was it.

"When I first met her, man, it was like I knew she

was the one." He stopped talking to accept his beer from the bartender. "I think love at first sight is an understatement. She's not the best-looking woman that I've ever dated, but she is beautiful—inside and out. She was like the missing piece to a puzzle that I had been without for a long time. She made me complete." He sipped his beer, happy to have met the woman that had his best friend contemplating such things. Casey must pack a powerful punch because Alfred swore he was never settling down again until he found *the one.*

"I don't know, man," Alfred said, staring at the television. "Do you ever think Jones will be able to set foot in the ring again?"

Quincy watched the two amateur boxers going at it on the screen. "I don't know. I hope so. I haven't been keeping up with boxing since the last fight party we threw at the house. So, what are you going to do?"

"I don't know," Alfred answered. "Maybe I should just back off the situation for a while."

"Man, you love that woman, so don't let her slip through your fingers. Do something, man. Let her know how you feel."

"I was thinking about giving her a call and apologizing."

"Is that all?" Quincy asked. "You basically told her to get out of your business because you are father of the year." He laughed. "You're going to have to do something better than that. Use your imagination."

"You're right. I'll have to think of something."

The waiter brought out their buffalo wings with celery and bleu cheese dressing. Alfred dug in. Quincy was more reserved because Marva was cooking dinner.

"Well, don't wait too long. Like my daddy used to tell me, study long, study wrong."

Alfred laughed. "I knew you were going to break out with one of his quotes. It never fails."

"Hey." Quincy took a bite of a celery stick. "Words to live by."

"That may have some validity to it," Alfred admitted.

"There's only one way to find out. You need to lay it on thick, and I'm sure you're just the man to get the job done. You're going to have to do some serious impressing."

"I think I can manage that." Quincy always had a way of making him see things from a better perspective. He was a true friend.

"Marva and I just want to see you happy. We want you to find whatever it is you're looking for. If you think this woman is it, let go. Maybe she's the one you've been waiting for."

"It's not that easy, and you know it. How can I let go with someone who I'm not sure is willing to do the same for me? It's just not that easy," Alfred replied

"Of course it is."

"I don't know, man. What if she's the wrong one?"

"There's nothing to it. Just do it." Quincy pulled out a twenty and placed it on the bar. "My treat tonight. You coming over for dinner? Marva's making her famous lasagna."

As appealing as it sounded, Alfred wanted to be alone with his thoughts. He had to figure out what to do about Casey James.

"Nah, Q. Not tonight. See you on the basketball court tomorrow?"

"Tomorrow." He placed a comforting hand on Alfred's shoulder. "You know the offer still stands for dinner."

Alfred waved it off, shaking his head. "The wings were enough for me."

"Hey, you don't have to eat, you can come socialize with us." Alfred wasn't budging. "All right, don't think too hard," Quincy said with a smile. "See you tomorrow. Be prepared to get taken to the hoop, my brother." He looked back before walking out the door. His friend had finally found true love and hadn't the slightest clue what to do with it.

Casey was a special lady, and Quincy was right. Alfred couldn't let her slip through his fingers. He had a long talk with Christie the night he'd argued with Casey. He realized that night that he didn't tell his daughter he loved her enough. Instead, he showered her with material things. All she had to do was say, *Daddy, can I have . . .* and it was done. Every night he thought about picking up the phone to call Casey and say he was sorry. But his stubbornness told him that he had nothing to apologize for. Minutes later, he would find himself with the phone in his hand dialing her number, only to hang it up before it rang. He was in a constant war with himself *Should I? Shouldn't I?* Lately, the *shouldn't I*s were winning. Not any more. He was going to take control of the situation and get the woman he loved back into his life.

Seventeen

It had been nine days since her clash with Alfred. She guessed it was really over. Not that she had put much effort into trying to find out where they stood. She couldn't bring herself to pick up the phone and call him. In her mind, it would have seemed that she was crawling back to him when he told her to get lost. No, she couldn't send herself through that kind of torture. She wondered if he sat up late at night thinking about her. She wondered if he missed the sound of her voice or the touch of her hand the way she missed his. It was kind of hard coming back to earth after she had caught a glimpse of heaven. Her old routine wasn't the same after she had gotten to know him.

After thinking long and hard, she decided to call Ms. Green and withdraw from the Big Brother and Big Sister program. She felt she had overstepped her boundaries, especially since Christie wished she were her mother instead of Kelly. Leaving the program was something she didn't want to do because it would be Christie who suffered in the end. Of course, she would call her from time to time to check on her. She had upset Christie's life enough, and she felt it would be best to break the ties now rather than later.

Casey kept reliving the afternoon she argued with Alfred. If she could go back to that day, she would do everything differently. She wouldn't have approached Alfred the way she had.

"I could have at least waited until he got out of the truck. But no, I *had* to go over there screaming at him. What was I thinking?" she asked herself.

This was the first morning that she actually had an appetite. She had been forcing herself to eat for the last couple of days. Everything was bland, like her life. She knew she should have trusted her first mind about him. Why did she allow him into her life when she knew what the outcome was going to be?

She was sipping a cup of coffee when she received a call from Liz. After seeing the number on the caller ID, she was hesitant to answer the phone. Did she have any news about her job? She was ready to go back to work just to keep her mind off her issues. Dealing with the problems of other people was more appealing than dealing with her own. Finally, she picked up the phone. Liz asked her how she was doing and wanted to know what she had been up to. They chitchatted for a few more minutes before Liz got to the point.

"We're having a meeting today. You'll know where you stand by this afternoon. So keep your fingers crossed," Liz said. "I'll do what I can. I'm going in there to fight for you. I don't want to see you go."

"Me either," Casey said. "It's good to know you're on my side. Thanks for calling, Liz."

Butterflies settled in her stomach after that phone call. Casey didn't know whether she was hoping to keep her job or to lose it. If she lost it, then she could devote all of her time to Home Sweet Home. If she could keep her job, then her own business would be on the back burner, and she didn't necessarily want her business to come last. If she put it off, she would probably never get things off the ground.

She poured the rest of her coffee down the drain. She noticed Petey running around in her backyard dragging his chain behind him. At least she didn't have to worry about him hanging himself. He'd climb back over the fence when he got ready to go home. She really wished her neighbors would do something about their dog. He was beautiful, and she couldn't understand why they had him outside. He belonged in the house.

Not being too fond of Petey climbing the fence, she put on her slippers and was about to go outside and take him back home when Punkin called, begging her to get dressed. He said he had the ideal place for Home Sweet Home. That was the best news she had heard in days. It seemed as if everything in her life had been going down the drain lately. Maybe her luck was about to change.

Punkin pulled his black Navigator into the driveway almost an hour later. He took in her appearance as she got into the passenger's seat. "You look like you haven't slept for days. Honey, don't have regrets for telling him the truth. If you ask me, I think he should be crawling on his knees and begging to get you back."

"Well," Casey said sarcastically, "he hasn't crawled or begged yet and that says a lot. I don't care if I ever see him again. It goes to prove that I was right about him all along."

Punkin masked his face with dark shades. Casey could be a Ms. Goodie-two-shoes when she wanted to. He wasn't about to let her go back to that life of boredom and depression just because her father was a poor excuse for a man. All she needed when it came to relationships was a little backbone. As far as business was concerned, she had all of the backbone she needed. Punkin was proud of Casey for having the courage to take a leap of faith and start her own business. She had a lot more courage than most of the people he knew.

"Well," Punkin said, "there are two people in a relationship. Have you done anything to make things right?"

She glanced out the window, not willing to answer his question. Punkin *would* have to play the devil's advocate, telling her things she didn't want to hear, but already knew.

"I saw your mother at the casino this weekend." Punkin laughed. "She had the nerve to have a date. Honey, he wasn't bad-looking either. Your mama waits until she gets old and wants to be getting her mack on."

"Oh, yeah?" Casey asked with vague interest. "She's not dead, you know. Nobody wants to be lonely. I'm happy she's dating. I've never seen my mother bring a man to the house." Now that she thought about it, her mother never seemed interested in dating. The only thing she was concerned about was taking care of her daughter.

"Yeah, but it was the strangest thing." He frowned. "When I looked at him, I kept thinking that I had seen him somewhere before. It finally dawned on me that I didn't know him but he reminded me of someone." He paused. "Actually, he reminded me of you."

Casey's eyes widened. "Punkin, what are you saying?"

Punkin didn't know whether he wanted to continue the conversation. "I don't know. He looked like a male version of you," Punkin said. "I got to putting two and two together, and I think that man was your father."

Casey's eyes closed. If by any slight chance that man was her father, it would be sheer coincidence that her mother saw him. "Punkin, my father is long gone. He was probably someone she met while she was there." At least she hoped so.

"You're right," he said. "It was just my imagination running away from me." He turned up the radio as they headed just outside of downtown. Casey suddenly seemed fidgety, and the last thing Punkin to do was upset her. He was beginning to regret he had mentioned her father. He already knew how she felt about him. Their usually carefree attitudes were replaced by tension. He could tell she was thinking hard about what he had said. *Man, I really know how to put my foot in my mouth!* Twenty minutes later, they turned into a parking lot, and Punkin drove around until he found a parking space. He turned off the ignition, but didn't move from the seat.

"Casey, I'm sorry I mentioned that. For a moment, I forgot how you feel about your father. I wasn't trying to be funny or anything, and I wasn't being careless about how you feel."

"It's okay." Casey looked at the dashboard. If she looked him in the eyes, he would know how she truly felt. "Don't worry about it." She forced a smile to her face.

"That's the building over there," Punkin said. "I think it's a good location."

They were parked across the street from a redbrick building with French accents. It was located just outside of downtown in an area that seemed to thrive with businesses. Casey finally focused and found that she liked the location.

They entered the building and walked through its plush lobby and caught the elevator up. When the doors opened, they stepped out onto marble floors, which glistened under the lights.

"It's must be this way." Punkin steered her to the right and headed down the long hallway. They rounded another corner and went to the office at the end of the hall.

They peered through the glass doors to a suite. From what they could see through the glass, there was one large office and four medium-sized ones. There was a large reception area that had a parquet hardwood floor. Casey could visualize a large oriental rug in the middle of the room. How the office would be decorated was taking shape in her mind. It was just what she was looking for. The office wasn't too large or too small. It was perfect. She couldn't wait for the Realtor to get there so she could get a better view.

"The Realtor said that the space across the hall is yours too, if you want it, in case you want to expand. There's a door that connects to the suite." The elevator bell sounded as the doors opened. "Hey," Punkin said, "let me go down to the truck. I left my cell phone, and I need to see if any clients have made it in. I'll be right back." He dashed for the elevator before Casey could offer to go with him. She didn't want to be hanging in the hallway by herself until the Realtor came. She hoped Punkin hurried back.

She knew she wasn't going crazy, but she thought she vaguely heard the sound of jazz music playing. She looked up at the ceilings, but there were no speakers around. Her ears strained to make out where it was coming from. Stepping closer to the door, Casey pressed her ear against the glass. It sounded as though the music was coming from inside. She turned the knob, and to her surprise, the door opened. Maybe the Realtor was already inside waiting for them to arrive.

She called out, but no one answered. *What kind of stuff is this?* She called out again, and still no one answered. He probably couldn't hear her because of the music. She followed the sound to an office in the back. The door was closed, so she rapped on it. Again, there was no answer.

She took a deep breath. Slowly, she turned the knob and opened the door. Now she could hear the music clearly. The room was completely dark, with the exception of a single candle. *That's strange.* She fumbled along the wall for a light switch, but stopped because she could feel that someone was there. The person stepped into the soft light thrown off by the candle and when the light cascaded across his face, words failed her. *It's Alfred!* She couldn't move from where she stood. He walked toward her and pulled her inside, closing the door. After straining her eyes, she could see that the room was completely filled with flowers. *What an apology!*

He kissed her softly on the lips. "It's good to see you again, Casey."

Her only response was to hold him close. She never thought she would see him again. Just when she thought it was over, he came back and reassured her he would be there.

"Please accept this as a gift from me to you," Alfred said.

"I'm not sure I'm following you," Casey said. Surely he wasn't talking about what she was thinking.

"Someone informed me that you've been looking for a place to start your own business." He stepped closer to her so he could see her eyes. "Let me help you."

As much as she would have liked that, she couldn't let him do it. She would feel indebted to him forever. He could see that she was about to resist, but he couldn't let that happen. She opened his eyes to some things he would never have known. The least he could do was give her a start at something she deeply believed in.

"I won't take no for an answer," he insisted. "Why didn't you tell me about your job?"

"Punkin has such a big mouth." Casey pretended to be upset. "It wasn't your fault that I got into trouble. I'm the reason I'm in this position, and I knew what I was getting myself into."

"All this time I thought you were just taking a vacation." He took her hands into his. "I want you to know how sorry I am for the way I acted. You were only concerned about Christie, and I should have listened to what you had to say. I also want you to know that I've been miserable without you, and my life hasn't been the same."

He could see tears begin to form in her eyes. He dried her tears with his fingers. "Marry me, Casey." He hadn't planned on proposing, but seeing her again and feeling this overflow of emotions made him want her in his life *forever.* "I love you, and I'm praying that you feel the same way about me."

"Are you sure you love me?" she asked with a shaky voice. "You aren't asking me this just because we argued, are you?"

"Yes, I'm sure I love you," he whispered. "I wouldn't make this decision just because we argued. I want to marry you. Let's get our license and get married this weekend."

He wanted to many her. He said he loved her, and if love felt this good, she wanted it for the rest of her life.

"Yes," she said, hugging him tightly. "I'll marry you."

Eighteen

Her mother was ecstatic when she heard the news. She insisted on cooking dinner for them, so she could meet Alfred. She called all of her friends and bragged about her daughter's engagement. She knew her daughter was in love when she came by sulking and dragging around. Casey had told her so much about Alfred, and she always said such nice things. She kept asking to meet him, but Casey always refused, saying she wasn't bringing anyone for her to meet unless he was *the one*. Well, finally, *the one* was coming to dinner.

Alfred was quiet on the drive to Casey's mother's house. He fumbled with the radio awhile before turning it off. His fingers drummed a beat on the steering wheel. Surely this powerful man, who could be a cutthroat businessman, wasn't worried about meeting her mother. Casey looked over at her husband-to-be and smiled. She grabbed his hand and held it.

"You think she'll like me?" Alfred asked nervously as they pulled into Casey's mother's driveway.

"Trust me." Casey gave his hand a reassuring squeeze. "She's going to love you."

She noticed a gold Chrysler parked in her mother's driveway. She hadn't seen that car before. Maybe someone dropped by for a few minutes. The front door swung open and her mother grabbed both of their hands and pulled them inside.

"Give me a hug. I finally get to put a face with the name," Casey's mother said to Alfred. She hugged him as if she had known him all of her life. "There must be something special about you because I never thought this day would come." She laughed.

"And you come here." She gave Casey a tight hug, rocking side to side as she embraced her. She touched her daughter's face. "I just can't believe it." Her baby was getting married! Casey was finally going to get the happiness she always refused to let herself have.

She ushered them to the den where an older gentleman was watching television. "This is, uh, Jay." Her mother quickly made the introductions.

There was something vaguely familiar about the man, but Casey couldn't put a finger on it. Maybe he just had one of those familiar faces. Jay stood and shook Alfred's hand and then Casey's. He was much taller than he first appeared. Her mother was standing in the doorway, with a hand across her chest. She seemed to be holding her breath.

Jay commented on what a beautiful woman Casey was. He stood there awkwardly gazing at her. "You look just like your mother," he said looking from Casey to her mother.

Casey could feel herself growing uncomfortable. She cleared her throat. "Well," she said, laughing nervously, "my family always said I looked a lot like my father."

Jay rubbed the back of his neck. He suddenly seemed to be stressing out. He turned his attention to Alfred and smiled. "I hear you're about to be a lucky man," he said.

"And a proud one, I might add," Alfred said. He began to scrutinize Jay closely. There was something about the way he looked at Casey that made him uneasy. He couldn't put his finger on it.

"Well," Jay said, slapping Alfred's shoulder, "let's talk politics." They headed to their own section of the room and became engrossed in their own conversation.

Casey noticed that her mother had disappeared into the kitchen, so she joined her there. Her mother never looked up. She was acting a little weird. Was she hiding something from her?

"Have I seen him somewhere before?" Casey asked her mother, who was busy fumbling around in the kitchen. "I've seen him somewhere before," she said, answering her own question.

"Well, they say we all have a twin somewhere in the world," her mother said without looking up from the salad she was making.

After washing her hands, Casey took a knife from the drawer and began peeling cucumbers. That was her job when she was a little girl. She peeled in silence. It was starting to irk her nerves that she knew this man, but couldn't remember where she'd seen him. Her mother was tense, and the silence wasn't making it any better.

"Where'd you meet him?" Casey asked as she crunched on a slice of cucumber.

Her mother took the sliced cucumbers and tossed them in the salad. She opened the refrigerator and placed it on the bottom rack. She sure seemed to be taking her time answering.

"The casino." She washed and dried her hands before checking the roast in the oven.

Casey began making up all sorts of explanations, yet none seemed to satisfy her. Why in the world would her mother meet someone at the casino and bring him home? *He looks like a male version of you.*

Nah, Punkin was wrong. He had no idea what her father looked like.

"So, you just met at the casino and now you're dating? Is that it?" Casey asked. suspiciously.

"That's it," her mother said as she placed the roast on top of the oven.

Casey wasn't too fond of her mother's clipped answers and didn't like the way she wouldn't look at her when she spoke. It was as if she didn't want her asking questions.

"How long have you known him? I mean, you don't just meet someone and bring him to your house. He could be a murderer or something." She looked behind her to make sure Jay was nowhere around. "Besides, I don't like the way he looks at me."

"Don't be silly." Her mother continued poking around at the roast. "Jay was just noticing how you and I resemble each other, that's all."

"You never said how long you've known him," Casey said.

Her mother was growing frustrated. She wasn't used to her daughter interrogating her.

"Casey," she said in the lightest tone she could muster, "this is *your* night. We can talk about me another time." She placed a pan of broccoli-and-cheese casserole in Casey's hands. "Let's set the table." Then she walked to the dining room, leaving Casey to her own thoughts.

Alfred kept trying to get her attention, but her mind was on her mother. After a while, Alfred gave up trying to get her in the mood. He had to prod her to tell him what was bothering her. She finally opened up and told him what she was thinking.

"I think both you and Punkin have an overactive

imagination." Alfred massaged her shoulders as they lay on the massive couch with oversize pillows in the family room. "You'd know your father if you saw him, and besides, your mother wouldn't keep something like that from you." He planted a kiss on her cheek. Even he had to admit that there was a strong resemblance. It was actually starting to make sense because Jay tried to get his life story from him in a matter of minutes. That could even explain the way he looked at Casey. If he was indeed her father, he wondered where he had been all those years.

"Every time I asked my mother about Jay, she was all tense, as if she didn't want to discuss it. She was acting strange. What if I'm right?"

"Then you deal with it. You have to find out why he wasn't there and take it from that point. Don't you have any pictures of your father?"

She pointed to her head. "They're in here. I burned all of his picture when I was a little girl. I wanted him out of my life altogether and I thought by burning his pictures I could make those thoughts go away, but I was wrong. Somehow, I can't really remember his face, it's a blur in my mind." She turned so she could see Alfred's face. "Don't let that happen to Christie. I know sometimes her mother frustrates you, but always leave the door open for her to visit her daughter."

"I promise," he said.

He knew that she was bothered by her father not being around, but he never knew it affected her in this way. If Jay was her father, it would only open an old wound which had healed on the outside only. Maybe this time, she could deal with her father and let the wound heal inside out.

Alfred agreed with her that her mother was acting strange. She kept dominating the conversation every

time Casey even acted as though she wanted to ask
Jay a question. She'd even jump in the conversation
if Jay had anything to say to Casey.

Casey wrapped herself in Alfred's arms. She wanted
to believe that Jay wasn't her father, but she was having a hard time. Alfred was right, she'd know her
father if she saw him.

Nineteen

"I knew you were nosy enough to follow the music." Punkin laughed as they priced one of Vera Wang's wedding dresses. "I'm glad you're not on a horror movie because you would be the first one to get killed. The nosy people always die first. Didn't you ever watch *Halloween* and *Friday the 13th?*"

"You're silly," Casey said.

"Honey, hold out that hand and let Punkin see that rock." He took her hand into his to examine the five carats Alfred had placed on her finger. "That's what I call love." He pretended to wipe a tear from his eye with his pinky finger. "Is that platinum?" he squeaked. "It's so beautiful I could cry and it ain't even mine. It has all the four Cs."

"What?" Casey asked.

"The four Cs." He repeated. "Color, clarity, cut, and what I think is most important of all, *carats*. So, what does your mama think?"

"Oh, she fell in love with him. He's got her wrapped around his finger."

"I can't believe we're finally getting you married off. You're going to be such a beautiful bride. I just can't believe it." He gave her a tight hug. "Now who am I going to call at three in the morning when I have a problem?"

"You can still call me." Casey laughed. "I'm just getting married."

She slipped into a dressing room to try on the gown. Punkin rooted himself outside the door. He felt privileged to be the first one to catch a glimpse of her dress.

"And you found a real prince charming too," he said through the door.

"I saw my mother's, uh . . ." She hesitated. *"Friend"* The only thing she heard was a grunt from him. She opened the door so he could zip the dress for her. "I know you're waiting for me to say it, but I think you're wrong."

"You *think* I'm wrong or you *hope* I'm wrong?"

Casey opened the door and stepped out. Punkin smiled appreciatively. She walked over to the full-length mirror. She fell in love with the dress. She stared at her reflection in the mirror and spun around a couple of times. Who would ever have thought she would be getting married?

"You look stunning," Punkin said. "Alfred is going to fall over once he takes a look at you coming down the aisle. You're so beautiful that if I were straight, I'd marry you myself. Alfred is lucky to have caught my best friend."

"Don't make me cry." Casey wiped her eyes. "The last thing I want to do is cry all over this dress before I buy it or get to wear it."

They spent the rest of the afternoon reminiscing over old times and discussing the future. She was getting the feeling that Punkin was more excited about her wedding than she was. It didn't matter what size the rock on her finger was. If Alfred had given her a diamond chip, she would have gladly accepted his proposal. She didn't measure love by the size of the diamond in her ring. Learning to love was a beautiful thing.

"I'm not going to say I'm not happy for you." Quincy rubbed chalk over the tip of his pool stick before tapping the right corner pocket. He raised up as he knocked the ball into the pocket. "When I suggested you apologize, I didn't think you would propose."

Alfred leaned over and aimed for the eight ball. "Believe me, proposing wasn't even on my mind." The eight ball went into the right pocket.

Quincy was happy that Alfred had finally found someone. Now maybe he could settle down and have the ideal family he never had with Kelly. "Oh, man, you really know how to pick 'em. She's a knockout. Casey is a pretty nice lady."

"Yeah, she is, isn't she?" Alfred asked.

"How has Kelly reacted to you getting married? You know, I think she always hoped you two would get back together." Quincy followed Alfred into the kitchen and sat at the table. He laced his fingers together and leaned back, folding them behind his head.

"I haven't talked to her. She hasn't bothered about coming around before, so what difference is it going to make?" Alfred asked. "She'll just have to deal with it."

"You haven't told her?" Quincy asked. "She's going to flip her wig."

"She'll be all right." Alfred joined Quincy at the table. "All she wants is someone to hold her hand financially anyway."

"That's what I mean, and she's going to see your new wife as a threat to the finances. And you think Casey's the right one?"

"Man, I *know* she's the right one." His tone was a little on the defensive side. Quincy's expression prompted him to soften his tone. "She's what Christie and I need and want."

"Man," Quincy said, "I don't want to play the devil's advocate, but this happened kind of suddenly. I just don't want to see you make the same mistake twice. If you recall, you did the same thing with Kelly."

"I know, and I really did love her at the time. Since I truly cared about her, I couldn't actually call it a mistake at the beginning."

"Now you want to get all analytical on me. Kelly was a mistake. Had you known how she really was, would you have married her?"

Quincy could see frustration written all over Alfred's face. He decided not to press the issue. Maybe Alfred knew what he was getting himself into. He went to the refrigerator searching for something to drink.

He smiled. "I think she'll make you a good wife. I have to admit, you two look good together."

"Thanks," Alfred answered. Why was Quincy questioning his judgment?

"I hate to rain on your parade, but you know Kelly is going to have a fit." Quincy sighed. "This could get ugly."

"Kelly will just have to accept whatever happens." He finally noticed Quincy still digging around for lemonade. "Man, look behind the milk. It's right where I always keep it."

Quincy poured himself and Alfred a glass of lemonade and returned to the table. "Yeah, Kelly is going to have to get herself a life."

"Kelly does have a life and that's been the problem. She rarely calls Christie to see how she's doing and

she stood her up for mother-daughter day at Six
Flags." He drummed his fingers on the tabletop.
"That was the last straw."

Quincy rolled his eyes toward the ceiling. "I don't
blame you. She wouldn't keep playing with my child's
emotions."

Quincy pushed back his chair and stood to leave.
"We all have a long way to go. Like I said, don't worry
about Kelly. I want you to be happy. If Casey makes
you happy, and you can deal with all of this other
mess, cool. Wanna play ball tomorrow, around six?"

"Yeah, six is fine. I'm supposed to go with Christie
and Casey tomorrow to find Christie something for
the wedding."

"Cool. I'll see ya later."

Alfred sat on the steps as Quincy drove off. What
if Quincy was right about him rushing into things?
Had he really done the same things before he married Kelly? Was he setting himself up for failure once
again? He hoped not, because this time, he knew what
to do differently. At least he hoped he knew.

Twenty

Casey glanced at her watch. It was the second time she'd checked it in the last thirty minutes. It was almost noon, and the restaurant was starting to fill up from the lunch crowd. Why Alfred chose that particular restaurant to have lunch, she didn't know. She preferred something that wasn't so ritzy. A vast majority of the people who walked in looked as if they spent most of their time on a golf course or at a day spa. She overheard two women discussing when they planned to get their next boob and nose jobs. She never felt so out of place in her life.

A sigh of relief escaped as she saw Alfred and Christie coming to the table. Christie hugged her, and Alfred gave her a peck on the cheek. Christie was excited about the wedding and the reception that was going to follow. They were busy planning the day's activities when a woman stopped by their table.

Her hair was slicked back into a chic chignon, which showed off the almost perfect bone structure in her face. Arched eyebrows highlighted her almond-shaped gray eyes. She tried to make her thin lips fuller with more lipstick. She moved with the grace of a runway model. She was chic and elegant.

She cleared her throat as she gazed down in Alfred's direction. Alfred, who seemed to grow uncom-

fortable, glanced back and forth between Casey and
the woman. As if by cue, he cleared his throat and
introduced her.

"Casey," Alfred said, "this is Kelly, Christie's mother."
Kelly looked down her nose at Casey as if she were
some creature from outer space. "Kelly, this is Casey."

"Hello," Casey said. "It's nice to meet you."

Kelly didn't even acknowledge her presence. She
glanced at Casey's hand. "I guess you've resorted to
dating married women."

This woman acted as though she controlled Alfred.
Casey could tell she was used to manipulating situ-
ations to fit her needs. She sauntered up to their table
as if she had the authority to make anyone do whatever she wanted. Casey's eyes narrowed. This was Alfred's situation, so she held her tongue.

Alfred groaned inwardly. Why did Kelly have to pop
up out of the blue? She was the last person he wanted
to see. *Why now?* He knew he was going to have to
deal with her sooner or later, but he didn't think it
would be this soon. He forgot she enjoyed dining at
this particular restaurant.

"No," Christie volunteered, "she's not married yet,
but she's gonna marry Daddy." She grabbed Casey's
hand and held it up for Kelly to see. "Isn't it pretty?"
she asked proudly.

Kelly's head whipped around in disbelief. Her eyes
darted quickly from Casey's hand to her face. "Christie," she said in a harsh tone, "how many times have
I told you not to speak until spoken to? Children are
to be seen and not heard." Christie shrank down in
her seat. "And sit up properly," Kelly snapped.
"Young ladies don't slouch." Christie became stiff as
a board.

Kelly turned to Alfred. "I knew nothing about you
planning to get married. Is this nonsense true?"

He closed his eyes, trying to blot out her words. Arguing with Kelly in public was not something he wanted to do.

"Just when were you planning on telling me? Am I not important enough to be informed until after the tragedy has taken place?" Her eyes changed to a bluish color. "Oh," she said loud enough for others to hear. "I guess you weren't going to tell me about this. I'm your child's mother, and I have a right to know. You couldn't make your first marriage work so why are you planning to jump into another one?"

Casey was boiling. How could this woman just walk up to them and start interrogating them? More importantly, why wasn't Alfred doing anything about it? People began whispering and discreetly pointing in their direction. Kelly continued her assault.

"I mean, I don't want just any woman off the streets having a relationship with my daughter. I mean, look at Christie's hair." She pointed to Christie's head. "The least you could do is find a wife who knows how to make a straight part."

Alfred took a sip of water before slamming the glass down on the table. Water splattered on the tablecloth. "You know nothing about my fiancée, and I will not tolerate you insulting her or our child," he said in a controlled voice. "I've had enough of this, Kelly. I'm warning you."

Her eyes flashed to Casey. "You mean you're actually defending her? She's not your type, Alfred." Her nose went up in the air. "She a little too *plain* for you." She leaned in front of his face. "You should have told me," she sneered. "I didn't know you were desperate these days. I never received the money you were supposed to have sent. Where is it?"

"Kelly." His voice cut into the silence of the room. "Leave!"

Kelly stood there glaring at Casey, as if she hadn't heard a word Alfred had said.

"You know," Kelly said. "you could have found a better replacement. Someone who is a bit more . . . *refined.*" She wasn't concerned about who heard her or if she made a fool of herself or anyone else.

Casey wasn't about to sit there and take any more of Kelly's insults. She pushed back her chair and stood. Apparently, Alfred wasn't going to take control of the situation. She cut her eyes at him before addressing Kelly.

"Look, if you and Alfred have issues you need to resolve, then by all means, resolve them. Just leave me out of it."

About that time, all eyes in the restaurant were on their table. The maître'd came over to the table. "Excuse me, but we've received some complaints from some of our guests, and I must ask you to leave."

He had never been kicked out of a restaurant before. Leave it to Kelly to have the pleasure of giving him the firsthand experience. Not only was that embarrassing for him, but it was an awkward situation for Casey. Although she didn't say anything when they were escorted out, he knew she was fit to be tied, and he couldn't blame her. Why didn't he do something sooner? He couldn't understand why Kelly had to make a big deal out of him getting married. Heck, she didn't want their marriage, yet she didn't want him to get married again. That woman made no sense to him. Maybe this was payback for what he had done to his brother.

He flicked the sterling-silver pendulum on his desk,

setting it in motion. He watched as it swung rhythmically back and forth. Quincy's words constantly ran through his mind. Was he making the same mistake he made with Kelly? Was he rushing into another marriage?

It was three o'clock in the morning, and he was sitting up second-guessing his decisions. He got up from the burgundy leather wingback chair that he loved so much. He always found that he could think better when he sat in that chair. He adjusted the thermostat to fifty degrees. After pouring himself a glass of scotch on the rocks, he went back to his favorite chair. The cool air began to kick in and with a click of the remote, a flame ignited in the fireplace.

Aah, he thought, *this is perfect.* He propped his feet on the matching leather ottoman. "How can I be sure that I love this woman?" he asked himself. Was there any validity to anything Quincy had said the other night? Was he rushing into another bad situation? Sure, Casey and Kelly were like night and day, but how did he know he wouldn't end up in another relationship that was destined to go down the tubes? He had to be sure for his sake and Casey's.

He began to make a mental chart of both women. Casey was an unselfish, giving woman. On the other hand, Kelly rarely gave anything unless she was getting something in return. Casey was motivated by love, whereas Kelly was motivated by money. He remembered when he first met Kelly. She was out with some of her girlfriends at a party a mutual friend was throwing. He went over and spoke to her, and she immediately stuck her nose in the air, saying that she was already spoken for. Yet, she started calling and one thing led to another. They started dating hot and heavy. She showed no concern for the so-called boyfriend of hers until he came back from the service.

Unfortunately, her boyfriend turned out to be his brother, Aldrich. By this time, Kelly claimed she was in love with him, and Aldrich couldn't take it. He thought Alfred had gone behind his back and stolen his woman, when Alfred had known nothing about his relationship with Kelly.

A few years later, Kelly's parents split up and the finances got rough. Her mother started pressuring them to get married and eventually they did. It didn't matter about the pressure from her mother because Alfred honestly loved Kelly. Later, he began to wonder if she really loved him or if she married him just because her mother wanted her to. In actuality, he knew the answer to that question. Besides, her mother didn't care which brother she married, as long as she got help with the bills. He'd never forget the look on Aldrich's face when he told him that he and Kelly were getting married. After that, Aldrich disappeared and barely kept in contact. Alfred tried to maintain a relationship with him, but Aldrich was cold and distant. They never had a chance to mend things between them.

He took a swallow of his drink and frowned as it burned his throat. Casey was independent and didn't need to define herself by someone else. This time, he was allowed the chance to pursue, instead of being pursued. Most important of all, he knew that the love he felt for her was reciprocated. The doubt that was once there began to subside, and he knew in his heart that Casey was the right woman for him.

Twenty-one

She tossed and turned all night. Slowly, she eased out of bed. After turning on the lamp on the nightstand, Casey saw that it was three-thirty in the morning. Something just didn't feel right. Her first inclination was to call Punkin, but he probably wouldn't answer the phone.

She found herself throwing on some jeans and a T-shirt. She didn't know where she was going, but she knew she had to think. Twenty minutes later, she found herself on Loop 610, which took her all the way around Houston and back. Finally, she made an exit. He would just have to get up because she needed to talk. He was going to be sore at her, but he would get over it.

Contrary to what she believed, Punkin was up. Before she could ring the doorbell, Punkin opened the door. He stood to one side so that Casey could enter. He closed the door behind her and took a long drag of his cigarette, blowing smoke rings into the air. "Well, it's almost four o'clock in the morning." He casually flicked ashes into a hand-shaped ashtray. "What's on your mind?"

Punkin was a trip. She never liked when he did stuff like that. His condo was like stepping back into time. They were sitting on pillows that were placed on the floor in front of the coffee table. Beads were strung from his bedroom doorway. Incense burned on the counter of the bar. To top it off, he had blue lightbulbs in his lamps. What was up with the mood lights? All he needed was a headband, and he would be ready to head to Woodstock.

"No, actually I dropped by to play spades," she said sarcastically. "Your significant other isn't here, is he?"

Punkin smacked his lips. "Honey, he doesn't get the privilege of spending the night. It doesn't matter whether he's here or not. You're always welcome in my home."

She scanned the room. "You know, every time I come to your place, I feel as if you should be reading my palm or something. You don't happen to have an old crystal ball lying around, do you?" she asked.

"Honey, I don't need no crystal ball to read your future. All you need to do is be you, and I'll do the rest. Punkin already knows something is bothering you, and I think his initials are A and W, okay?"

Punkin looked totally ludicrous with his big, masculine hand holding a Virginia Slim cigarette. "I'm sorry about coming over so late. I just couldn't sleep, and I didn't want to wake my mother."

"Well, I wouldn't be your best friend if I was never here for you, would I?"

"I guess not."

"I was actually over here waiting for the phone to ring. If I didn't hear from you by tonight, then I was on my way to your place to give you a piece of my mind."

"You are cruel." Casey laughed. But she couldn't feel the warmth of the moment because all of her troubles were starting to pile up.

"You know you don't have to tell me." He looked

at her with a strange expression. "Let me see your hand."

Casey laughed. "What? Why do you want to see my hand?" A chill rippled through her. Punkin had never looked at her like that before.

"Give me your hand," he commanded. "I know you've heard the rumors."

"What rumors?" Casey asked.

"You already know what I'm talking about. The rumors that I'm strange—gifted." He put out his cigarette.

"You know I don't pay any attention to rumors. Besides, I don't believe in that kind of stuff anyway."

"Just because you don't believe in it, doesn't mean it doesn't exist. My mother was gifted, as was her mother and her mother's mother. Somehow I picked it up. I've always had it, but for years I didn't know what to do with it. Now I do." He held out his hand to grasp hers.

He was scaring her. This was a side of Punkin she had never seen. He almost had this ethereal semblance about him. Casey was sure it was the blue lights in the place. It had to be the blue lights, right?

Reluctantly, she gave him her hand. He closed his eyes, as if he were in a trance. "I see two people, a man and a woman," he said. "Wait, there's a little girl. She lying down in the backseat of their car. She's sleeping. There's rain, so much rain. There's an accident. Now, all I can see is this little girl. Something happened. Where are the man and the woman?" He paused for a moment to watch Casey's expression. He closed his eyes again. "Now I see a woman, a young woman. A dark shadow is always close behind." He swallowed hard.

Casey sat with an astonished look on her face. A thin veil of perspiration covered her forehead.

Punkin continued, "This shadow is growing stronger and is closing in on her. It engulfs her. I can't see her anymore. She's being swallowed up, and the only thing not covered by this shadow is her hand. There's a thin chain with something gold hanging down from her hand. It falls into this cloud of darkness. Slowly, her fingers are being sucked in. But wait," he said, breathing, "Just when she thinks it's all over, a hand reaches for hers. It's a strong, determined hand—a man's hand. On his finger is a gold ring with a star." His eyes popped open.

Casey's eyes were as round as saucers. Some of it made sense, but the other part meant nothing to her. What did the rest of it mean? She was terrified. Tears were streaming down her face. *What does it mean? What's going to happen to me?*

"Punkin! Don't you ever do that to me again," she yelled as she snatched her hand away. "Don't you ever do that to me again!"

"I'm sorry, I didn't know you would be terrified by this. I didn't mean to scare you, girl. It was probably nothing." He tried to calm her. He didn't think she would react the way she had. "You want some water or juice?" he asked. She probably needed a stiff drink after what he just saw.

"Juice," she answered as she wiped tears from her face.

Punkin went to the kitchen and brought back a glass of fruit punch. "Girl, don't worry. It probably means you are going through some sort of metamorphosis or something." Casey was going through a metamorphosis all right, but not what he was saying.

She took the juice. "Yeah, right." She waited for her heart to resume its normal pace. "I'm not letting you do that again."

"Who were the people in the accident? Any idea?" Punkin asked.

"I don't know, Dara's parents maybe. How do you do that?" Casey was still in shock.

"Honey, I don't do anything. I get this feeling, and I see things. Sometimes I see things I don't want to see." Punkin seemed relieved to finally tell someone details of his gift.

"Like what?" Casey didn't think she wanted to know anything else about herself

"Just things," Punkin answered.

Just then, Punkin's sister, Rene, walked out and stopped in front of Casey, pointing her index finger at her. Then she said to Punkin, "She looks like she might know about my benefits."

Punkin hurried over to Rene. "Girl, close your mouth. Don't nobody know about your benefits."

"You know about my benefits, don't you?" she asked Casey. "Yeah, you know where my money is. Who got my money? You tell them people I needs my money."

It was one bizarre morning. It seemed like something out of *The Twilight Zone*—it didn't make sense. Casey stuck her feet into her sandals and headed for the door, purse in hand.

"I think I've had enough for one evening. This is a little out of my league. Talk to ya later," she called out behind her.

Punkin leaned against the door after closing it behind her. He was right when he said that sometimes he saw things he didn't want to see. His hands clutched his chest. He willed what he saw not to come true, but his dreams were never wrong. Sometimes one had to learn to prepare for the inevitable, but could that person accept their fate?

Twenty-two

The rhythmic sound of raindrops against her windowpane was lulling. Casey piled the covers over her head and snuggled deeper into her pillow. She overheard the weatherman saying that there was a sixty percent chance of rain in the forecast. That was good sleeping weather, and it would be even better if she were nestled in Alfred's arms.

She could hear a dog barking in distress. "Petey!" she said as she buried her face into her pillow, "don't tell me you're over the fence again."

She sprang out of bed and put on her slippers. If Petey was back in her yard, she was keeping him. She knew it would be stealing, but apparently her neighbors didn't want their dog. She pulled back the curtain, and it was just as she figured: Petey was hanging by his chain once again. Casey had spoken with her neighbors several times about Petey climbing the fence, and they hadn't bothered to move him.

The rain was coming down hard, and she searched all over for her umbrella, but she couldn't find it. She grabbed a plastic trash bag and covered her head before running out to the fence where Petey was gasping for air. The worst probably would have happened because her neighbors rarely looked out of their back door. She unhooked Petey's collar and rubbed his neck. It didn't take much for Petey to follow her into the house. He didn't seem to like getting wet any more than she did. He stood at the back door shaking water all over the floor.

She dried him with a large towel. "Well," she said to Petey, who was busy checking out his new space. "Hey, just don't mark anything. This is my territory," she warned. "I guess I'll see if the paper is here."

The dog followed close behind her while she opened the front door to see if the paper was lying in the driveway. She noticed a cream envelope taped to the door.

"This is strange, Petey. Someone left a letter for me." Petey barked happily in the background. She closed the door and sat on the floor next to Petey, rubbing his spotted coat. "Let's see what's inside, shall we?" He yelped his approval.

Her name was neatly printed on the front, and the back of the envelope was sealed with tape. She pulled the tape off and took out the paper, which matched the envelope. A letter inside read:

Casey,

I cannot tell you how sorry I am to have to tell you this. I've thought this over and I've decided that our marriage would be a mistake. After seeing Kelly again, I realized that I'm not completely over her, and Christie really needs her mother in her life. This is for the best. Please don't try to contact me as I will be out of town for the next few weeks.

Alfred

Her first reaction was anger, but ten minutes later, as the tears fell on the cream paper, she knew she was hurt. What a chicken way out of a relationship. He didn't even have the decency to tell her on the phone or in person. Her knight in shining armor was nothing more than a fraud. Petey lay next to her with sulking eyes.

"A stinking letter. My feelings weren't even worth a face-to-face visit." Casey crumbled the letter. "I trusted and believed in him, and all I get is a letter."

She had to admit that he had timing. The day before one of the biggest days of her life. Why? For Kelly? She had about as much personality as a rock.

Hours later, Casey lay in bed, stuffing herself with butter-pecan ice cream. *Sleepless in Seattle* had just ended and *You've Got Mail* was beginning. She had used a whole box of Kleenex by the time the first movie ended. After calling her mother several times and getting no answer, she finally left her a message saying that the wedding was off.

The phone began to ring off the hook. Casey pointed the remote at the television, turning up the volume. She didn't want to be bothered with anyone. All she wanted was to be alone. When the phone rang again, she turned off the ringer. Her butter-pecan ice cream and Petey were all the company she needed.

Alfred had been running around asking if anyone had seen Casey. It wasn't like her not to call or to disappear. Caterers were busy bringing in food and chairs were being set up for the guests. He called her house several times, but got no answer. He was about to call her mother when Aunt Maggie rushed into the study.

"I think you might want to read this," she said. "Casey's return address is on the envelope so I thought it might be important."

He anxiously took the envelope and cut it open

with a letter opener. He thought his heart would stop beating when he saw the words scribbled on the page.

Alfred,

By the time you get this letter, I will be on a plane going to Anywhere, USA. I've thought this over, and I've decided that our marriage would be a mistake. I'm not what you need in your life. This is for the best. Please don't try to contact me as I will be out of town for the next few weeks.

Casey

He collapsed into his favorite chair. Aunt Maggie kept asking what was wrong, but he was in a state of shock. She pried the paper from between his fingers. He vaguely heard her saying she was sorry.

He stormed out of the study and went through the house yelling for everyone to get out. People began scattering out of his way. He was like a madman on a rampage. Just when he was finally sure that he didn't propose to Casey because he didn't want to lose her, she called everything off. He was never going through this again. He locked himself in his room. Minutes later, Quincy was calling out to him, twisting the door handle.

Somehow, Quincy managed to open the door. Alfred could see the paper hanging from his fingers. "Man, I'm sorry," he said. "I don't know what to say."

"What is there to say?" Alfred said with a maniacal laugh. "She split."

"Man, maybe she got cold feet or something." He placed a hand on Alfred's shoulder. "The day isn't over yet, she might show up. So don't go tossing everybody out by their heels just yet."

"What's the likelihood of that? One in a million?" Alfred rubbed the bridge of his nose. "She's not going through with it. She probably left because of Kelly's performance the other day. I knew I should have done something. Anything would have been better than nothing."

"Don't do this to yourself. You can't take the blame for someone else's actions."

"Never again," he vowed. "Never again."

There was nothing Quincy could say. Only time would be able to fix this mess, and there was no telling how long that would take.

Twenty-three

In the weeks that followed, Casey busied herself finding another location for Home Sweet Home. Liz had kept in touch and gave her the number to someone she knew who was leasing a space. By this point, she was desperate. She had to get things moving or she would put everything on the line. But when she saw the place, she liked it and it was a done deal.

She felt a strong sense of pride on the day she opened the doors to Home Sweet Home. It seemed as if this was the day she had been waiting for since she started her career. *This* is what it all boiled down to. People had their own personal definitions of success, depending on what their goals were. If Casey could make this business work, she would declare herself a success. She was starting off small but was hoping her business would grow large.

She couldn't hide her surprise when a dozen yellow roses arrived. She didn't know why she hoped they were from Alfred. More than likely she would be receiving many tokens of good luck from well-wishers. She held her breath as she opened the card. A sigh escaped her lips as she found out the flowers were from her mother and Jay. Though she was a little disappointed, she was still pleased.

"Those are beautiful roses," said Mrs. Potter,

Casey's new secretary. She took the roses from Casey and headed to her office with them. "And they smell wonderful too."

"They do smell lovely," Casey answered. They probably would have seemed more fragrant if Alfred had sent them.

"Someone sure seems to be sweet on you," Mrs. Potter commented.

A look of sadness crossed her face. Casey was quick to clear up the misconception. "Those were from my mother and her friend."

Mrs. Potter smiled sweetly. "Well, the day isn't over, you might be surprised."

When Casey interviewed Mrs. Potter, she liked her immediately. She was an older woman with a bubbly personality that matched her features. She was full-figured with a round face that was full of warmth. Her smile could tell a person many things. Just seeing her smile made Casey feel that everything would be all right and that every day was special. The only other person who made her feel that way was her mother. Maybe that's why she hired Mrs. Potter on the spot.

"Yes, sir," Mrs. Potter said, "I think things are going to run smoothly. Can you feel the excitement in the air?"

Mrs. Potter's enthusiasm was contagious. "Yes, I do feel the excitement. This is really it." Casey smiled as she scanned the room.

"Oh, I forgot to give you this." Mrs. Potter handed her an envelope.

Casey carefully opened the envelope that was addressed, TO MY BEST FRIEND IN THE WORLD. It read: GOOD LUCK NEW BUSINESS. I KNOW YOU WILL SUCCEED, LIKE YOU ALWAYS HAVE. She was happy to have a friend in Punkin. He was as thoughtful as they came. Casey's thoughts drifted to Alfred and her mood sobered. What would he have given her?

"Is something wrong, Ms. James? You don't look too good." Mrs. Potter touched Casey's shoulder, jolting her from her thoughts.

"I really don't know." She passed the card to Mrs. Potter. "I'm fine, Mrs. Potter. I've just been going through some things, and I'm trying to deal with them the best way I can."

"I see," Mrs. Potter said. "You know, I learned a long time ago that sometimes you have to start living for the moment. Life is too short to dwell on the past. Before you know it, life will have passed you by. If it's a grudge you're holding on to, it will make you bitter. Then you will end up looking like this all of the time." She puckered her lips.

"Ugh, I definitely don't want to look like that." Casey laughed.

"You know what holding in all of that pain and frustration is like?"

"I think I have some sort of idea, but what do you think?" Casey asked.

"It's like playing a videotape and putting it on pause the moment you get to a part in the picture you don't like. You never press play or fast forward. Your life is on hold."

"I've been living. I wouldn't go so far as to say that my life has been on hold."

"Well, if you've honestly been living for yourself and making all of the accomplishments in life for *yourself*, then I guess you have been living."

Casey was busy looking down at her shoes. Everything Mrs. Potter was saying struck a nerve. "You're right."

"Then you know what you need to do, don't you?" Mrs. Potter asked.

"Yes, I know." Casey smiled. She felt as if all of the pressure and depression she felt all of those years was washing away.

"Then get busy living."

"Thanks, Mrs. Potter. I really needed to hear that."

Mrs. Potter threw a hand up, shaking her head. "Don't thank me. If I can keep someone from making the same mistakes I've made, then that's thanks enough."

Yes, it's time to start living.

Twenty-four

Punkin was starting to worry about Casey. She was looking a little on the thin side. Casey could feel his eyes on her as she drove through the Saturday morning traffic to G Town.

"What?" Casey sighed in agitation.

"Have you looked in the mirror lately? What are you doing to yourself?"

"It's nothing. I've been a little stressed by everything. I'll be okay." What good would it do to talk about it? It still wouldn't change the way things were in her life.

"Well, I hope so," Punkin said. "Why haven't you told me about what happened between you and Alfred? I'm your best friend, and you've been keeping me in the dark."

"There's nothing to talk about. It's over and done with." She turned on the radio to listen to early-morning jazz on KTSU.

"The heck it is. Hey"—Punkin patted himself on the chest—"it's me, Punkin, you're talking to. You haven't been the same. I call you and don't hear from you for days at a time. I almost thought I was going to have to come to your place and kick the door in just to check on you."

"I've been busy with Home Sweet Home. That's the

one thing I have control over. I make or break that agency."

Punkin watched as Casey stiffened behind the wheel. It wasn't like her to stay on the defensive. Alfred really messed her up in the head. Now she was going to start blaming all the men in the world for her problems. Punkin was thinking hard about having a little talk with Alfred for kicking his best friend to the curb, especially after she spent all of that money on that wedding dress. She could sue him for the cost of the dress.

"Your momma is walking around like she is on cloud nine or something. She looks like she just had a Coke and a smile, and everything is dandy," Punkin said to break the silence. This was not the kind of fun he was expecting. Usually when they hung out, they had a ball, but this was like going to a funeral.

"I know, and it's all because of this Jay person," Casey muttered more to herself than to Punkin. "I will be too through if he's who I think he is." Her feet became heavy on the pedal as they sped past Texas City.

A smile slowly crept across Punkin's face. "Well, if you really want to know who he is, get his license plate number and then on Monday, we'll go down to the county and look him up on public records. You game?"

Casey nodded her head. "I'm game."

"What are you going to do if he is your father? I mean, the least you could do is hear his excuse."

All the years of struggling and watching her mother have to work two jobs was heart wrenching. Casey thought about how they lost their home and were forced to live in a one-room apartment. No, she could never forgive him for deserting them.

"Did you hear what I said?" Punkin interrupted with annoyance in his tone.

"I heard you," she answered. "No excuse he could give would be sufficient enough."

"Never is a long time. You've got to put those ghosts behind you and start dealing with the here and now. One day you might look up and wish that you heard his excuse, but at this rate, you'll never know. He owes you that much. He was never there for you, and I think you deserve to know what happened." Punkin peered over at the speedometer. The needle was holding at eighty-five. "And if you don't slow this matchbox down, the men in blue are going to have a few words for you. I know the Germans say these cars are safe, but I don't really want to find out first-hand."

Casey eased off the pedal. Leave it to Punkin to rationalize things. But as good as his closing argument sounded, the jury was still out and leaning toward a guilty verdict against her father.

"I hope this seamstress is a good one, seeing how far we have to drive to get to her," Casey said lightly. "Where is she located anyway?"

"Don't try to be slick and change the subject," Punkin said slyly. "I'm hip to your game. Anyway, she's located on the Strand." Punkin decided to let his interrogation drop for the moment.

If nothing else, at least the weather was nice enough to get a clear view of the gulf, not that the gulf was something spectacular. Suppose she was one of the players on *Survivor,* and she was stranded on Galveston. If she was challenged to jump in the water and take a swim, she'd lose. That's how bad she thought the water was. People were walking along the beach and frolicking in the water. Casey and Punkin pulled up in front of a small shop with several cars parked nearby. Punkin spotted a couple of other stores that he wanted to check out later, so he planned to meet her back at Altha's.

"Welcome to Apparels by Altha. Do you have an appointment?" the receptionist asked.

"Yes," Casey answered. "I have a two o'clock appointment."

The receptionist checked her appointment book. "Ms. James?"

"Yes, that's me."

"Would you like something to drink?" the receptionist asked.

"Yes, that will be fine," Casey answered.

The receptionist went to get their drinks, while Punkin and Casey took a seat.

"Altha will be with you in a moment," the receptionist said politely as she handed them their drinks.

"Thanks," Casey and Punkin responded in unison.

"I'm sure happy that we made an appointment," Punkin said as he sipped his drink. "I've heard that this place is always packed, and if you were a walk-in, you would have a long wait."

"Well, I guess it's good that we had an appointment," Casey responded aloofly.

Punkin took in Casey's cool attitude and decided that he may have been too hard on his friend. "I'm sorry for jumping on your case about your father. I know how you like to wear your feelings on your sleeve. I didn't mean to hurt your feelings, and I hope you will accept my apology." He playfully nudged Casey on the shoulder.

Casey looked at him smiling. "Okay, I'll forgive you this time."

Altha turned out to be a dream. She designed a dress that she thought would be flattering on Casey. She then took a roll of material and draped it around her so that they would have some idea how the dress would look.

Altha believed that Punkin should wear an outfit that would stop people in their tracks. She wanted to give him something to match his outgoing personality. Punkin already had some idea of what he wanted—a black tux sprinkled with rhinestones!

"Honey, I want to make a statement. I want people to look at me and remember me when I come back next year." Altha agreed that Punkin would be making a statement, but Casey didn't know if she meant that in a positive way.

"You have beautiful legs," Altha told Casey. "You should wear a dress that will show off your legs. I have just the thing in mind for you. All I need you to do is pick out your material."

Before they picked out their material, Altha took their measurements. Punkin decided later that he wanted to get away from the traditional black tux and go with navy blue.

"I'll have to look for shoes later," Casey said after they left the shop.

"Sounds good to me," Punkin answered.

They walked on the Strand and ventured into some of the stores there before stopping by a café for a quick bite to eat.

"It's been a long time since I've visited Galveston," Casey commented as they waited for their seafood. Now she was happy that Apparels by Altha was located on the Strand.

"Me too. Nothing seems to bring me this direction anymore." Punkin answered before biting into a cheese stick.

"I know what you mean. When we were younger, going to Galveston was the thing to do. Now it's just a bunch of college kids running around at beach parties." Casey motioned to just beyond the café's door to a crowd of teens walking on the boardwalk.

"Oh, honey, you ought to see them running around at that beach party they have every year. Those little hot mamas are all scantily clad and everything. Half of them look like they walked straight out of a pornographic movie." Punkin waved a hand in disdain. "Men running around in leopard-print bikinis with boas hanging across their bare chests, lookin' like Tarzan about to rescue Jane." He fanned himself with a napkin. "But, I have fun there every year, and I'll be back on the beach this year. I bet those kids go every year too."

"It wouldn't surprise me. Actually those kids look like they are in high school." Casey squinted through the glass.

Punkin suddenly became serious. "Are you ever going to tell me what happened?" He was never going to let her live it down. Why was she keeping it a secret from him?

Although Casey found the situation embarrassing, she knew Punkin would never laugh at her. Up until that moment, everyone thought she called off the wedding. She pulled the crumpled piece of paper out of her purse and handed it to him.

Puzzled, Punkin unfolded the paper and began reading the note. He threw the paper on the table. "That's just a trip. I can't believe he would stoop so low. I never would have thought he would go out like that. What a loser."

He was so busy verbally abusing Alfred that he almost didn't notice Casey dry her eyes. He caught himself "I'm so sorry, Casey. I can't begin to imagine how you must feel."

"It's all right, Punkin." She sniffed as she threw the paper back into her purse. That letter was going to be a constant reminder that she couldn't allow herself to be vulnerable to anyone.

"I guess I've met someone who made me feel that way. It wasn't the same situation, but it was the same kind of pain. Everybody promises to take you to heaven and half of the time you don't even get off the ground. Always promises of giving you the moon and stars." He seemed to reminisce. Punkin shook his head. "About the only way I've ever come close to seeing stars is on the American flag." He laughed. "Oh, say, can you see . . ."

Casey tapped Punkin on the arm. "You are too silly. You and your significant other have been together for a while. Obviously something is keeping both of you there."

"Everything that glitters ain't gold. He's only about five-carats, but he's still gold. So, I'll keep what gold I've got because I might give it up for something that looks like gold, but isn't."

"Nah, you know he's da bomb." Casey laughed.

"Whatever." Punkin cackled. "He's probably a scud. What about Michael Jefferson? Remember him? You just refused to give him the time of day."

"Do I?" Casey shook her head. "Now, he's a scud. Talk about losing a natural high. Michael just isn't innovative enough for me. He seems so predictable."

"That may be what you need," Punkin said. "Predictability may mean stability, and there's nothing wrong with that."

"Well, it's a little too late for that," Casey said.

"Casey, relationships aren't always bad. Why don't you give Michael a chance? He could escort you to the benefit."

She flat-out refused. Oh, no, she wasn't about to go down that road any time soon.

"I heard that if you start going out with someone

else after you break up with your boyfriend or girlfriend, that it doesn't hurt so bad." He stuck a fork
into her plate and grabbed a fried crawfish.

"I guess I'm going to have to suffer because I'm
not following that advice, Dr. Love Jones."

Punkin laughed. If she followed all of the advice
he had to offer, there was no telling where she would
end up. "What you need is passion in your life."

"I've experienced passion, but I don't want anymore."

"*P-lease*. There's nothing wrong with wanting passion. Maybe Alfred wasn't the right fuel for your tank.
Maybe instead of regular unleaded, you need super."
He laughed. "Or propane. There's nothing wrong
with alternative fuel—trust me, I know!" He busied
himself with his food.

"This is not about some man. This is about me,"
Casey said defensively. "I'm sure your friend Michael
couldn't fuel anybody's flame."

"You didn't have to go there. If you're definitely
not interested in Michael, I'll let him know when I
see him again."

"Thank you very much. How long will it take for
it to finally get through your head that Michael isn't
my type?"

"Well," he said, pointing his fork at Casey. "Since
Alfred has turned your life upside down, maybe you
should find out what's really going on with him."

Casey stuck a piece of fish into her mouth. "I don't
know, Punkin. He asked me not to contact him, and
I have to respect that."

Punkin's brows rose inquisitively. "Just because he
said that doesn't mean he meant it. He's probably
over there hurting just as bad as you are."

"I don't know about that, and I'm not trying to

find out. He's probably reconciling with Kelly," Casey said.

Punkin shook his head. "If she's as bad as you've said, I can't see why he would go back to her. I mean, for crying out loud, they've been divorced for four years and now he wants her back? Something just doesn't add up."

"Maybe that's the problem," Casey said. "We always try to rationalize how we feel. I have a theory on men."

"Oh, Lord." Punkin casually waved her off. "Another one of your theories."

"To me, all men are placed into the lie, cheat, and steal category until they prove differently. If he proves that he isn't a liar, he's upgraded to the cheat and steal category. That's the level where most of them fail. They steal your heart and then let you down by cheating."

"I don't know, Casey." Punkin placed his fork on his plate. "Your theory may not be foolproof. There are a lot of men who don't cheat. So where do those men fit in your male model theory?"

"Rest assured, they all fit into the model somewhere. If it's not about another woman, it's about how he truly feels about you. Some men will never love you for who you are." Casey wiped her mouth with her napkin.

"Sometimes I don't get you, Casey. Sometimes you have this sadness about you that I can't explain."

Casey tried to keep things on a light note. "Ah, it's all in your imagination. We all have our moments."

"You're right, but yours is a little different." He could see that Casey was under pressure. "But, on the Alfred situation, all I have to say is for you to follow your heart. That's all any of us can do."

Casey would have loved to take that advice, but sometimes following your heart wasn't the smart thing to do.

Twenty-five

Casey marked another red X on her calendar. It was the end of another week. It seemed as if the days and nights had been passing, and she had nothing to look forward to. When she was a kid, she wished the months would rush by because she looked forward to the summer. What did she have to rush for now? Nothing. She didn't have to rush home. Most of her days were spent around a lot of people, and she was happy, but when nighttime came, her friend, loneliness, kept her company. And what a faithful friend it was. It was there in the mornings and late at night. It was there as she drove down the street or went shopping. Who could ask for a more faithful friend? Well, tonight, she was going to allow herself to have a good time and not worry about him.

"You can do this," she said as she pushed the stud onto the back of her earrings. "Your life was boring before him, and you were fine. You'll be fine after him."

Casey ran her fingers over the silky material. Although she approved of what she saw in the full-length mirror, Alfred wouldn't have the opportunity to appreciate her appearance. She sat on the edge of the bed and buckled her strappy sandals. Why did she still care what he thought? He wanted Kelly, not her.

She couldn't get herself to stop expecting a phone call or something. She kept kicking herself for even caring, for even hoping. There *had* to be more to love than what she was experiencing.

It was nine o'clock when she heard Punkin honking outside. Casey checked to make sure that her business cards were in her evening bag before closing the door behind her.

Had Punkin gotten a new car? She couldn't see what color it was, but she did know it was a sleek big-body Mercedes. A man with a receding hairline stepped out of the car. She could have choked when she realized Michael Jefferson was standing in her driveway. What in the world was he doing there?

Michael nervously stepped to her. "Paul couldn't make it." He began wringing his hands and shifting from one foot to the other. Fat beads of sweat suddenly popped out on his forehead. "Richard, ah—his significant other, decided to go with him. He didn't want you to have to go alone so, ah, he asked me to go with you."

Ah, man! How could Punkin set me up like this? It's okay, I'll just lose him in the crowd. Casey remained silent, forcing Michael to become even more uncomfortable. Finally, he fell silent. They both stood there gawking at each other.

"It's okay," she finally said. "Thanks for coming." It wasn't his fault that Punkin devised this plan.

Michael seemed a lot more at ease. He opened the passenger door for her and closed it after she got in. "You look your usual spectacular self," he commented as he sat in the driver's seat.

"Thank you," Casey replied. She gave Michael a quick once-over. "You look nice yourself," she said.

In actuality, he looked as if he was about to choke to death since his necktie was way too tight. His head looked as if it might explode at any moment. Apparently Michael thought he was still the same size he was in college.

"Why thank ya." Michael said in his best southern drawl, which she found to be a bad imitation. He kept glancing over at her thigh, which was revealed through a high slit. "You really look ravishing."

"Thanks," Casey said.

"I heard about your relationship." He took his right hand from the wheel and planted it on her exposed knee. "I'm really sorry it happened. But, when one door closes, another one opens." He gave her knee a squeeze.

She politely placed his hand back on the steering wheel. "Thank you. I can agree with what you just said, but right now, that door is still closed." She smiled sweetly.

"Oh," he said, laughing. "I'm sure some lucky fellow will change your mind." His hand returned to her knee.

Why won't he take the hint? I know he's not as stupid as he's pretending to be.

"I doubt it very seriously," she said with a nasty stare.

The expression on her face was enough to make him remove his hand. Michael turned up the radio and was a perfect gentleman the rest of the drive.

The Sweet Water Country Club was an excellent place to have a party. Cars were parked everywhere. There was a row of trees on either side of the driveway that led up to a massive, white, three-story house that served as the club.

"I should have known that anything Marva touched was going to be exquisite. Just look at this place. It's amazing," Casey said as Michael eased the car behind another one waiting for valet parking.

"Oh, it'll do," Michael said. "I'm a member here, but I was thinking of changing my membership." He looked her up and down, and Casey felt the hairs on the back of her neck rise. "Maybe you can meet me here sometime."

"No, thank you." She smiled with an artificial sweetness. "Oh, look over there. There's a lake." She pointed to the far left of the house.

"Yes, I know. The firm had a picnic here last year. You know I'm an attorney, right?"

"How could I forget?" Casey said. Michael was getting on her nerves. She and Punkin just might lose their friendship over this.

"Well, you know," he boasted, "I've just made partner, and the benefits are excellent."

Casey was too happy when their doors were finally opened by two young men. Casey heard one of them whistle as she stepped out of the car.

"I must admit," Michael said, "we make a lovely couple." He smiled broadly.

She didn't even bother to answer. They were directed to the room where the party was in full swing. There was a live jazz band playing in front of a crowded dance floor. People were milling all about.

Marva spotted them and immediately came over. She gave Casey a hug and shook Michael's hand. "I'm so happy you made it." She smiled. Marva was stunning in a royal-blue outfit.

"Thanks for the tickets," Casey said. "This is a nice place for a party."

Michael stood there idly rubbing the bald spot at the top of his head. Just looking around made him wish he had joined the hair club. He even thought about joining a health club after seeing all of the men his age who were fit and trim.

"Yes, thanks for inviting us. You've really outdone yourself this time," Michael said to Marva.

Marva engaged in a brief conversation with Michael before spotting her husband.

"Oh, there's Quincy." She motioned for him to come over. "I want you to meet him."

Casey's mouth went dry as Quincy headed in their direction. *Oh, no! It's Alfred's best friend. Alfred must be here.* She had to give it to Quincy. He was an attractive man. He had a fine body, a handsome face, and a good head on his shoulders. What was there not to like about him?

Both were surprised to see each other. "It's good to see you again. You look splendid. Let me get you a drink." He retrieved two champagne flutes from a passing waiter. He gave a glass to Michael and one to Casey. He looked at Michael, as if sizing him up. "Is this your date?" he asked Casey.

Michael didn't give her a snowball's chance in hell to answer the question. "Yes." He extended his hand. "I'm her date."

"Well," Quincy said as if in shock. "It's a pleasure to meet you."

Quincy promised to visit with them later as he took Marva's hand and disappeared to the dance floor.

"I'm all about business tonight," she said to Michael.

"Me too." He looked greedily at her.

She wasn't thinking along the same lines as he was. Though she planned on losing him in the crowd, he stuck by her like Krazy Glue. *I should have driven myself!* She began rubbing her arms. *Please don't let me break out in hives. Please!*

Casey gave the crowded room the once-over. Was

Alfred coming? Was he still out of town? She was dying to ask Quincy about him, but she didn't have the nerve. As quickly as she thought of Quincy, she saw him standing with a group of men talking. He looked in her direction and gave her a slight smile. It was one of those *it's such a pity* smiles. Michael came to the table, shoving a drink in her face. She gave him a rude look before taking the drink and setting it on the table.

Punkin finally came over to the table with Richard. She wanted to laugh because they looked as if they were going to the prom. They were all color-coordinated.

He began explaining why he couldn't pick her up and why he didn't call. Casey was steaming under the collar at him, but she wasn't going to ruin her night.

"So what do you think of my outfit?" He twirled around so she could get a three-hundred-sixty degree view. He dusted off his sleeves. "What about the sparkles?"

"Bling, bling!" Casey shielded her eyes with a hand. "You're a regular rhinestone cowboy! I'm going blind over here."

Punkin whooped. "I know that's right, girlfriend." He sat down next to Richard, who seemed as if he'd rather be at home sleeping or reading a good book.

Michael butted into the conversation, as if he had to remind everyone he was there. "Well, I must say that I think the fund-raiser is a success."

He continued gawking at Casey as if she were on the menu. He grabbed her by the hand and insisted she dance with him. To her disdain, it was a slow song. Why couldn't he have picked something faster, so she wouldn't have to touch him?

He got her on the floor and smashed her next to him. Every time she received a compliment from someone, he held her close. She was getting pretty tired of his behavior. His hand slid down her sides, holding her to him by her hips. She tried to pry herself loose, but his arms were like vices.

"Why haven't you called me?" he asked against her ear. His lips felt cold and clammy. She was starting to feel things crawling on her skin. "I've been asking about you every day. That's okay, now I've got you."

Now he's got me! What in the world is this wacko talking about? He gave her a squeeze that could have knocked the breath out of her and repeated himself. "Why haven't you called me?"

"Michael, I have been busy. As you know, I was planning a wedding," she said hoarsely.

"Well, the wedding's off," he hissed in her ear. "You won't have that excuse anymore. Oh, baby, I'm going to make you very happy, starting tonight!"

Her heart leaped into her throat. What was he talking about? "I don't want to dance anymore. As a matter of fact, I'm not leaving with you!" she snapped. She looked around, but no one seemed to notice because they couldn't hear her over the music. "Don't put your hands on me again!"

He remained on the floor, rubbing his balding head. He couldn't believe she was trying to show him up. Things didn't work that way in Michael Jefferson's world.

Casey went back to the table, but Punkin and Richard were mingling with other guests. What else could go wrong? To her horror, she spotted Kelly working the crowd. She was weaving her magic on all of the men surrounding her.

Kelly spotted her from across the crowded room. Their eyes made contact, and Kelly looked away as if she were a mere figment of her imagination. A mixture of hurt and jealousy found its way into her heart.

Kelly looked in her direction again and gave her a vicious smile. Casey returned the smile and tried to make a grand exit, but Michael latched on to her like a leech looking for blood.

She was completely sick of him. "Why don't you go get us another drink," she suggested.

"I will," he said, taking her by the hand, "but you're coming with me."

Michael finally ran into some of his friends from *the firm* and went to talk to them. Within an hour, Casey met several business contacts, as well as two potential associates for Home Sweet Home. When Michael went off to mix and mingle with a couple of his colleagues, one guy finally convinced Casey to dance. After a couple dances, Casey decided to head back to her table. Just as she sat down, she saw Alfred walk into the room. Her heart seemed to stop for a moment. He went over to Quincy, and they shared a laugh or two. Seconds later, Quincy nodded in her direction, and both of them glanced over at her.

Alfred looked stunning. She could only imagine what he would have looked like on their wedding day. She knew he would come. She knew it. At least she found herself hoping he would come. He looked at her with hurt in his eyes before he looked away. There was something in his demeanor that didn't seem right.

Suddenly all of the lights in the room were dimmed, and a large spotlight began to spin. A woman's sultry voice could be heard on the microphone. The spotlight focused on the glass ceiling above. A fast-paced beat began to play.

"Prepare to be amazed," the woman said. "Let me introduce you to Agent 800." A man dressed all in black began to descend from the ceiling on a thin rope. "His mission is to take back the three hundred thousand dollars that thieves have stolen from the city."

Agent 800 descended to the floor and was immediately assaulted by a band of ninjas. They began hand-to-hand combat. For a moment, it seemed as if Agent 800 was on the losing end. There were oohs and aahs from the crowd as they were mesmerized by the agile moves of the ninjas and Agent 800. The bandits had the agent on the floor, pressing a sword against his neck. After a series of suave moves, 800 got the upper hand. Several more ninjas swung across the room, making attacks. They used several weapons to show their agility. Again, the crowd was in awe. As the scene began to unfold, they went through a series of obstacles. With a final blow to the last enemy, Agent 800 did several back flips to land at the podium where the announcer stood. He handed her the check, and the crowd parted as a black sports coupe slowly rolled to the front of the room. Agent 800 had done a hard day's work, returned the stolen check, and got the beautiful girl in the end. What a day. The applause was astounding.

"Ladies and gentlemen," the announcer said. "We'd like to thank you for surpassing our goal of two hundred thousand dollars. Please, give yourselves a hand." The crowd kept applauding. "I'd like to present this check to Marva Johnson, chair of the fund-raising committee."

Marva accepted the check on the behalf of Big Brothers and Sisters of America and made a short speech. Then the party went back to full swing.

"I'm leaving," Alfred told Quincy. "I can't stay here with Casey in this room."

"Man, don't leave!" Quincy begged. "Don't leave me to the wolves. You know I can't deal with all of these phony people by myself. I need my partner with me tonight." He looked at Casey. "She sure doesn't look like a woman who would do what she did, especially not for Michael Jefferson."

Alfred's brows rose with interest. "Michael Jefferson? Is that who she's with?" He took a hard swallow from his glass.

Quincy shook his head. "Yeah, and he's been all over her. He won't let her breathe. She didn't look like a happy camper to me."

"Michael Jefferson?" Alfred asked again.

"Michael Jefferson," Quincy confirmed.

It wasn't long before Kelly eased her way over to Alfred. Casey's blood began to boil. Somehow, she knew that woman would be her nemesis. Alfred was busy talking to Quincy and didn't notice Kelly until she was at his side. He gave Kelly what Casey deemed to be a phony hug. There were some definite family problems. She didn't know if he was just performing for the audience or if he was really being standoffish with Kelly.

"Why, Alfred, I didn't know you were going to be here." Kelly smiled.

"Hello, Kelly. Quincy was kind enough to get me a ticket." Alfred's first thought was to make a quick exit. Irritation momentarily flashed across his face, but instead of leaving, he took a sip of his champagne. He was sure she was going to go on a "save our family" campaign.

Quincy's face reflected his surprise that Kelly was there. She walked over to Quincy and embraced him. "It's been a long time."

Quincy smiled. He knew Alfred must have been uncomfortable in Kelly's presence. They had been fighting like cats and dogs over the past few years, and Quincy wasn't so sure things had changed. He noticed that Alfred's free hand was shoved into his pocket. He kept shifting from one foot to the other.

Alfred barely gave Kelly a second glance. If she didn't hurry up and wander off on her own, he would leave. He scanned the room until his gaze rested on Casey, who was staring in his direction. When their eyes locked, flame immediately ignited between them. *Should I go over to her or should I stay away?* He decided to test the waters before swimming out to the deep end. He slightly raised his champagne glass in a mock toast. When she did the same, he decided it was safe to go to her. He excused himself from Kelly and Quincy. Kelly did her best to hide her frustration.

Suddenly, out of nowhere, Michael appeared. He even went as far as to kiss her on the cheek. "Did you miss me?" he asked, fully knowing the answer to the question.

She looked at him for one second and when she turned around, Alfred was nowhere to be found. *Where is he? What happened? He was coming over, I know he was!*

"I've got to go to the ladies' room," she lied. "I'll be right back."

She went to grab her evening bag, which was lying on the table, but Michael reached it before she did. "Why don't I watch this for you? Let's call it collateral, shall we?"

She sneered at him before walking off. Who did he think he was? Who did he think *she* was for that matter? Punkin was nowhere to be found. She was leaving, but she didn't have any money. Michael held her purse as ransom. Marva couldn't leave until everything was over, and she didn't really want to impose. *Think, girl, think!*

Twenty-six

Michael was growing impatient. Where was she? She'd better not have run out on him or else she was going to pay. He didn't waste his gas driving to pick her up for her to not leave with him. He had plans for her. He was going to drop her off at home and invite himself in. She would try to fight him off, at first, but once she felt him in action, she would soon change her mind. He had the music to sooth the savage beast, and tonight, she was going to be his.

He stood and looked around the room. Just thinking about his plans made him want to pack her up and leave right then. He was giving her five more minutes and then he was going to find her. When he sat down, his eyes widened as he noticed that Alfred had joined him at the table.

"Looking for someone?" Alfred asked.

Michael shifted uncomfortably in his chair. "Yes, as a matter of fact I am."

Alfred knew Michael was up to no good, and as Quincy was saying, something wasn't right about this situation. Michael's eyes were glazed over and a thin veil of perspiration was on his forehead.

"Well, I just saw your date get into a cab and leave." He leaned closer to Michael. "Now, why would your date run out on you like that?"

Michael became a bit cocky. "That's my business. You're not in her life anymore, so all's fair in love and war. If it's war you want, I'm willing to comply," he said boldly. Alfred Willingham may have scared others, but Michael wasn't going to back down that easily. Since he had enrolled in that TaeBo class, he knew how to defend himself, and he didn't mind doing it. He was still in the beginner's class, but it was effective enough to use on Alfred.

"You don't want that," Alfred said. "Stay away from her. I know what you're up to."

Michael gave a hard laugh. "You don't know diddly-squat. You're just a sore loser. She doesn't want you, just accept it. It's me that she wants. That's what's wrong with all of you so-called pretty boys. You can't stand losing to the average guy. Well, let me tell you something. I might be average looking on the outside, but I'm superb in the areas that count. That's why she's with me."

Alfred knew damn well that he hadn't touched Casey like that. Just imagining his hands all over her pushed all of the wrong buttons. Before he knew it, he had Michael by the lapels of his jacket. "Listen, Jefferson. You heard what I said. Stay away from her. This is my last time telling you." He snatched the purse from under Michael's grip. "I'll take this."

Alfred straightened his jacket and casually strolled away from the table. Michael shot darts into his back. *No one insults Michael Jefferson and gets away with it. No one!*

Casey stalled in the restroom. She decided she would just to have to hang around until Marva got ready to leave, but she wasn't leaving with Michael. She opened the door of the ladies' room and stepped into the hallway. A man she thought she'd never see again was standing on the other side of the hall waiting for her.

When she saw Alfred's face, all of the residue from the anger and embarrassment she felt melted away. She wanted to run and wrap herself in the arms she'd grown to love.

Alfred looked her up and down. *He did get to see my dress!* He swallowed hard. How he'd missed her. He never knew how much until she was in front of his face. "I thought you might need this." He held up her purse.

She was overwhelmed, relieved, and most of all elated to see him. He was her knight in shining armor. "Yes, thank you so much," she said, sniffing. She turned her head so he couldn't see how much she was overcome with emotion.

He wanted to be angry with her for standing him up. He wanted to lash out at her for making him feel like a fool, but most of all, he wanted to feel her in his arms again. He stood behind her and turned her to face him. The tears that rolled down her cheeks were proof enough that she loved him. When she looked into his eyes and saw tears that matched her own, she knew that he loved her.

They held each other as if they had been apart for years. When his lips touched hers, the flames were rekindled.

"You look wonderful," he said as he wiped her face with the back of his hand.

"Thanks. So do you." She wrapped her arms around him. "How did you know I was having a hard time with Michael?"

"Well, a little bird pulled my coattail, and I watched." He pressed his lips against her hair. Most people he knew never lived their fantasies, but at that particular moment, his fantasy had come true. He had her in his arms again.

"We need to talk, Casey." He pulled back to look into her eyes. "Don't we?"

Casey smiled. "Yes, we've got a lot of talking to do."

"I don't know what it is that I've done, but can I make it up to you sometime?" He just didn't know that he could make it up to her over and over.

"Yes," she answered. "You can start making it up to me tonight."

He wasn't sure he was following her lead too well. "Really? Any special requests?"

"I'm sure you've already got things figured out," she answered.

His hand idly caressed hers. "I know how I'd like to make it up to you, but I don't know if we're ready for that. We've got a lot of wrinkles that need to be ironed out."

"I know, but since you've been away, I've had time to think about things and I realize that I love you just as much as you love me and that's all that matters. But tonight, I want to be wrapped in your arms until the sun comes up."

"Are you sure?"

She tilted her head to one side. "Are *you* sure?"

He let out a soft groan. Just thinking of making love to her made him ache with a pleasure he thought he'd never know again.

"I am," he said honestly. "But I want you to want the same thing I do." He pulled back the sleeve of his jacket to check his watch. It was well after midnight. "We've been here long enough. We have our own networking to do."

The familiar tingling that ran up her spine every time he touched her returned. She saw Punkin talking to a couple of acquaintances. Where had he been all of that time? She mouthed, *I'm leaving.* Punkin noticed Alfred at her side and nodded. He blew a kiss in their direction before returning to his conversation. Casey scanned the room quickly for Michael, but she didn't see him anywhere. Just as they were about to head outside, Michael mysteriously appeared out of nowhere.

"Just wanted to say good night." He smiled deceptively.

"Good night," Alfred said curtly. He grabbed Casey's hand and started toward the entrance.

"Well, ain't that something?" Michael said to a group of his colleagues. "She's so major that she can come with one man and leave with another." He laughed. "But, I guess that's what sluts do."

Alfred stopped dead in his tracks and stepped in Michael's face. "What did you say? I must have a hearing problem because I know you didn't say what I *think* you said."

Michael puffed up his chest. "You don't have a hearing problem at all. You heard correctly, *brother.*"

Casey could see where this was going. She quickly grabbed Alfred by the arm. "This is exactly what he wants. Don't stoop to his level. Let's just leave."

At first, Alfred resisted Casey's tugs on his arm. Then he realized that she was right. Michael Jefferson wasn't worth it. He backed away and waved Michael off. Why blow his night?

"Where are you off to so soon?" He asked boldly. When Alfred kept walking, Michael kept talking. "I thought so."

Alfred gritted his teeth to keep from retorting. Just knowing that Casey was by his side was enough for him to forget about Michael.

Michael seemed sad as he watched them walk out the door, but she didn't care. He acted like a complete heel. Alfred slid his arm around her waist as they waited for his car. Casey relaxed.

Twenty-seven

"What are you thinking about?" she asked.

Alfred drove in silence a few more moments before answering. "Us." Though he was happy to be with her again, he needed answers. Deep in his heart, he knew this woman loved him, but why would she leave him on their wedding day?

Her pulse quickened. Was he having a change of heart? "What about us?"

He seemed indecisive about the whole situation. He hunched his shoulders. "I don't know, Casey. I think we really need to sit down and have a talk before we go any further."

"All right. I believe that's fair to both of us."

They both fell silent. Maybe they needed more time to sort things out before falling into each other's arms. He had to know what happened and why. He wasn't going to set another wedding date only to be made a fool of again.

Casey closed her eyes. She didn't feel tired, but the next time she opened them, they were pulling into Alfred's driveway.

"I almost forgot how beautiful this place is."

"It's not half as beautiful as you are." He planted a light kiss on her lips.

"Watch your step," he said as they headed through

the front door. He took her by the hand and led her down three steps before crossing the living room to the stairs that led to the second floor.

The last thing he wanted from Casey was a one-night affair. He wanted to make sure she wasn't going anywhere before he committed himself to her heart and soul.

He led her up the stairs. The only light in the living room was from a large fish tank in the corner. Blue incandescent lights lined the handrails that led upstairs.

It burned him up to see Michael Jefferson dragging her around as if she were a piece of meat. He literally assaulted her. She didn't have to worry about that ever happening to her again. He couldn't resist taking her into his arms, holding her gently. She lifted her head, anticipating the warmth of his lips against hers. He had to oblige the lady, didn't he?

His lips sought hers, commanding her tongue to respond to his. When he felt his own body beginning to respond, he released her from his embrace. "What happened to us, Casey?" His voice was pain filled. He sat in the chair next to the window. He knew that if he sat on the bed, no talking would be done.

"I honestly don't know," she said as she unbuckled her sandals and sat Indian-style on the thick carpet in front of him. All of the hurt began flooding back in. "Nothing like this has ever happened to me before. I've never been so . . ." Her voice broke.

"Confused?" Alfred suggested. She nodded in agreement. "Neither have I," he said. Alfred gripped the arms of the chair as he recalled their wedding day. "I mean, to just stand someone up on their wedding day."

"That's the thing that gets to me the most," Casey said. "That's something I'll never forget. It's possibly something that changes how I feel about marriage for a long time."

At least she sounded remorseful, Alfred thought. But he kind of got the feeling that she was more of a victim of her own actions than he was.

"I thought we agreed to talk about this later," she said. She stood up and slowly unzipped her dress. "I've missed you—in more ways than one." The gown dropped to the floor.

His mouth went dry. Oh, she really knew how to change the subject.

Twenty-eight

Was love beautiful or what? Everything was finally going her way. Home Sweet Home benefitted greatly from the fund-raiser. Business was good. Love was good. She was wearing her engagement ring again. Alfred kept asking her to set another date, but she hadn't given him one yet.

Was there any truth to the saying that all things happen for a reason? Maybe that sleazeball Michael Jefferson was brought into her life to bring Alfred back to her. She'd have to thank him if she ever saw him again. He would surely love that.

Her mother was busy rushing them to set a date because she wanted grandchildren, but Casey was going to give their marriage some time. It wasn't that she didn't trust Alfred, but she had to be sure that he wasn't going to up and leave her and then she'd be forced to explain to their child why his daddy wasn't there.

Casey's mother and Christie got along beautifully. She was already claiming her as her granddaughter. They were road buddies. She liked to drive and Christie liked to ride. They were always going to antique stores and outlets. Casey was starting to think Aunt Maggie was getting lonely. She constantly asked about Christie when she wasn't home.

Jay was a constant presence too. Her mother was

happy, so she should have been happy for her. He seemed like a nice man, but Casey wasn't feeling him. He asked a lot of questions about her. She guessed he was just trying to get to know her. Her mother was putty in his hands. *Oh, Jay, do you want tea? Well, I have Earl Grey, Constant Comment, Cinnamon, English Breakfast* . . . She literally catered to him.

One night, when she and Alfred joined them for dinner, Casey beat Jay to the punch. He thought he was going to get to ask all of the questions, but she had news for him.

"Your mother makes the best meat loaf I've ever tasted," Jay said as they all helped themselves to dinner. He carried on and on about her mother's cooking. Casey found herself frowning. Her mother's cooking was good, but it wasn't all he was making it out to be.

"So, Jay," Casey said as she helped herself to some rice, "Have you ever been married?"

He seemed pleased that she was taking an interest in him. He smiled. "I'm widowed. My wife passed away a little more than a year ago."

"I'm sorry to hear that," she said. "Do you have any children?"

"Yes, I have two children. I have a son and a daughter."

"That's nice," Casey said.

Alfred gave her a strange look. He never thought she would show an interest in Jay. She must have been getting at something.

"My son lives in Chicago. He's practicing medicine there, and my daughter lives here in Houston."

"Oh," Casey said. "Does your son get to Houston much?"

"When time permits." He picked at his food. "He's a very busy man."

Casey began quizzing him on his daughter and found that all of his answers were general. Her mother kept trying to get into the conversation and change topics, but Casey would steer it back to Jay's family.

Alfred tapped her on the knee under the table. She gave him an annoyed glance and continued her interrogation. He could see that Jay was becoming weary and uncomfortable. Alfred didn't know how much he could take without cracking under the pressure. Casey should have been an attorney. After ten more minutes of listening to Casey scrutinize Jay, Alfred finally excused himself and Casey from the table. He steered her by the elbow, and they stepped outside on the front porch.

"What's with you?" he asked. "If you want to find out if he's your father, this is not the way to do it."

Casey went to the porch swing and gently swayed. When she didn't say anything, he joined her. There was a look of distress on her face. She tilted her head back and watched the ceiling move back and forth as they rocked. Alfred took her left hand into his and toyed with the ring that rested on her finger. He had to admit, he had picked a good one.

"You still think he's your father, don't you?" He braced his foot on the porch to stop the swing from rocking.

She continued staring up at the ceiling. "I don't know what I think."

"Well, you made it pretty obvious that you thought something, and everybody else seemed to think so too." He gave her hand a squeeze. "Don't look for something that's not there."

Why couldn't he see what she saw? If Jay was her father, why was he resurfacing now? What did he want?

Twenty-nine

Casey hated driving downtown. All the construction work made a driver's life miserable. She wedged her car into a parking spot in front of a meter. She just had to run into the county building to find out some information on a couple of the kids' parents. She finally got to the computer and found nothing. She tried several more avenues before giving up. She opened her notebook to make sure she had the correct spelling of their names. Just as she was about to close it, Jay's license plate number fell out.

A debate began. Her fingers nervously drummed on the counter. *Should I? Shouldn't I.* She closed the notebook and prepared to leave. But curiosity wouldn't let her. Finally, she gave in. She pulled up public records and entered Jay's license plate.

"Well, well, well," she said. "What do we have here? Mr. Edwin James—my father."

She didn't know whether she was angry or hurt. She knew she was angry with her father, but she was hurt that her mother didn't tell her. Where had he been all of this time?

Punkin was completely shocked when Casey told him about it. He had to take a seat, he was so surprised.

"Honey," he said, his hand covering his heart, "You know how I like to run my mouth. I didn't think

there was much to it. Jay is your *father?*" He pulled
out his Virginia Slims and began puffing away.

"I can't believe my mother didn't say anything."
Casey went into the kitchen and sliced the apple pie
Punkin had brought with him. She put it in the mi-
crowave and warmed it enough to melt the vanilla ice
cream just a little. Punkin took his pie, and they both
sat on the floor in the living room, as they always did
when they had things to talk or gossip about.

"The only thing I can do is go over there and talk
with both of them. Do you know I have a brother?"
It was something, knowing that she had a brother out
there somewhere in Chicago who probably knew
nothing about her.

She spent that evening trying to decide how she
was going to deal with it. What could she do?

"I'm sorry that you had to find out this way." Alfred
stroked her hair after another session of passionate
lovemaking. He knew something had been bothering
her because she had been standoffish all day. He
could ask her a simple question, and she would darn
near bite his head off.

She snuggled closer to him. All of those years she
wished she could give her father a piece of her mind
and now that she had the chance, she didn't know
what she wanted to say.

"Me too," she said. "I'll never be able to forgive
him for leaving us."

He kissed her cheek. "Well, if your mother can forgive him, can't you? Apparently his reason was good
enough for her."

"I don't want any of his excuses." She pulled the
covers over her head. "Let's not talk about him anymore."

"Okay," Alfred said. "Let's talk about setting a date." He heard her groan. "So, when?"

"Alfred, let's not rush into setting a date. We have plenty of time to get married."

"Why can't we just circle something on the calendar?" he asked.

She threw the covers off and sat on the edge of the bed. "Alfred, please don't rush me. I'm under enough pressure as it is," she said in agitation.

He sprang out of bed and jumped into the shower. After dressing, he picked up his keys and headed for the door. She was sitting in the living room in a chair with her feet tucked under her. She looked like a lost little girl.

"Why are you putting this off? I'm not going to wait forever." He sighed. "Maybe you need to think about whether you really want to marry me or not. You know how I feel about you. Ask yourself if you feel the same about me." She flinched as the door closed behind him.

She wanted to scream, "I do feel the same way you do," but the words wouldn't leave her mouth. She asked herself why she didn't want to set a date, and for the life of her, she didn't know.

Thirty

Alfred leaned back in his seat. His heart hammered against his chest. *What are you doing,* he asked himself. *The woman of your dreams is sitting inside that house, and you've just given her an ultimatum. Either she sets a date or you walk. How reasonable are you being?* He started the car and headed toward home.

He knew Casey was upset about her father, and all he did was add more pressure. How supportive was he being? She needed to deal with her family before she could deal with him. But at the rate she was going, nothing was going to be resolved and both of their lives would be on hold. That was something he didn't want. Four years was long enough to put his own happiness off, and now that he found it, he wanted it right at that moment. Not next year or the year after. What he did want was for the both of them to live happily ever after.

This was going to end tonight. He turned the car around and headed in the opposite direction. Minutes later, he found himself in Casey's mother's driveway. He sat in the car a moment, debating whether he should go through with it. He had come all this way, so there was no need to leave now. He rang the doorbell, and her mother answered the door. She seemed surprised to see him without Casey. Just as he

expected, Jay was there. They invited him to join them
in the den. Alfred waited until they were both seated.

"We just finished dinner, would you like some?"
Casey's mother asked. Jay folded the newspaper he
had been reading.

"No, thank you. I think you know why I'm here."
They looked at him as if they hadn't the slightest clue
as to what he was talking about. "Look," he said to
Casey's mother. "I love your daughter and right now,
she's going through some things that she shouldn't
be." He looked at Jay.

"What do you mean?" Casey's mother asked. "I'm
not sure we're following you." Jay held her hand.

Alfred was tired, he was angry, and most of all, he
didn't want to see Casey suffering the way she was.
They were really trying to keep this thing under
wraps. How long did they plan on keeping up their
little charade? This wasn't just about them, it was
about their daughter too.

"Look, she knows what's going on," he said. "She
knows you're her father, Jay. She found out everything."

Casey's mother's mouth dropped. "Oh, no," she
said. "We never wanted her to find out like this."

"Why didn't you just tell her?" Alfred couldn't hide
his anger. He felt someone should be angry with
them, and since Casey hadn't bothered to confront
the situation, it may as well be him. They were literally
deceiving their own daughter.

Her mother was about to explain, but Jay held up
his hand, indicating that he was going to do the talking.

"I just wanted to give her time to get to know me."
He stood and began pacing back and forth across the
room. "I was hoping that maybe she'd like me

enough to give me a chance. I didn't want to just spring all of this on her all at once."

"All this talk is about you," Alfred said. "What about her? You're up here worrying about how to make things easier for you, but either way it goes, this won't be easy for her." He turned to Casey's mother. "Casey is *very* hurt that you didn't come to her with the truth. I even told her that you wouldn't keep something like this a secret from her. I just hate that I was wrong."

Her mother broke down into tears. "I was going to tell her. We were going to explain everything. We just needed some time to figure out how to tell her."

Alfred stood to leave. He didn't want to hear any of their excuses. "I'm a selfish man. This is holding up my marriage and tearing the woman I love to pieces. I suggest both of you get your acts together and tell her something—preferably the truth."

He stood there looking at them. They were nervous wrecks. But they brought it on themselves. Had they been upfront about all of this, they could all be in the healing process by now. He excused himself and went to his car. Now that he had gotten that out of the way, maybe his life would have order restored.

As he drove away, he could see Casey's mother and father standing in the doorway. They had a lot of thinking to do, and something told him they weren't going to get much sleep that night.

Casey should have gone to the office, but after checking in with Mrs. Potter, she realized there was no need to rush in. She instructed her to call her at home if there was an emergency. She went back to sleep and didn't get up until it was well after noon.

Petey began barking and then the doorbell rang.

She opened the door and looked up to see Jay standing on her steps. His presence told her a lot. Somehow he found out she knew his cover had been blown.

"Jay, this is a surprise." She remained in the doorway, holding on to the knob.

"Can I come in?" he asked. He appeared nervous. She knew why he was there, but she wasn't ready to have it officially validated yet.

"Right here is fine." She stepped out on the porch and closed the door behind her.

"Case." He moved toward her.

"My father used to call me that before he walked out on me and my mother," she said angrily. "But since you're not him, call me Casey."

"I'm sorry." He went to touch her arm, but she shrugged away. "I was young and made some bad decisions.

"All of those years." Her voice cracked. "All of those years I wished you were there. All of the birthdays and graduations that you missed. You missed the biggest part of my life and now you're here. All of those years, I watched my mother work two jobs because of you."

Jay's head was down. "This isn't easy for me either."

"All I want to know is why you left us. Why am I seeing you for the first time now?" Casey swallowed the sudden lump in her throat. Why did she have to get close to tears now? Since when did her anger turn into pain? She cleared her throat.

"Casey, I've wanted to talk to you for many years. I just—"

"Then why didn't you come see me?" she asked. Tears stung her eyes. This was totally out of the plan. She had practiced being tough as steel when she told him how she felt. Now she was standing there falling apart. "Where were you when I needed you?"

"Casey, I was at every important event in your life. You just didn't know it. I attended all of your graduations—even your college graduation. I bought you gifts every year for your birthday."

"That's not true. My mother never said you sent me anything. What gifts were you supposed to have sent to me?" She couldn't believe what she was hearing. It was all lies.

"For your college graduation, I bought you a gold watch with diamonds around the face." He continued to ramble off a list of the things he bought her.

She pulled back the sleeve of her shirt. It was true. "Why didn't you say anything? Why did you let me think that you weren't around all of these years? None of this makes any sense," she said, sobbing.

"I know it doesn't make any sense, but I'll explain everything. I promise. I know that saying I'm sorry isn't enough, but I really am." He held her hand in his. "Please find it in your heart to forgive me."

She pulled her hand away. "I don't know. This is too much for me. I need time to think." She bustled back inside and closed the door. It wasn't until she heard Jay's Chrysler start up, that she broke down crying again. Nothing was as it seemed. Nothing.

Thirty-one

Her mother sat next to her drying her eyes. Casey waited rather impatiently for her to gain her composure. Casey noticed that her mother seemed sad and aloof, or would worried have been a more appropriate description? She sat on the sofa next to her.

"I thought we had a better relationship than this. You are all that I have, and if I can't trust you, then who can I trust?"

"You can trust me. This was just something difficult to tell you, and I didn't want you to turn your back on me."

"You still love him, don't you?" Casey asked, looking down at the carpet. "After all of these years, you still love him."

Her mother's only response was silence. She stood and began arranging her favorite collectibles on the shelves. She picked up a duster and wiped furniture that was already dust free.

"Why?" Casey begged for understanding. She went over to her mother and stilled her busy hands. "Why?" she asked again. There was a strange gleam in her mother's eyes that she had never seen before.

Her mother threw her dust rag on the coffee table and sat on the sofa. "Now that you've found the right man, you know where I'm coming from. Edwin was my best friend." Her mother sighed. "What we shared was love—*real* love. We had a love like no other."

"Apparently that love wasn't enough to make him stay," Casey said with bitterness.

Her mother ignored her comment. "He made me feel like I was the only woman in the world and the most beautiful," she said with a dreamy smile. "We were so intertwined that we could communicate without words. All we had to do was look at each other and we knew what the other was thinking. I could start a sentence, and he could finish it for me—that's how close we were.

"And, baby, when you come to know *real* love, you won't settle for anything less. *Real* love can stand the test of time." She smiled. "So, yes, I still love your father, and I will continue to love him until the Lord calls me home."

Casey could not believe what she was hearing. She was at a total loss for words. Her leg, which was crossed over the other, bounced up and down in agitation. Was love her mother's only excuse? *Your father and I are in love and that's why I let him come back after all the years he was gone.*

"I know you don't understand right now, but you will. When you meet the man who believes that the sun rises and sets on you, you'll know what I'm talking about." She took a tissue from the box on the table and dabbed her eyes. "Yes, you'll know what I'm talking about."

"Yeah, right," Casey said almost inaudibly. She wasn't about to spend her life pining away after some man. Finish her sentences—right! That had to be one of the most ludicrous things she had ever heard. She loved Alfred, but there wasn't any sentence finishing going on. She knew he loved her, but there were no sunrises or sunsets as her mother described. She was starting to believe her mother needed her head examined.

How could her mother make her deserter father sound like some kind of superhero or something? Well, from what she could tell, there was definitely no *S* on his chest, and he never answered the calls of distress. So what kind of superhero was that? He was just an impersonator wearing a hero's disguise.

Casey convinced Punkin to meet her at Memorial Park for a power-walk. There were a lot of people out walking and jogging. She checked her watch. Punkin was fifteen minutes late. Fortunately for her, it didn't get dark until eight-thirty. Finally, Punkin strolled up wearing a tank top, warm-up bottoms, and a bright yellow headband that matched nothing he had on. She glance down at the tennis shoes he used to wear back in 1985. Just looking at him made her want to laugh in spite of her mood. They started off walking a couple of laps around the park.

"So, basically," Punkin began, "you don't know where he's been."

"No," Casey replied as they picked up the pace. "She went into the spiel about loving him and true love and all of that nonsense. She sounded like something out of a Kelsey Anderson romance book. She was talking about stuff that just doesn't exist."

"Major accomplishment," Punkin said sarcastically. "Your mama would have to go off the deep end at the wrong time. But, at least that's a start."

"A start? That was the beginning of the end," Casey replied. "I don't think I can stomach any more of their explanations. I don't even want to know. It doesn't matter anymore."

"No, don't be so pessimistic about the situation,"

Punkin said, panting. "That is the beginning of finding out the truth."

"Well, they say that sometimes the truth hurts." She picked up her pace once more. "I'm through hurting."

"What does Alfred have to say about all of this?"

She shrugged. "I haven't talked to him."

"Well," Punkin said, "either he's understanding or you've fallen out."

"It's the latter," Casey answered as they headed over to a bench to rest. "He keeps bugging me about setting a date."

Punkin took off his tennis shoe and began rubbing his foot. "And? What's the problem?"

"I've got a lot on my mind, and I don't want the added pressure."

He slipped his foot back in his shoe. "Do you love Alfred?"

She frowned. "What kind of question is that? Of course I love him."

"Then what's the problem?" he asked as he tied his shoe.

"There is no problem." She wiped her face and neck with a towel.

"I think you're afraid because you think Alfred is gonna leave you like your father did." He pointed to his head. "You'd better think hard before letting him slip past you. That man loves you, and I don't think he's going anywhere unless you make him."

"Yes, but he is the one who called off our wedding," she interjected.

"True, but there has to be more to that than you think. Honey, all this walking and stuff ain't for me. I'm fine enough." He laughed. "You can keep walking if you want, since you have more junk in your trunk than I do."

Casey closed her eyes and tilted her head back. "He said he bought me gifts for all of my birthdays. At first I didn't believe him. I thought it was all a crock of lies." Her fingers touched her watch. "I now know that's why Mom never said anything negative about him."

Punkin's hand covered his mouth in surprise. "I always wondered how your mother was able to afford that expensive Rolex."

"I don't know which way is up or down anymore. I would have given anything for my father to have taken those gifts back and been there for me in body, not spirit."

"I know what you mean. These men go around fathering kids and never take an active part in their lives. Some of them would rather pay child support than to spend any quality time with their offspring. Then when that child makes something out of his life, they're the first ones to holler, 'That's my kid!' They have the nerve to want to stick their chests out then. It's sad."

Casey smiled at Punkin. "I've never told anyone this, but I worked so hard to be the best that I could be so that my father would say, 'That's my girl.' I honestly wanted to be something that he could be proud of. When I made my speech at my high school graduation, I pretended that my father was in the audience. I wanted desperately to believe that he was out there cheering for me and calling my name. I swore I could hear him calling. Now, I know that he really was out there somewhere calling my name." She shrugged. "It wasn't my imagination after all."

"Come here, sister." Punkin moved over to Casey. "You sound like you could use a hug." He held her so close that she could hardly breathe.

"Thanks, I needed that." She turned her head so that Punkin couldn't see the mist forming in her eyes.

"I'm sure that Alfred can give you a lot more of what you need." Punkin laughed.

"Yeah, well, I need to work on that." *He's probably furious with me, but we'll be okay.*

Thirty-two

Casey stood in the mirror, brushing her hair. Alfred lay at the foot of the bed with one arm propped under his chin, watching her. He'd seen her do that so many times, and it seemed as if she liked it. But, tonight, there was something different. He thought she would brush every strand right out of her head. She was stressed. He jumped out of the bed, pulled up a chair, and asked her to sit down. He took the brush from her and began stroking her hair.

She smiled at his gesture. She closed her eyes as the brush ran through her hair. Alfred never knew brushing her hair would be so stimulating. It was almost like stroking an exotic animal. He was going to have to do this more often, especially when she wore those skimpy bedclothes he'd grown to love.

"This is a nice change," she said. "A girl could get used to this."

"Want me to polish your toes, too?" he asked. He leaned over and kissed her on the lips.

"What are you trying to do, spoil me?" She laughed. She opened her eyes and looked back at him. He was looking down at her as if asking "what?"

"I intend to," he said seriously. He gently turned her around so he could resume his task.

"This is a wonderful start." She smiled. All too

soon, she heard him place the brush on the dresser. Just when it was starting to feel good, it was over. He rambled around the dresser.

"Pick a color." He stood in front of her with several polishes. He quickly changed his mind. "That's okay, I'll choose."

Surely he wasn't serious about polishing her toes. He had actually flipped his wig. She stood and felt his forehead with the back of her hand. "Are you feeling well?" She laughed.

"Yes. Sit down so I can handle my business." He sat on the floor in front of her, placing her foot on his leg.

"What color did you choose?" She leaned over, trying to see.

He held up the bottle. "This one."

Jasmine. How funny that he would pick her favorite polish. She watched as he diligently polished each of her toes. Well, at least she didn't have to worry about him polishing her skin. He was doing a wonderful job.

Surprise was on her face as she laughed. "You must have—" He was already shaking his head.

"No, I've never done this before," he said. "I was a nail polish virgin. You were my first."

"I'm flattered." She moved her foot off his leg and pulled him by his T-shirt toward her. She kissed him fervently on the lips.

"When are you going to realize that I want to be everything to you?" He caressed her cheek. "I want to be your protector and your lover. I want to be the father of your children and your best friend."

He pulled her to the floor, next to him. "Let me explain something to you, Casey." He looked in her eyes, which were becoming moist. "When you hurt, I hurt. When you're stressed out, so am I. Sometimes you may not say anything, but I know when something is bothering you. I can't explain it. When you're happy, I'm happy. And when I see you cry, it rips my heart out." He took her hand into his and kissed her palm. "The only time I ever want to see you cry is when you're happy. I plan on making you happy for the rest of my life."

Oh, my God! This man makes me feel as f the sun rises and sets on me! She knew what her mother was talking about. Alfred had been there for her through everything. It was then that she gave him a date for the wedding: the following Saturday.

Thirty-three

"Do you want me to go with you?" Alfred asked. "You don't have to be alone."

She placed a kiss on his lips. "No, I think this is something I need to do alone." She headed out the door. "Just knowing that you're here makes all of the difference in the world."

Today was going to be the beginning of the rest of her life. It didn't matter whether her father was in her life or not. It was time for answers, and she was going to get them.

Her mother and Jay met her at the door when she arrived. She chose to sit in the living room because there were no barriers between them there. If they sat at the kitchen table, it would be between them, and she didn't want to miss one gesture or movement.

An uncomfortable silence filled the room. Oh, how she wished she would have let Alfred come with her. Everyone seemed to be waiting for someone to break the ice.

Finally, Casey cleared her throat. "Uh, why don't you tell me the truth. I want the truth from both of you."

Jay went to speak, but Casey's mother patted his hand, indicating that she would start.

"Are you sure?" Jay asked her mother.

She nodded yes. "Edwin and I met and immediately fell in love," she began. "Little did I know that he came from one of the most prominent families in town. I was from the wrong side of the tracks." Casey listened as her mother continued. "They came from old money. Every male in his family was a doctor, which was a tradition. Edwin was in med school at the time and told his family that he had met someone and wanted to get married."

Then Jay broke in. "My family was outraged and was dead set against me marrying your mother. I continued medical school and then your mother found out she was pregnant, and we had you." He sighed. "Again, my family was outraged and said that I was disgracing the family because your mother and I weren't married."

"His family came to me, offering money to get out of his life. But I turned them down," her mother said.

Her mother and father were never married? She was learning more and more every day.

"Eventually," her mother said, "they threatened to disinherit him and cut funding for medical school. I couldn't let him lose everything because of me. He didn't want to go. As a matter of fact, he flat-out refused."

"But your mother insisted," Jay said. "Finally, I gave in because I knew I could take care of you if I didn't rub my family the wrong way. I promised your mother that she would never have to work, and I stuck to that promise, because I loved both of you."

If it were under other circumstances, she would have laughed at her parents because they looked like two children who had been sent to the principal's office. "But, why did we move? Why were you working two jobs?" Casey asked.

"We moved because I wanted to conserve the

money Edwin had given us. He didn't know when he would get his hands on that kind of money again. So, I used it wisely. As far as working two jobs went, I wanted to keep my mind occupied. We were never without, Casey."

Casey could feel her mouth starting to get dry. This was starting to overwhelm her. All of this time she had been hating her father for no reason.

"His family already had someone in mind for him to marry," her mother said. "She came from one of the wealthiest families in Houston, and she would be an asset to their family. It was like a business deal. Of course, I didn't want that to happen, but I knew it was for the best. I couldn't deprive him of what was rightfully his, and I encouraged that to happen."

Jay held her mother's hand. "I wanted to see you and spend time with you, but your mother didn't want you to think ill of me. She knew you wouldn't understand why I couldn't come around. And I decided that was best for her too because I didn't want you to think less of your mother since I had married another woman."

"However," her mother said, "I did say that it was okay for him to send you gifts or attend special events in your life, but we agreed that he would stay out of sight."

"We're sorry, Casey," Jay said. "We thought we were protecting you, but it seems as if we've done you more harm than good."

That was an understatement. "What about your son? Does he know about this?"

"He does now and as expected, he wasn't too thrilled about the situation. But he came to grips with it and wants to meet you."

She didn't know what she was going to do. She had no idea what to say or think. Her parents had just

dropped the biggest bomb of her life on her. It wasn't
the bomb that was the problem; it was how to deal
with it.

Thirty-four

Casey began working long hours to keep her mind off her parents. Besides, she wanted things to be in tip-top condition at Home Sweet Home before the wedding. Alfred didn't really approve of her working long hours, but he didn't force the issue. Since she was working late, he offered to pick her up. He wasn't too fond of her walking into a dark parking lot to get into her car.

After stopping off for dinner, he took her home. When they turned into the driveway, they noticed a brick had been thrown through the back window of her car, and all her tires were flat. Alfred told Casey to stay in the car while he looked around.

"You must've really ticked somebody off," Alfred said as he opened the door for Casey.

The police came out and took a report. Then a wrecker picked up the car and took it to the dealership.

"Don't worry," Alfred said. "It's probably some teens in the neighborhood. I'm sure it's no one you know. Why don't you stay over at the house tonight?"

She objected. "I'll be okay," she said. "Petey's in the house."

"If you stay, I'm staying. I don't feel comfortable leaving you alone."

"Alfred, really, I'll be fine. If I need you, I'll call. Besides," she said, "you and Christie have an early flight in the morning."

He didn't seem to be buying it. There was no need for him to get up extra early just to catch his plane.

"I'll be fine. I promise," she said as she hopped out of the car. Alfred walked her to the door.

He didn't like the idea one bit. "All right. Call me if you need anything."

He and Christie were going to California to visit Dara, who had been placed with her grandparents. After visiting for a couple of days, they were bringing Dara back with them for the wedding.

After showering, Casey dressed and hopped into bed. She was asleep as soon as her head hit the pillow. She was awakened by Petey's barking.

She reached down to the foot of the bed and rubbed his back. "It's okay, Petey," she said sleepily. "Go back to sleep."

She laid her head back on the pillow, but Petey kept barking and ran out of the room. She followed Petey to the back door, where he yelped and scratched at the bottom.

Through the thin material covering the glass on the window, Casey could just make out the outline of someone standing on the other side of the door.

"Who's there?" she called out. The person answered by twisting the knob. Casey ran to the phone and dialed 911. She realized with rising panic that her phone was dead. The man began twisting the doorknob harder. She ran to the alarm system and hit the panic button, but nothing happened. The glass in the door shattered and the intruder's hand crept inside and unlatched the dead bolt lock. As the door swung open, she ran for the front door. She could hear him running behind her.

She screamed as he grabbed her shirt before she could unlock the door. A struggle ensued and Petey began to attack the intruder. He struggled with the dog as he continued to attack him. Eventually, the intruder ran out of the back door and into the night.

Fortunately, Casey's alarm was attached to the phone line and when it was cut, the police were automatically dispatched. She called Punkin on her cell phone and asked him to come pick her up.

"Girl, I just can't believe that this happened to you," Punkin said when they got to his apartment. "Do you think there's a connection to the car incident?"

"I don't know," Casey said as she stretched out on his couch. "I told the police about it, so we'll see what happens."

Punkin lit a cigarette. "Alfred is going to be upset. You already know he didn't want you staying alone anyway. You need to tell him about this," he advised. "You should be on the phone calling him right now."

"No," Casey said. "He won't go out of town if I tell him. Besides, I don't want to hear him fuss."

"Well, he needs to know, and you know it." Punkin smashed the remainder of the cigarette in a nearby ashtray. "He's going to question why you haven't told him about it, and I'm going to agree with him."

"I know, I know," Casey said in frustration. "I'll tell him when he gets back."

"All right, but my name is Bennett and I ain't in it," he said.

Casey frowned. "I get the point." She propped a pillow behind her head and pulled the blanket over her. "I said I would tell him and I will—when he gets back."

"All right, Ms. Thang. Have it your way. I don't have nothing else to say about it."

"Good."

"Fine."

Thirty-five

"There's a gentleman here to see you," Mrs. Potter said as she poked her head in the door. "He's interested in adopting a child."

Casey's back was to the door while she typed on the computer. "Could you show him in please?" She cleared the screen and swiveled around in time to see a tall, attractive man enter the door.

She went to stand to shake his hand, but he told her that wasn't necessary. As hot as it was outside, he wore a pair of leather gloves. He introduced himself as Byron Marsh. He reeked of money—from the expensive suit to the link bracelet he wore on his wrist. Casey knew he was used to being in charge.

Something in his gaze made her uncomfortable. He kind of reminded her of a volcano that could explode without warning. Though he was an attractive man, he seemed as though he had a dark side. She could feel him crowding her space.

He provided her with information about himself and said that he wanted to adopt a newborn son. Casey informed him that they had just received a newborn baby girl, but he was adamant about a son. She almost felt as if he thought women were inferior beings.

"No," he said. "A girl would never do. Girls are

too much trouble. Besides, a son could carry out the family tradition."

"Well, Mr. Marsh," Casey said, "we'd love to assist you."

He seemed like another Michael Jefferson, but in a nicer package. Like Michael, Byron made her skin crawl. It was eerie.

He was quick to answer her questions and when she explained that he would have to attend parenting classes and training for adoptive parents, he flat-out refused. He said he didn't have time for such trivial things. His schedule was hectic, and he wasn't changing his plans for some silly old class. After reaching into his coat pocket, he pulled out a checkbook and a pen. He casually threw a check for fifty-thousand dollars on her desk.

"That should take care of my training," he said briskly. He looked around her office. "It appears that this business needs the money, so think hard before you make a decision."

This man just didn't get it. Money couldn't get people out of everything. She slid the check back across the desk to him. She broke down the process of adoption and how they had to comply with state rules.

He seemed rather bored, as he gave a fake yawn while she explained things to him. "I'm good friends with the governor. I'm sure he can pull a few strings here and there for me."

Casey laughed under her breath. "It doesn't matter who you know, Mr. Marsh. Home Sweet Home is *my* business, and if it's found that I'm not in compliance, this business could be shut down. Frankly, I'm not willing to lose everything I've worked so hard for just because some man walked in off the streets and tried to get me to bend the rules. It doesn't work that way with me. You either comply or say good-bye."

Byron stood and tore his check to pieces. "Well," he said in a nasty tone, "I'll just have to take my business elsewhere."

"Have a nice day," Casey said.

Just like that, he walked out of her office. How could he just walk into her office and try to bribe her? She didn't know him from the next person. He could have been trying to set her up for all she knew. Home Sweet Home could have used the finances, but Casey wasn't taking any under-the-table money.

"Well, Mr. Marsh," Casey said to herself, "you'll learn that money won't buy you everything."

Casey walked hurriedly to the rental car. It was another late night at work again. How she wished Alfred were there to pick her up. She threw her appointment book on the seat and started the engine.

In her business, she was going to come across a lot of people, but she didn't think she'd ever meet anyone like Byron Marsh. She couldn't get that look that stared straight through her out of her mind. How could she best describe it—mean? He seemed like a crude person. How could he think he could just throw her a check and that would be all she wrote? Well, she showed him. Actions spoke louder than words.

The alarm company came out and restored her service, and Casey had another door put up that day. The police said that there had been a string of robberies in the area and that she probably didn't have to worry about the intruder coming back. She was still a little leery, but she wasn't about to be forced out of her home. She felt better knowing that the police would tighten up patrols because of the crime spree.

While the police were there, the neighbors spotted Petey running around and decided to claim him. They hadn't worried about that dog since he was gone, and suddenly they wanted him back. If it weren't a shame, Casey would have made them pay her for room and board. They had the nerve to look at her as if she were a thief. Had they come around looking for the dog? No. Had they posted any pictures of him? No. They just wanted him back for added protection. If the break-ins hadn't been going on, they would have remained unconcerned.

Casey was really going to miss that dog. She turned on the alarm as she entered the house. After changing clothes, she stepped out on the back porch and called for Petey, but he wasn't there. *Now they want him to be a house dog! Imagine that.* She closed the door and sighed, making sure the dead bolt locks were engaged.

Alfred called to see how she was doing. He said he and Christie were having a wonderful time and that Dara couldn't wait to see her again. His cell phone began to break up. She asked what he was doing and he said that he, Christie, and Dara were out and about. He promised to see her soon, and they hung up.

Thirty-six

Alfred was pleased with himself Casey was going to be surprised that he and the girls were back. He couldn't wait to see her again. It seemed as if they had been apart forever. Dara's grandparents were flying down in a couple of days in time for the wedding. They were going to take Dara back with them.

He opened the box that was in his pocket. Casey was going to love her wedding band—at least he hoped so. He had such a good feeling about them. Hopefully, Casey could forgive her father and they could start over. Alfred didn't agree with her parents' decision, but he could honestly say he understood. Love could make people do crazy things.

After trying to sleep with the lights off, Casey ended up turning on the lamp at her bedside. It was eleven-thirty, and she was wide awake. She pulled out a new book she had started and hoped she would eventually fall asleep. Things weren't the same without Petey around. She picked up the phone just to make sure it had a dial tone. Satisfied, she hung it up.

As sleepy as she was, her eyes popped open every time she found herself drifting off. She looked at the clock every time she woke. She leaned over and

looked out the bedroom door. She could see the light
on the alarm, which told her that it was still activated.
Casey picked up her book from her lap and continued where she left off. The next thing she knew, the
book was reading her. When she woke again, it was
one o'clock. Her hand went to the lamp and clicked
it on. She went to the kitchen and poured a glass of
water. As she stood by the counter, it dawned on her
that she hadn't turned her lamp off before she went
to sleep. She froze. Slowly, she turned to the alarm.
To her horror, the red light wasn't on, which meant
the alarm wasn't activated.

Where was he? Inside the house or waiting for her
on the outside? She'd do better on the outside because she might have a chance to scream and have
someone hear her. Her brain kept saying *run,* but her
feet wouldn't obey. *Breathe, Breathe.* She could feel
someone's presence in the room. Her heart began
beating rapidly. She felt as though she was going to
faint. *Don't you dare! You're going to the door, and you're
getting out of here.* Hairs began to stand up on the back
of her neck. Finally, her feet were willing to move.
She slowly began backing toward the door. Suddenly,
from out of nowhere, a large hand covered her
mouth and nose. The sound of her glass hitting the
floor was the last thing she heard as she drifted into
darkness.

A strong odor aroused her. Casey's head ached mis-
erably. She almost gagged on the cotton material that
was shoved down her throat. After struggling to move
her hands and feet, she found that they were tied.
Strong arms sat her upright on the couch. *What's going on? I'm going to die. I'm going to die tonight!*

The intruder remained out of her sight. She could
hear something dragging along the floor. Finally, he

pulled a chair in front of her and took a seat. Surprise showed on her face.

"Well, Ms. James," Byron Marsh said as he crossed one leg over the other. "I think I'll call you Casey. Tell me if you mind if we refer to each other on a first-name basis." His dark laughter cut through the silence. "Well, since you have nothing to say, I'll have to call you Casey.

"Guess you wished you would have taken my check now," he said darkly. "Next time you'll watch how you treat your clients." He took off his gloves to reveal a scar on his left hand.

It was Byron who broke into her house the first time. Why didn't she pick up on it earlier? How she wished Alfred were there to protect her. She should have listened to him and stayed at his house. But who was to say that he wouldn't have done the same thing there? Then Aunt Maggie would have been in jeopardy. She didn't want that to happen. It was best that she was alone.

"Let me start by introducing myself," he said politely. "My name is Kenneth Smith. I know that name doesn't ring a bell, but I'm your father's late-wife's son." He took a cigar out of his pocket and lit it. Rings of smoke filled the air.

He watched as she tried to cough. "Don't worry, you won't gag to death. I'll make sure of that." His voice was without pity. "As I was saying, my mother was married to your father." He stood and paced in front of her. He stopped occasionally to look into her eyes. She actually thought he was trying to terrify her.

The man seemed to be driven by hatred and fury. With each word he spoke, his anger heightened. He slammed his fist into the palm of his hand. "He made my mother miserable. She loved him with all of her heart, but his heart wasn't in it. They were a couple in marriage only. My mother was the laughingstock of society and why?" he asked. "Because he loved some woman who could never give him the kind of happiness my mother could give. Oh, he was polite, but all she wanted was his love. Sometimes I wished he would have walked out on her instead of staying with her and making her miserable."

"Well," he said, "you should be happy that he deserted you. What if the shoe were on the other foot? How would you feel to see your mother with a man who didn't love her?"

He stopped in front of her, watching as tears flowed from her eyes. "Stop crying!" he yelled. "Your tears mean nothing to me. My mother cried more tears than you could ever imagine." He looked down at her. "You are a poor excuse for a grown woman. You probably cry at the drop of a hat."

He leaned close to her. "What's wrong? You've never had an intruder in your home before?" He laughed. "Well, don't worry your pretty little head about it. I'll be in and out before you know it."

Casey shook as tears racked her body. Why was he making her pay for her father's mistake? She was hurt just as much by this as he was. But he was relentless. He seemed as if he was high. He jumped from subject to subject, sometimes not making any sense. It was as though he had so much to say but everything wanted to come out at the same time.

"He killed my mother, you know? She died of a broken heart. They said it was a heart attack, but it came right after your *father* told her about you and your mother." He extinguished his cigar.

"That's why I vowed to make things right. It's about time that he knows what it is to suffer." He placed a finger under his chin, thoughtfully. "At first, I thought about getting rid of your mother, but then,

I decided you would be a better prize. Who knows? Maybe I'll get two for the price of one."

He went to his jacket, which was lying on the arm of the couch, and pulled out two syringes. "It's such a shame," he said. "You're a beautiful woman, and I hate that I have to do this." He shrugged his shoulders. "I guess that's life though." He pulled the top off one of the needles, thumped its side, and squirted some of its contents in the air. "Maybe you'll get a chance to meet my mother when you cross to the other side, if you end up on the right side of the road. You might be going the opposite direction." He looked down at the floor.

"This is going to be painless, I promise," he said. "I want to hurt your father, not you. You won't feel a thing." He moved toward her. "The first shot will put you to sleep, and the second will slow your heart down until it eventually stops."

She began to struggle desperately. *Oh, my God! This is it. This is really it!* His strong hand gripped her arm, and she could feel the needle pinch as it went in. The cool liquid poured into her veins.

She tried to scream, but nothing came out. She'd never see her mother again. She would never hear any more of Punkin's funny stories. Most of all, she'd never see Alfred or Christie again. The relationship that could have been with her father was never going to be. *Oh, Alfred, I'm never going to see you again.*

Thirty-seven

He couldn't wait to wake her up with a kiss. He pulled into her driveway and got out of the car. After going to the front door, he remembered that she usually kept the chain on it. He definitely didn't want her thinking someone was breaking in on her so he went around back.

He unlocked the door and went to punch in the code, but the alarm wasn't activated. *That's strange,* he thought to himself. This was totally unlike Casey.

A light was on in the living room so he headed toward the front. He could hear someone sobbing. "Casey?" he called out. Just as he entered the living room, he saw a man standing over Casey with a syringe in his hands. Her head was leaning to one side, and her eyes were low. She seemed to be barely hanging on to consciousness.

"What in the hell is going on here?" he yelled at the man, who seemed startled to see him.

Kenneth whipped around and then he headed toward Alfred and a struggle ensued. Casey knew she was dreaming. Alfred was in California, wasn't he? It must have been the drug making her hallucinate. But that hallucination was there struggling with the deranged man who was trying to dispose of her. She could see that Kenneth had a syringe in his hand and was trying to stab Alfred with it. She was fading fast and would be unconscious at any moment. She maneuvered herself around so her feet, which were still tied, were pressed against a window. Alfred and Kenneth bumped against the walls and knocked things off the shelves.

Things weren't looking good. She had to act quickly. She willed herself to kick against the windowpane. It didn't want to give. She kicked again and nothing happened. Sleep was overcoming her. She glance up to see that Kenneth had Alfred pinned against the wall and was trying to press the needle toward his chest. *Alfred needs me!* She breathed as deeply as she could and gathered all of her strength. This was her last effort. It was now or never. She would be the difference between life or death for the both of them. She drew her feet back and gave her final kick. There was a sharp pain in her left ankle as the glass shattered. The alarm began blaring. It must have caught Kenneth off guard because he looked toward her, and Alfred's fist made contact with his jaw, knocking him to the floor.

Her eyes were heavy as a hand removed the gag from her mouth. She remembered seeing a gold ring with a star on it before her eyes closed.

Alfred ran over to Casey and untied her hands and feet.

"What did he do to you?" He leaned over her sobbing. "Please don't let it be too late," he begged, looking up at the ceiling. The sound of an ambulance could be heard in the distance.

Several faces hovered over hers. Everyone was smiling down at her. Alfred's hand held hers tightly. Her mother and Punkin were wiping their eyes. Her father's face was filled with worry. *Well, at least I'm not dead!*

"You had a lot of us worried," her father said. "We're happy you're still with us, thanks to Alfred." He patted Alfred's shoulder. "Thanks for saving her for us."

"Trust me, it was purely for selfish reasons," he said as he kissed her cheek. "Besides, she helped me help her."

Casey tried to move her legs, but a sharp pain caused her to wince.

"Don't try to move," Alfred said. "You've got stitches in your left leg."

He looked terrible. His eyes were red. Had he been crying? "I don't know what I would have done if I had lost you." He kissed her hand. "You did some quick thinking. There's no telling how long we would have struggled if you hadn't distracted him."

"I was scared," she said. "All I knew was that I had too much to live for. Where's Kenneth?"

"He's in jail," her father said. "He'll probably be there for a long time. I never knew he hated me so much. Apparently, he's been in Houston for months trying to figure out how to get next to me. I thought he was working at the hospital, but apparently he'd become so engrossed with his vendetta that the hospital referred him to a psychiatrist. He couldn't practice again until he was better."

"He confessed to damaging your car and to stalking you," Alfred said. "The officer who patrolled your neighborhood said he had seen his car parked in front of your house late at night on several occasions. He thought the car belonged to you."

"That's not all he planned to do," Casey said. "He planned on hurting you too, Mom."

"What?" Jay said. "I've put both of you in danger,

and I didn't even know. If anything had happened, I would never have forgiven myself"

Casey looked at Jay, who really seemed to blame himself for everything that had happened.

In spite of the circumstances, it was nice to see all of her loved ones—even her father—surrounding her. Her experience made her love for life grow. She learned the hard way that life must be lived to the fullest each and every day.

She was released from the hospital the next day. Alfred insisted that she stay with him until the wedding. He sent someone over to move her things out of her house and place them in storage. Christie and Dara ran out to meet them as they parked the car. Christie hugged her tightly.

"I'm so happy you're okay," she said.

"Thanks, Christie. I'm happy too." Dara was eagerly awaiting her turn to be hugged.

After hugging Dara, she heard a loud bark as Petey came running from around the corner. She rubbed him behind the ears.

"How did you manage to get Petey?" she asked Alfred.

"Your neighbors found out what happened and decided that you needed him more than they did. So, I opened the car door, and he hopped in."

Alfred spread a blanket on the floor and turned the thermostat down. They both lay by the fire, watching the flames. It was ironic that Alfred would show up when she needed him the most, *again*.

"I've got to tell you something," Casey said.

"What's that?" he asked as he held her close.

She turned to face him. He was lying on his arm watching her. The flames danced across his face and made his eyes sparkle—a sparkle she thought she'd never see again.

"The night you and Christie left for California, someone broke into the house."

His head popped up. "Why didn't you tell me?" he asked. "I told you I wasn't comfortable leaving you alone after the car incident."

"I know, I know," she said. "I didn't want you to stay home on account of me. This was the first trip you and Christie had together in a long time and I wanted that."

"Thank God I came back when I did. That's twice that I could have lost you," he said with an edge in his voice. "Don't ever hesitate to call me when you need me. That's what I'm here for. How can I take care of you if you won't let me?"

"I know. You don't have to worry about that anymore."

"Good," he said. He stared into the fire. It was just starting to hit home that this Kenneth man had been trying to kill his fiancée. How could someone be so bitter that he would take his pain out on someone who had nothing to do with his problems? Maybe in Kenneth's mind everything was logical.

"You know, your father really cares about you," he said a short time later. "He was sitting up there bawling like a baby. What are you going to do about him?"

Casey sighed. "My mother loves him and from what Kenneth was saying, my father was just in that marriage because he had to be. He made his wife miserable right along with Kenneth. I thought I was on the losing end, but you know," she said thoughtfully, "I kind of feel sorry for Kenneth. He blames my father for his mother's death."

"And what do you think?" Alfred asked.

"My father may have been responsible. He didn't

physically touch her, but I believe he broke her heart."

Alfred pulled her close. He was never letting her go. "Speaking of broken hearts, why did you stand me up for our wedding? We could have had this out of the way the first time."

She looked surprised. She laughed. "I didn't stand you up. You're the one who taped a letter to my front door and told me not to try to contact you because you would be out of town."

He looked at her as if she had been taking too many pain pills. "I did no such thing. The day of our wedding I was calling around for you and then Aunt Maggie handed me a letter from you. That letter asked me not to contact you."

"I wonder who wrote that." They both fell silent, wondering where the mysterious letters came from.

"Well," Alfred said, "that goes to show that you can't stop love."

"You want to know something strange?" Casey began picking at the edges of the blanket. Alfred turned on his back and pulled the blanket over both of them. The room had grown cold.

"Everything has been strange lately," Alfred said.

"The night I thought you called off the wedding, I drove over to Punkin's house." Alfred had a weird expression on his face. She laughed. "He had this 'dream,' about this dark shadow following me. He said that it was trying to engulf me and just as I was about to be sucked totally in, a hand wearing a gold ring with a star on it reached in and pulled me out."

Alfred was staring intently at her. He didn't like supernatural stuff. "Anyway," Casey said, "the night you struggled with Kenneth, I saw that ring on your finger. So, before I blacked out, I knew everything was going to be okay."

Alfred studied the ring on his finger. "This was my father's." He took the ring off and handed it to her. "He gave it to me before he died. It was his father's and when we have a boy, I'll give it to him. Oddly enough, I found myself rubbing that ring on the flight back. I don't know why, but I felt like I had to get back to see you that night. Weird, huh?"

"Yeah, weird, but I'm happy you made it back." She smiled.

"From now on, tell Punkin to keep his revelations to himself" He laughed.

"That, I will," Casey said.

Thirty-eight

Casey dropped by the agency to give Liz an invitation to the wedding. Liz was pleased to see her and said that she planned to attend.

"There's something I think you should know," Liz said. Casey waited for Liz to tell her what was on her mind.

"I probably shouldn't be discussing details of Vicia's departure with you, but I'm sure by now you've figured out that she was the one who reported you to our program director." She leaned back with a look of disappointment on her face. "Anyway, Vicia was fired not long after I got word that you had to leave. It wasn't that you weren't a good worker, but everything is very bureaucratic around here. You were meant to be the example. Unfortunately, there was nothing I could do."

It wasn't really a surprise that Vicia was gone, however. Casey thought maybe she'd quit before getting tired. She never really cared about what happened to the children anyway.

"Why was she fired?" Casey asked.

"Well," Liz said, "she had been falsifying documents. She was pretending to go and see the children on her caseload, when in fact she hadn't seen them in months. We've had some angry foster parents calling and making complaints. Most of these complaints made their way to the ombudsman's office. So, the agency launched an investigation and began auditing her time and leave. Several times she had been known to be at the beauty shop getting her hair and nails done. This meant she was also falsifying travel and getting mileage for fabricated trips." She threw up her hands. "The thing I thought would interest you the most was this." She opened her drawer and pulled out two pieces of paper. "I found these when I cleaned her desk out."

Casey took the sheets from her. The familiar words that had turned her life upside down were back in her hands—the fake letters written to both her and Alfred, calling off the wedding.

"Why would she do this?" Casey asked. "I've never done anything to her."

"Sometimes you don't have to do anything to anyone. She always envied you," Liz said. "She envied your dedication. The case involving your fiancé's niece was assigned to someone else, but Vicia took it upon herself to try to take the case. I don't run that kind of ship." There was disbelief in her voice. "I told her several times not to contact that family, and I later found out that she did what she wanted to anyway. It was like she was blatantly disregarding my authority."

"After all of my hard work, I get let go," Casey said. "Regardless of what anyone may think, I loved this job. I poured my heart into each and every one of the families I had to work with. I mean, for four years this job was my life, and I make one mistake, and it's see ya later, bye, bye. I can't believe they let me go so easily."

Liz's tone was soft. "You're no more surprised than I am. I've known people who have done worse than

Vicia, and they are still employed at this agency right now." She smiled. "Maybe it was time for a change. Where would you be if you were still here? Now you have your own business, and you're about to get married. Maybe this job was yours just so you could meet your husband. Who knows? Just count your blessings and keep going," Liz advised.

Casey explained to Liz how her relationship with Alfred hadn't been easy. Liz was appalled to hear of Kenneth's devious plot. It seemed like all of the odds had been against her. Yet Casey overcame them all. She didn't even know Vicia had been out to get her, but good prevailed. She guessed there was something true about those who do wrong getting theirs in the end. She was glad that their plans for her didn't go through or else she probably wouldn't have been around to see them get theirs.

Casey sat flipping the channels on the television while she waited for Punkin to pick up the food from Little China Restaurant. She kept flipping the channel until it landed on *Animal Planet*. It was the next best thing to the Discovery Channel. The Crocodile Hunter was in a far-off land searching for an animal that was believed to be extinct.

"I thought you were ordering takeout, not making dinner," Casey said as she joined him in the kitchen.

"Honey, I got us a full-course meal. You know this Chinese food don't fill you up."

They both opened the bags and took out their food. "Girl, what are you watching—Animal Planet?"

"Yes. You know how I like nature shows," Casey answered.

Punkin laughed as The Crocodile Hunter climbed into a tree to escape a charging rhinoceros. "Girl, that Crocodile Hunter is going to fool around and get himself killed playing around with all of them dangerous animals who have bad tempers. He goes crawling after them like they are pets or something. He's going to learn the hard way."

"I hope not. Then I'll have to find another show to watch. Besides, what lesson will he have learned if he's dead?"

"Child, that would be his final lesson, and I'm pretty sure that he'll be thinking that over when he realizes there is no antivenom on the way." Punkin slurped his wonton soup. After sipping a couple more spoonfuls, he turned to her. "Now, let's get down to the good stuff. I know you couldn't talk much today, but you have got to tell me about this Vicia woman. I told you I didn't trust her. Why did she despise you so much?"

Casey frowned in thought. "I don't know, we never really clicked in the first place. She liked to get over too much. I think it has something to do with the night I met Alfred at Bennigan's. We got along much better before then."

"I can't believe she'd go through so much trouble just because Alfred gave you his number instead of her." He frowned. "She has to learn that everything in life ain't going to go her way. We all win some and sometimes, we lose some. She knows that the world doesn't revolve around her."

"I don't know. I think she has some kind of hang-up. She probably went through some things and couldn't get over it," Casey said.

"I hate to say this, but you women can be conniving." Punkin pointed at the television and whooped. "Will you look at that Crocodile Hunter? He done grabbed that snake by the tail and it's just wigglin'.

See," he said, "the thing tried to bite 'em. He gonna learn."

"What is that supposed to mean?" She gave him a sideways glare.

"Just what I said. Women can be devious. You see another woman who did whatever it took to get where she is, and you get jealous and want what she's got." He shook his head. "Some women feel that if they can't brag about what they have, nobody should."

"That's true, but I never thought Vicia would feel that way about me," Casey said. "I just thought we were cool."

"Cool, smool. Girl, just because you're cool with someone doesn't mean they are truly your friend." He sucked his breath in surprise. "You mean what's-her-face actually got to you?" Casey nodded. Punkin set his food on the coffee table. "Girl, don't worry about that because the truth prevailed. She just needs someone to pray for her. Maybe I'll get Rene to do a little something for her." He laughed.

"Talk about her being crazy. There's no telling what Vicia might be doing when Rene gets finished with her. She might be standing over someone in the middle of the night quoting scriptures."

"You have to start thinking about your big day, which is right around the corner."

"I know," she said. "I'm actually excited." She followed Punkin to the kitchen.

"Have you spoken with your daddy since the Kenneth saga?"

"No. He called, but I didn't answer the phone. I wasn't ready to talk."

"Girl, you better quit being silly and drive your behind on over there and resolve this mess." Punkin went back to the living room to make sure he hadn't left anything behind. "You've got to come to terms with all of this."

Casey gave Punkin a hug. "You always tell me what's best for me, and you're right. I do need to resolve this, and I will."

Punkin smacked his lips. "Okay, now when you go over there, be on your best behavior or you're gonna end up in time-out."

"Okay." She laughed.

They sat around watching television for a little while before Casey received her phone call from Alfred.

"I'll talk to you tomorrow," Casey said from the door.

"Hang in there," Punkin said. "And take some of this Chinese food with you. I can't eat all of this stuff."

"I'll pass. Talk to ya tomorrow."

Thirty-nine

Alfred couldn't believe that another day had gone by and nothing out of the ordinary happened. He found himself holding his breath as the days grew closer to the wedding. Each day, he kept expecting *something*. That *something* hadn't showed its ugly face yet, but he kept expecting it. He tried to shrug it off, but that feeling stayed with him. Maybe he was over-reacting to all of the things he and Casey had gone through just to get where they were. *We're almost there. Just a little while longer, and we will be a family.*

He looked out the window to see Casey and the girls in the garden. Never in a million years did he think his life would be back together again. He didn't expect to be happy again until Christie was a grown woman. Casey was pointing out different flowers to Christie and Dara, who both seemed very interested. She was so good with his daughter. She was the mother Christie had been missing. Of course Aunt Maggie was there, but she was more of a grandmother figure. It wasn't that Alfred didn't appreciate Aunt Maggie's presence, because he did. There was no way in the world he was ever going to learn how to comb all of that hair on Christie's head. He had no clue as to what the latest craze was for little girls. If she were a boy, he could do all of the manly things with

him, like teach him to fish or take him camping. Not
that a girl couldn't do those things, but he definitely
didn't want Christie to end up being a tomboy.

Alfred leaned against the glass, intently watching
the three of them. They were touching each flower
as if its petals would disintegrate in the palms of their
hands.

As if she could feel his eyes on her, Casey turned
toward the window and smiled before returning to
her flowers.

Her flowers. It was amazing to Alfred how that garden had suddenly become hers. He knew she loved
living in the house, but it wasn't fair that they had
to make new memories in a home that held too many
from the past. She deserved more; as a matter of fact,
they all deserved a new beginning. He wasn't about
to let their future be overshadowed by his past.

Hours later, the girls begged Aunt Maggie to let
them go with her to the market. He overheard them
asking if they could stop by the mall, and since Aunt
Maggie turned to putty in their hands, he was sure
they would be gone for a while. Since it was just the
two of them at the house, Alfred persuaded Casey to
go for a drive. "Let's just get out and see where we
end up."

"All right." She loved his spontaneity. She liked to
ride, but she hated to drive.

They drove around town for hours. The Galleria
was one of their first stops. Alfred didn't mind shopping, but he didn't like staying in one store too long.
Casey was indecisive about what she wanted. Then she
saw something for Dara and Christie. After he finally
pried her from the mall, they stopped by Baskin Rob-
bins and got praline pecan ice cream with hot praline
syrup on top. The day was nice enough to ride

around with the windows down. Casey relaxed in the seat with her head reclined.

Twenty minutes later, they drove into a nice neighborhood where the yards looked like something out of *Better Homes and Gardens*. They turned into the driveway of a house that was simple but elegant.

"I was thinking about selling this house to a young couple," Alfred said as he unlocked the front door. "Do you think they might like it?"

Alfred remained where he stood, while Casey wandered from room to room.

"Do you mean for us?" she asked. "Oh, Alfred! This is it! This is perfect." Casey could hardly contain her excitement. She found herself running up to him and hugging him around the neck. "This is everything I've wanted."

"I'm glad that you like it," Alfred said, looking down into her eyes. One hand remained around her waist, while the other smoothed back a strand of hair covering her eye. "I think I've finally found everything I've been wanting also."

As his lips touched hers, time stood still. His hand moved from her face and entangled in the mass of hair hanging below her shoulders. Her kiss was sweeter than any other. It was more than sweet, it was electrifying. Wandering hands moved over the silky skirt to bare skin that was equally as smooth.

The arms that held her steadfast loosened their grip. Alfred couldn't mistake the expression on Casey's face for anything other than what it was. It was desire. He smiled at her with a devilish grin.

"Why don't we break in our house? You know," he said, nuzzling her ear, "get a feel for it?"

She wrapped her arms around his neck. "You read my mind." She smiled.

"I know. There are a lot of things I can do if you

let me." His lips greedily claimed hers. "How about trying each room?"

She looked around them. "That's a lot of rooms to cover."

"That's okay," he said as her pulled her to the carpeted floor. "If we don't make all of them, we have the rest of our lives."

"Girl, you won't believe who I saw in the beauty shop today!" Punkin was in a frenzy. He could hardly get a cigarette in his mouth quickly enough. "My blood just boiled, but I said that it ain't my fight, and I would be wrong to just walk up to that person and slap the taste out of her mouth." His index finger went up. "Mind you, I had a mind to do it. Trashing you like that."

He began pouring ice, frozen lemonade, and Tequila into the blender. Casey waited for him to turn off the blender before trying to figure out what he was talking about. She took two glasses and dipped the rims in salt. After stopping the blender, Punkin poured a generous amount of his homemade margaritas in each glass. He then went into the living room and began lighting incense.

Punkin was acting as if he were about to perform a séance or something. Casey waited patiently for him to join her on the floor. She took a sip of her drink and licked the salt from the rim of the glass.

"Punkin, who are you talking about?" She smacked her lips from the salty taste.

Punkin took a long slurp from his glass. "Alfred's ex-wife, Kelly." He set his glass on the table. "At first I didn't recognize her, but then I remembered her face from the fund-raiser."

"How do you know she was talking about me?" Casey asked.

"Be-*cause*, she kept saying Alfred's name and looking in my direction." He held up his hand. "Stop interrupting and let me finish. She and a couple of her high-society friends came in and got the works. I'm talking about full-body massages, manicures, pedicures, and hairdos. Okay? Since they were spending money, and I was benefitting from it, I felt obligated not to throw them out."

"Whatever, Punkin. What was she saying?"

"Oh, she went on and on about how her ex-husband had really started slumming. How he had called off the wedding after she told him what a mistake he was going to make by marrying you." He paused to sip his drink. "She went on to say that she was the better woman and that you would never be happy with him if she had anything to do with it."

"Now, see?" Casey's temperature began to rise. "She's not even concerned about her daughter. All she's worried about is me being with the husband she let go. Why make life difficult for the next woman because you didn't want to be there?"

" 'Cause she's trifling like that," Punkin said. "She even went as far as to say that she'll never have to work because Alfred would never let the mother of his child suffer."

"Is that right?" Casey asked with interest.

"That's right, girlfriend. And if I were you, I would let that hussy know which way is up. I would wring her bony butt out like a wet towel, okay?" He propped his feet on the coffee table. "After she embarrassed you at the restaurant and got you kicked out, honey, please. She deserves a good old-fashioned be-hind whipping." He whooped. "I started having flashbacks and if it wasn't a shame, I would have laid down my womanhood and picked up my manhood and beat the stuffing out of her narrow behind."

Casey laughed so hard that she spilled her drink on the floor. "Punkin," she said through her tears of laughter, "you are the best friend a girl could have." She leaned over and hugged him.

"I know, girlfriend." He fanned his hands in front of his face to dry the tears that were forming. "I just wish I could be your maid of honor. You think I could make it if I dressed in drag?"

Hours later, Casey's cell phone rang. It was Alfred wondering if she was okay. Punkin knew it wouldn't be long before she made her excuses and left. Jealousy was starting to creep up on him. He was used to being the person she relied on. Now that was changing. Minutes later, just as he knew she would, Casey was up and out the door. Punkin watched through the curtains as she drove away. He breathed deeply. Happiness was in his heart for his best friend. Yet, part of him was afraid that things wouldn't be the same. Would they still be able to hang out as they used to? Would they remain best friends or would they drift apart? He sighed. He was starting to miss her already.

Forty

"I really need to see you," Kelly pleaded on the other end of the line. She smiled to herself. She should get an Academy Award for all the acting she had done. Broadway was starting to sound kind of nice. She was a natural. Maybe acting was the one thing she could do for a living.

"I don't think that's a good idea, Kelly," Alfred said. "Why don't you just tell me what the issue is over the phone. It'll save both of us some time."

"You know," she said, pretending to sob, "I never thought I'd see the day you'd turn your back on me. You were always there for me when I needed you." She added an extra whimper for good measure. That always used to work.

He remembered a time he couldn't stand for her to cry. He would do anything to make her happy. She didn't have that effect on him anymore, and he was quite pleased about it.

"Well, people change," Alfred said. "Maybe you should consider changing too. It would probably do you some good."

"Don't be so heartless," she said, blubbering. "I know you're getting married, but there's no need for you to treat me like this." *Oh, I'm too good at this. I actually have a real tear in my eye!*

"Well," Alfred said, "how do you think I felt when you got us, including our daughter, kicked out of a restaurant? You were pretty heartless when you insulted my fiancée and talked to our daughter like you were out of your mind. I think you owe me an apology, not to mention my fiancée and Christie too."

"You know I didn't mean it. I just saw you sitting there and I-I lost control." She continued to sob. "That's not fair, and you know it. Please, I need to see you. I won't bother you again if you just see me this one last time."

He paused for a moment in consideration. "All right, Kelly." He sighed. "Where do you want me to meet you?" She immediately cheered up and gave him the name of a restaurant and the directions. He promised to meet her there in twenty minutes.

He was playing with fire meeting Kelly. There was no telling what she wanted. Probably money. He debated calling Casey and telling her he was meeting Kelly, but he decided to tell her about it later. There would be no secrets between them. He wasn't starting his marriage off like that.

Kelly clicked off her cell phone as she eyed Casey, who had just arrived at the restaurant. Kelly was about to leave until she saw her walk in. What a nice coincidence that she would pick the same restaurant to have lunch. She was sure her little hairstylist friend had filled her in on her conversation about her. He kept pretending to have to see if his client's hair was dry just so he could get an earful. She played him like a puppet on a string. This was going to work out perfectly. If Alfred didn't want her back, then he wasn't having anybody at all.

Her eyes turned into slits as she watched Casey from a corner in the restaurant. There was no way that little twit was going to waltz into Alfred's life and

ruin her good thing. Although Alfred had basically
written her a check and said good-bye, whenever she
needed financial assistance, he would eventually help
her if she whined long enough. Another woman in
the picture would cut her funds short.

She continued to watch Casey over the top of her
menu. Whenever Casey would happen to look in her
direction, she would raise the menu to keep from being seen. As much as she didn't want to, she had to
admit that Alfred's fiancée was attractive, though not
as beautiful as herself. Once she married Alfred,
Casey was sure to be quickly accepted into society.
Kelly's friends would soon become the new wife's
friends. Where would that leave her? It didn't really
matter because most of her friends couldn't wait until
she was out the door before they tried to get into the
bed that was still warm from her body.

Even at the benefit, she had noticed how men with
power took an interest in Casey. Usually, when she
and Alfred happened to attend the same social event,
he would come over and make his presence known,
but not that night. He and Quincy were too busy
watching Casey struggle with that slimeball, Michael
Jefferson. Kelly found it rather amusing that Casey
was trying to get away from him all night.

Ms. Goodie-two-shoes was sitting at the bar with her
nose stuck in a book. She was probably voted most
studious when she was in school, while Kelly was Ms.
Popularity. Yes, Alfred had to be turning her loose
with the gold card because her choice of clothing was
improving. The Dolce & Gabanna T-shirt and jeans,
Kate Spade bag, and Prada shoes were an expensive
casual ensemble. If there was one thing Kelly new
about, it was clothes. She wrinkled her nose in jealousy as the bartender kept hovering around her. He
examined Casey's hand as she showed him her en-

gagement ring. She seemed genuinely happy. She was beaming. Love was written all over her face as she probably began to talk about Alfred.

Why hadn't Kelly appreciated Alfred when she had him? Why did she have to give up everything? She had been in the same position and she blew it. So why was she trying to make his fiancée's life miserable?

Alfred scanned the room until he saw Kelly beckoning him to the back of the restaurant. He went over to the table and joined her.

"I can't stay long," Alfred said as he took a seat.

"It won't take long," Kelly said. She began squeezing a lemon into her water. She nervously sipped it. Alfred seemed to be impatient. Kelly was relieved that his back was to Casey, who still hadn't spotted them.

"I have to be honest with you," she said. "I was going to get you here just to cause trouble between you and your fiancée." She looked into his face for some kind of expression. It remained passive.

"Why doesn't that surprise me?" Alfred asked as he leaned back. "Nothing you can do will ever surprise me."

"Well, she's here. Over there," she said, pointing, "at the bar."

Alfred found Casey. He had walked right by her and didn't know it.

As if she could feel his eyes on her, she looked in his direction. At first, it was a pleasant eye contact with a smile, until she saw him sitting there with Kelly. The smile melted away, and she immediately headed toward them. *Oh, no, I'm not going through this mess again.* What in the world was Alfred doing there with Kelly? This woman was working on her last nerve. She went to the table and pulled out a chair. After placing a kiss on Alfred's lips, she turned to Kelly.

"I have had enough of you and your silly games," Casey said in a low voice. "Unlike you, I'm not going to make a scene and get us all kicked out of this restaurant."

Kelly's face went pale. "I, uh," Kelly began.

"No, let me finish," Casey interrupted. "You've had your chance. Now it's my turn. I understand and respect that you and Alfred have a child together. But you have to respect that I'm going to be Alfred's wife. He will no longer be supporting you when you have hard times. Do like everybody else does. Go out and get yourself a job."

Alfred let Casey have her say. He sat back quietly with a smirk on his face. Kelly had been asking for this, and he was going to let her get what she deserved.

"I'm not trying to replace you as Christie's mother," Casey continued. "But I will be a mother to her while she is in our home. That's *your* child, and you need to start being a mother to her. She loves you and she needs you. You are welcome in our home any time to visit your daughter, but you *must* respect what we have."

Kelly was close to tears, though this time, she wasn't trying to earn an Academy Award.

Casey wasn't buying it. Too many bad things had happened to her already, and she was about fed up with all of the nonsense. It was about time for her to be on top for a change and today was that day.

"You will not come to our home disrespecting me or my husband. Visits like this one you've concocted today will not happen without my knowledge. If there is something you want from *my* husband, you will ask me first. Do you understand?"

Kelly nodded. "I'm sorry," she said. "Now I know

that you really love him and he loves you. I know you won't mistreat Christie." She sniffed. "You'll probably be a better mother to her than I ever could be. I don't want to make your lives miserable. I honestly want you to be happy. Maybe I should just get out of Christie's life altogether."

"No," Casey said. "That's taking the easy way out. Christie loves you too much for you to bail out on her like that."

Casey stood to leave. She looked down at Alfred, and he immediately stood. "I trust that I won't be hearing any more secondhand information about you having a problem with me, will I?"

Kelly vigorously shook her head. "No, not at all." She couldn't look Casey in the eyes. Guilt was written all over her face.

"Good." Casey took Alfred's hand and left Kelly to her meal.

"You don't have to look so smug. I was just protecting my interest." Casey stood on her tiptoes and kissed Alfred. They both glanced back when they heard the doors of the restaurant swing open. When they realized it wasn't Kelly, they focused on each other.

"Oh, I like a woman who takes charge." He smiled as he took her by the hand and walked her to her car. He waited until she was behind the wheel before he squatted by the door so he could see her clearly. He studied her face as if in amazement.

"What's up with you?"

"It's just déjà vu." He shook his head. "The first time we met, I stood by your car and asked if I could call you, and you said no. You remember?"

A smile crossed her face. "Yeah, I remember. Who would have ever thought?"

"I watched as you drove away, and I never thought

I'd see you again. This time, I'm not losing you. I'm never letting you go."

"Good," Casey said, "because I don't plan on going anywhere."

Forty-one

Casey pulled into the driveway of the house she used to call home. A strange sadness overcame her as she opened the door. She was there to make sure all of her belongings were out before she decided to sell or rent it out. This house had been a haven for her for a little more than four years. It was kind of hard to say good-bye to the only thing that she could call her own.

In two days, all of this would be behind her. This place had been her safety net, her comfort zone. When she came home from work, this was the only thing she knew would be the same. Now she was leaving for the unknown. She was exploring uncharted territory. Who would have known that *she*, a woman who needed structure and couldn't adapt to sudden changes, would be making the many changes she had made in her life?

Casey sat on the windowsill, placing one foot over the other. The ominous question that loomed in her mind was, could she forgive her father? Could she forgive her mother? All of those years of unnecessary pain could have been avoided if her parents had been truthful. Not to mention the lives her father destroyed by pretending to love another woman. Were money and status more important than true love? Not in her book. At the same time, she couldn't let the cycle continue. After all, her father hadn't truly abandoned her, had he? There was so much about him she didn't know and wanted to find out. She never knew her grandparents, and she wanted to know what they were like, even if they didn't want her mother or herself in their lives. Could they still be alive? *There's so much I've been cheated out of!*

Casey went through the house checking the cabinets and closets. After making sure the refrigerator was unplugged, she took one final look and opened the door and stepped outside. As she closed the door of her old house, she bade a fond farewell to an old friend. As the evening sun shone on her face, she welcomed a new beginning. If she planned on starting anew, that meant starting fresh with everything, including her mother and father.

She found her father in the evening shade, cutting her mother's grass on a riding mower. He finished cutting the row he was working on before turning off the mower as he saw her pull into the driveway. Why hadn't she seen it before? Eyes that matched her own observed her in the same manner in which she observed him. He stood there as if he didn't know what to do next. She went to the porch and sat on the top step. Jay waited to see if she was going to invite him to sit next to her. When she patted the cement next to her, he went over and took a seat.

He grunted as he sat down. "These old knees ain't what they used to be. Well," he said, "in a couple of days, I suspect Alfred will be a very happy man." He wiped his face with a towel. They both looked down at their hands and began nervously fidgeting with their fingers.

"I hope so," she said sincerely. She focused on the sky, which had fluffy white clouds lazily drifting across it. " 'Cause I'm going to be one happy woman."

He leaned back placing the palms of his hands on the porch behind him. "You know, he loves you a lot."

Casey smiled to herself "You think so?"

"I *know* so." He chuckled. "I knew that from the moment he came over and set your mother and me straight."

"What?" Surprise was on her face. She knew nothing about Alfred talking to her mother and Jay.

"That's what I'm talking about." He slapped his thigh with his hand. "A real man. He didn't even go back and tell you about what he did."

"Well, are *you* going to tell me?"

Her father seemed to be in his own world. He was shaking his head in appreciation. "Yep, he's going to make a good son-in-law. He's a man who knows how to hold his peace."

"Daddy, are you going to tell me?"

Her father paused when he heard her call him daddy. It was something she hadn't done since she found out the truth. He could tell she recognized her slip of the tongue, but she didn't take it back and that meant the world to him. Instead, she scooted closer to him, the way she did when she was a little girl, and draped his arm across her shoulder and held his hand. Had she found it in her heart to forgive him? He silently prayed to God that this was what it meant.

"Yeah, Case, I'm going to tell you." He took in a deep breath. "Yeah, that fellow of yours came over here and told your mother and me that we needed to get our acts together because we were seriously hurting you. He said that he wasn't going to watch you suffer because of our stupid mistakes and that we better tell you the truth. I knew right then how much he loves you."

He looked at his daughter's hair. He remembered when she used to have one big ponytail at the top of her head. She had such beautiful hair. He was pleased that she hadn't gone through one of those phases and whacked it all off, trying to imitate those models who graced the cover of magazines. All of those years he missed and would never be able to get back.

"You know, I've really missed you, Casey," he said after a while. "I truly am sorry for the decision your mother and I made. I've suffered right along with you."

"You know," she began, "at my high school graduation, I gave my speech to the class and do you know what I was thinking?" She paused. "I was thinking that I bet my dad would be proud of me if he were here."

Jay's head hung low. He regretted every moment he was away from his daughter. He was a fool for thinking that she couldn't miss what she never really had. He was wrong; she missed him a lot.

"Through all of the applause I actually thought I heard you calling my name."

"I—" his voice broke. "I was calling your name, and I was very proud of you. I still am."

Casey patted his hand. "Thanks for being there. It really means a lot knowing that you supported me." She dried her eyes. "It's too bad about Kenneth. Everything that he's worked all of these years for is gone down the drain."

"Yeah, I feel sorry for him. I can't help but take responsibility for some of his hostility."

"There's nothing wrong with being angry, but to throw his whole medical career down the drain is a complete waste." She noticed the look of sadness on her father's face. "It's not your fault. You didn't make him do what he attempted to do."

"I know," he said softly. He rubbed his hands on his jeans. "So where do we go from here?"

"Well," she said thoughtfully, "we've been at the bottom so we have no place to go but up. They say that you don't know where you're going until you know where you've been." She smiled. "I know where I've been, and now I'm ready to go forward."

Her father smiled genuinely. "Does this mean I get an invitation to your wedding?"

"Dad!" She laughed. "I can do better than that. Do you think you might want to walk your daughter down the aisle?"

"I couldn't be more honored to give my daughter away to a man who truly loves her."

They sat on the porch catching up on the things they had missed until the streetlights came on. By the time her mother came out to join them, they seemed as though they had never been apart. She couldn't say that she agreed with what her parents did, but since she had Alfred in her life, she knew the true meaning of love. She didn't know if her love for Alfred would ever grow to what her parents shared, which was a self-sacrificing, unconditional love. She wasn't about to literally give her man away as her mother did, and if the love she had for Alfred wasn't returned, she would have to stop giving.

It wasn't long before Punkin drove into the driveway pulling a trailer behind his truck. There was a barbecue pit on the back that had thick smoke coming out of it. He went to the pit and shoved some wood around in it before closing it.

"Where are you going with that pit?" Jay asked. "The police are going to pull you over for polluting the neighborhood."

Punkin replied with one of his usual crazy remarks, and Jay told him that he was going to have to show him how to 'cue. Punkin opened the pit and showed off his brown ribs and homemade sausages. Her father swore up and down that he could out-'cue Punkin any day. Eventually, he went into the house and brought out some well-seasoned meat and threw it on the pit. Her mother ended up calling Aunt Ressie, who came over to join the fun. Casey called Alfred, who brought Aunt Maggie and the girls over. Pretty soon, some of the neighbors caught a whiff of the barbecue, and they brought side dishes and then it was a full-fledged party. Music was playing, cards were being thrown, and dominoes were being slammed down on the table.

A celebration wasn't something they had planned, but it felt good to come together with family and friends and have a good time.

Forty-two

Punkin had been acting strange all evening. Casey knew he was up to something. Every five minutes, his cell phone was ringing. Not that this was something out of the ordinary because he received calls all of the time, but this time was different. He frequently whispered on the phone and seemed to be talking in code. He called himself keeping her mind off the wedding. His efforts were good, but his behavior only reinforced the nervousness she felt. Casey would have sworn he worked for the secret service.

"Now, girlfriend, don't you worry about tomorrow," he said as he drove to his apartment. "Everything is going to be fine. You are going to be simply radiant, and your hair will be picture perfect."

"I hope so," she said. "My hair is the least of my worries."

Punkin opened the door and they went inside. He had an armful of bags they had gotten while shopping earlier that day. They had stopped by the beauty supply store to pick up some hair products so Punkin could do her hair for the wedding.

"Girl, just do what you always do while I put this stuff away." Punkin headed to the bedroom and changed into a black sequined shirt, blue jeans, and black loafers.

"Where are you going?" Casey asked. She sat there looking him up and down. Punkin had strange taste in clothes, but that was his style, and the clothes looked good on him and him only.

"Can I just get comfortable? You know I don't like sitting around looking to-up-from-the-flo-up," he said, snapping his fingers at her. When the doorbell rang, a look of surprise crossed his face. "Oh, I wonder who that could be." He sang.

He took his time going to the door and when he pulled it open, in came about fifteen of Casey's friends and acquaintances. They dropped various gifts at Casey's feet as they all carried all kinds of dishes and trays of food. Punkin came out of the room with balloons and gifts he had bought for her as well. Casey's mouth hung open. She was genuinely surprised to know that she was at her own bachelorette party. They sat around laughing, drinking Margaritas, and listening to music until there was an abrupt knock at the door. Casey jumped back when a fireman rushed inside carrying a fire extinguisher.

"Someone told me there was a fire in here that needed to be put out," he exclaimed. "If I'm not mistaken, it's a three-alarm, so I'm going to have to call for backup." He stood to the side to allow an entourage of six other firemen to come in. Punkin turned on a CD and all of the firemen immediately pulled off their slickers and began gyrating to the music. The women went wild as the men showed off their G-strings.

Casey sat in a chair in the middle of the room, and all of the men danced around her. She had never experienced anything like this before. As much as she enjoyed seeing the men running around half naked, they couldn't compare to Alfred in her eyes.

* * *

Alfred and Quincy sat out by the pool at Quincy's place enjoying the meal that Marva had prepared. Several torches burned, giving the place a tropical atmosphere. Unlike his first wedding, Alfred didn't have jitters, but he was excited. After all they had gone through, marrying Casey was the ultimate reward. The prize was well worth the effort.

Alfred noticed that Quincy was in a very good mood. At first, he took it that he was happy because of his wedding, but he was a little too happy. Every time he looked at Marva, his eyes lit up. That's what Alfred wanted for him and Casey. He wanted to love her more and more each day. Marva came out and told Quincy that she was on her way to Casey's party and that she would see them later.

Quincy was tripping all over himself to open doors for her and see her to the car. He came back all smiles. Alfred found himself grinning as well. It was contagious.

"Man, what gives? Why are you so lovey-dovey?" Alfred finally asked.

Quincy turned his back to the pool and gave a happy shout before falling into the water. He came up splashing and laughing. "Your boy is gonna be a father," he yelled. "I'm going to be a *daddy.*"

Alfred's excitement matched his friend's. Quincy and Marva had been trying for a while to get pregnant, and it finally happened. His best friend was going to know the joys of fatherhood.

"Me and Marva want you and Casey to be the godparents. Do you accept?"

"Man, you already know the answer to that." Alfred laughed. "I'm sure Casey won't mind either."

They spent the night hanging out and discussing

the baby and going over old times. Quincy wanted to throw Alfred a bachelor party, but he refused. One bachelor party in his lifetime was enough. Besides, that was one title he was ready to let go of.

Forty-three

The day started out cloudy. Casey kept running to the window looking out. She swore it was going to rain on her big day. She called Alfred several times to make sure he was going to show up for the wedding. She didn't want to risk another catastrophe before she got her chance to walk down the aisle.

Her mother was at her side the entire day. She was on the verge of crying all afternoon. When Casey wasn't busy running around trying to tie up loose ends, she finally asked her mother if she was okay. It was then that the tears flowed, and her mother apologized for keeping things from her. Casey hugged her mother and assured her that they could work things out. Her mother helped her into her gown and gazed at her. Although she had tried the dress on, she never imagined what she would actually look like on that day.

"Well," her mother said, "they say you should have something old, something new, something borrowed, and something blue." She went to her purse and pulled out a piece of velvet cloth. "These are for you." She placed the cloth in Casey's hands.

"What is it?" he asked curiously.

"Open it." Her mother smiled.

Casey opened it and found a strand of pearls. Her

breath caught in her throat. "These are beautiful. Where did you get them?"

"Those were your great-grandmother's." She took the strand from Casey's fingers and clasped it around her neck. "That's something old."

Punkin, who had come in to finish her hair, interrupted the conversation. "I've got something blue. I don't know about the borrowed stuff, but you can use this." He pulled out a garter. "Gimme your leg, so I can put this blue garter on it. I'm sure Alfred won't want to throw it to the men." He laughed.

Punkin asked Casey's mother if she would excuse them for a moment. It was only ten minutes before the wedding, and he had something he needed to get off of his chest. After her mother had gone, he closed the door.

"There's something I need to tell you," he said. "I hope you won't be mad at me, but it all worked out in the end."

Casey hoped it wasn't something dreadful that would take years for her to get over. If that something turned out to be like the something her parents had, she didn't know if she could bear it.

"What is it?" she asked as calmly as she could. Wedding jitters plus all of this other stress wasn't a good combination.

"Well, it's about Michael Jefferson." He laughed nervously.

"Oh, come on, Punkin. You know I don't ever want to hear that name again."

"Well, I deliberately let him pick you up for the fund-raiser."

Casey's mouth fell open. She knew it all along, so why was she surprised?

"I knew you and Alfred would be stubborn so I figured that if I threw him into the equation, both

of you would want each other back. You were sick of
Michael, and Alfred was sick of seeing you with Michael, so it all worked out."

"Punkin, what if Alfred hadn't come? What would
have happened then?"

"I wouldn't have let him take advantage of you. I
was watching from a distance." He smiled.

She hugged him tightly. "Thanks. If you hadn't
done that, there's no telling where Alfred and I would
be right now."

Jay was proud to walk his daughter down the aisle,
and he was even more proud of the fact that he was
giving his daughter away to a man who cherished the
ground she walked on, just as he did her mother.
This was truly one of the happiest days of his life. He
was sure that Casey and Alfred would like the trip to
Greece he gave them as a wedding present. At least
he hoped so.

The next morning Jay and Casey's mother watched
them disappear through the doors to board their
plane. He never thought he'd see the day he could
tell his daughter to her face that he was proud of
her. He could finally say that he'd gotten one of the
things he wanted most in his life, his daughter's love.

She dreamed of a simple wedding where she married the most marvelous man she could ever have
imagined. She dreamed that the man of her dreams
was holding her in her arms, assuring her that he
would never leave her side. When she woke, she realized that her dream was only an extension of reality.
The man of her dreams was actually holding her in
his arms. He was real. She could feel his breath on
her bare shoulders. She could touch his skin and feel
its warmth. No longer was this man a figment of her

imagination or an image in her dreams, he was tangible and he was hers.

Some people believed in fairy tales. Others pretended to live the fairy tale. But she knew what it meant to sacrifice. She knew what it meant to struggle. When all of the odds were against her, she overcame and endured. It would be no easy road, but it was one they would travel together, forever.

Epilogue

It had been a year since they said "I do" and things couldn't have been better. Casey was sad to say good-bye to the garden she had grown to love so much, but she was growing fond of the garden she started at their new house. Christie even took to helping in the garden. It was becoming a favorite pastime for both of them.

Home Sweet Home was doing better than she'd anticipated. Though business was good, the down side was the simple fact that there were so many children who needed to be adopted for various reasons. Her company expanded to include foster homes who could take in children at a moment's notice, sort of like an emergency shelter with a homelike atmosphere. There just weren't enough foster parents or people willing to adopt children with special needs. Everyone had the idea of adopting the perfect or problem-free child when that kind of child actually didn't exist.

Her mother and Jay finally tied the knot. Casey gave up on trying to capture the past and concentrated on the present and the future. They couldn't regain all of the years they'd lost, but they could make new memories with each passing day. Now she had both parents to worry her about producing a grandchild. They wouldn't have long to wait.

Punkin was now a cochair on the fund-raising committee for Big Brothers and Sisters of America. He also operated his own psychic hot line. He was getting into hot water telling people things they didn't want to hear, but he was accurate. He became so popular that the local radio station gave him a weekly spot on the morning show. The newspaper was trying to recruit him for the daily horoscopes, but he wasn't interested in anything so general. Casey was starting to think he liked delving into people's personal lives and telling them what they could expect. He kept trying to find out what was in store for himself, but his future was blank to him. To his relief, the feeling that he and Casey would grow apart was unjustified. They were as close as they had always been. Instead of losing his best friend, he gained another one in his best friend's husband.

Quincy and Marva had just had a little boy, Quincy Jr. Casey and Alfred were the proud godparents. After seeing the baby, Alfred started hinting around that he wanted another child. She was quite content helping to raise Christie, but she promised him that they could start working on it. He was pleased with her answer and waited patiently.

One afternoon, while waiting for Alfred to join her for lunch, she spotted Vicia, who noticed her and looked the other way. Casey made it a point to go over and see how she was doing. She had gone down since Casey saw her last. Her hair wasn't in its usual form, and she wore no makeup at all. She seemed tired and run down.

Casey pulled up a chair, not to confront her, but just to talk to her. She really looked as though she could use a friend. She listened as Vicia told her how she had met a man and they ended up getting married. They hadn't known each other for long before they decided marriage was for them. From what Vicia understood, he was supposed to be from a well-established background. At first things were going well, and they bought a house and traveled the country. Because she knew so little about her husband, she knew nothing about his gambling habits or his explosive temper.

She noticed that they were behind in all of their bills and the lights and gas kept being cut off. Then they foreclosed on the house. Her husband left her and married a woman who could sustain his lifestyle. Her wishing well had run dry. She had to file bankruptcy and owed creditors a lot of money. She was tired of working to pay bills and neglecting herself. The reason she was at the restaurant was that she wanted to spend some money on herself for a change. She could barely look Casey in the face.

"You look well." Vicia said. "Life is good to you." She fumbled with her napkin.

Casey was at a loss for words because she would be telling a lie if she said that Vicia looked well. She settled for a simple thank-you.

"I know you know about what I tried to do," Vicia said. "I can't begin to tell you how sorry I am. I've been meaning to apologize to you, but I never had the nerve to face you."

"Apology accepted," Casey said. She had to admit, when she first found out about what Vicia did, she wanted to strangle her, but everyone had to pay for their wrongdoing. Vicia was paying the price as they spoke and was probably paying for other things she had done to other people.

"All I want to know is why you did it," Casey said. Vicia was silent for a moment and shuffled her silverware. This woman was a far cry from the Vicia who used to burst into people's homes and throw her weight around. This woman seemed to lack self-esteem and confidence.

Finally, Vicia explained how she hid her insecurities behind her makeup and clothes. She worked hard to keep up her appearance so that people would like her. She also hid behind her job so that people would think she was important. She met Casey's eyes as she told her how things always seemed easy for her. Casey was surprised to hear that all the guys liked her and paid little attention to Vicia. Casey never knew of any men who were interested in her.

"That's just what I'm saying," Vicia said. "You were oblivious because you didn't care about any of that stuff. They were afraid to approach you because they knew you wouldn't go for any of their BS."

"Well, I didn't go to work to socialize, I went to do my job," Casey said.

"You always seemed so sure of yourself," Vicia said with a slight smile. There was a sadness in her eyes that Casey had never seen before. "I, on the other hand, was very insecure."

Talk about insecurities. Casey knew what it meant to be insecure. Instead of sharing them with the world, she kept them to herself. She explained to Vicia how she thought her father had abandoned her and her mother, and how she didn't want to go through the same things again.

Vicia was surprised to find out that Casey buried herself in her work to keep from dealing with her personal problems. "Yeah, but you ended up with a wonderful husband. All I ended up with was a loser."

"Stop looking for the wrong things in a man," Casey said. "Money doesn't make the man. Just because he is well off doesn't mean he knows how to

treat you. You should look for a man who is caring
and considerate. Someone you feel would be a good
father and most of all, he should be someone who
can be your best friend. And once you find that, my
friend, all of those other things will fall into place."

Vicia could see Casey's far-off gaze and knew immediately that her husband was all of those things to
her. For once, she was envious for the right reasons,
but deep down inside, she was truly happy that Casey
had found the happiness she deserved. From listening
to Casey, she knew that the right man would come
along soon enough for her. *My friend.* After all that
she had done to her, Casey still considered her a
friend. Casey never said a bad word to her and Vicia
truly believed that she honestly forgave her.

She had the house all to herself. Alfred was at work
and Christie had gone with her mother for the weekend. There was nothing else to do, so Casey walked
along the freshly laid cobblestone walkway that led to
her favorite part of the grounds, the garden. She sat
on the bench, which was strategically placed in the
center of all of the beautiful flowers. From where she
sat, she had the perfect view of a dazzling sunset. She
felt euphoric surrounded by beauty that was one hundred percent nature's doing.

A shudder went through her as she thought that a
year earlier, she could have been gone if Alfred
hadn't saved her from Kenneth. Yet, it all worked out
and she was thankful for every day her eyes opened
to see another sunrise and sunset. She never would
have imagined that she would be as happy as she was
at the moment. If someone would have told her two
years earlier that she would be happily married, she
would have told him he was out of his mind. She

broke a flower from its stem and smelled it before spinning it around. Maybe she would take some fresh flowers with her when she went inside.

Alfred was relieved to see that Casey's car was there as he pulled into the driveway and parked. He went inside, but she was nowhere to be found. He knew exactly where she was. He walked softly down the cobblestone walkway to the garden. He stopped short of rounding the corner and just looked at his wife sitting there with a flower in her hand. Every time he looked at her, it was as if he were seeing her for the first time. He fell in love with her more and more each day. He never knew love could be this good the second time around. Sometimes, he found himself wishing that they would have met a long time ago. Then again, his marriage to Kelly made him grow up a lot, and he learned from that experience. He hoped to be a better husband to Casey than he had been to Kelly. He watched as she looked down at her stomach and gave it a rub before smiling to herself. He could have jumped for joy. He certainly hoped that meant what he thought it did.

"You wouldn't happen to be stealing any of those flowers, would you?" he asked.

Casey seemed startled before smiling at him. He sat next to her on the bench smiling broadly at her. Now that he thought about it, she had been looking exceptionally beautiful lately. He took the flower from her hand and tucked it behind her left ear.

She gave him a light kiss. "How long have you been standing there?"

"Not long," he said. He continued smiling as if he had just won the lottery.

"What are you smiling for?" she asked suspiciously.

"Nothing." He laughed. "Can't a man just be happy to see his beautiful wife?"

"Sure, he can."

They both sat there grinning at each other. Casey was sure he was up to something.

"So," he said, "do you want some ice cream or a pickle or anything?" His eyes were on her stomach.

She burst out laughing. "You know, don't you?"

"Know what?" he asked innocently.

"You already know we're expecting." She smiled. "I wanted to surprise you."

He pretended to be surprised. "I *am* surprised." His countenance turned serious. "Are you happy about it?" The last thing he wanted was for her to feel the way Kelly felt about her pregnancy.

"What kind of question is that?" She placed her hand in his.

"I just want you to be happy."

"I *am* happy. I'm as excited about this as you are."

"I love you, Mrs. Willingham."

"I love you too."

ABOUT THE AUTHOR

Rochunda Lee lives in Houston, Texas. She is a graduate of the University of Houston with a degree in Social Sciences. She has always enjoyed writing because it allows her to be creative and use her imagination to the fullest extent. She enjoys going to the movies, visiting with friends and relatives, and traveling.

Do You Have the Entire
SHIRLEY HAILSTOCK
Collection?

__Legacy

0-7860-0415-0 $4.99US/$6.50CAN

__Mirror Image

1-58314-178-2 $5.99US/$7.50CAN

__More Than Gold

1-58314-120-0 $5.99US/$7.50CAN

__Whispers of Love

0-7860-0055-4 $4.99US/$6.50CAN
